Don't Eat the Parakeet

Charisse McAuliffe

 THREE SKILLET

DON'T EAT THE PARAKEET, McAuliffe, Charisse

First Edition

 THREE SKILLET

www.ThreeSkilletPublishing.com

Cover design by Farley L Dunn

ISBN: 978-1-943189-28-1

Don't Eat the Parakeet

Chapter 1

KAREN WYCLIFF twisted the wand on the blinds just enough that she could see outside, but certainly not enough for anyone in her yard to see her looking through. That would not do. After all, she would be turning thirty-nine at her birthday party in three weeks, and this man outside her door must be close to a decade younger.

Then, with a gasp, she saw him turn her direction, and without a moment's hesitation, her hand desperately flipped the wand she still held in her fingers. With the revealing blinds closed, and leaning her head against the wall, she drew in a deep breath and enjoyed the pounding of her heart. It made her feel alive again, and she needed to feel something good. Brad had been gone just three months, and his sudden departure from her life had devastated her. After all, they had started building this pool together, and then he had bailed out to go to Mexico with his secretary, leaving her with all the headaches of the life they'd built.

No, she didn't need this man outside her window to know she was alive. She had far too much of *life* all around her every day. She just needed something besides a seventeen-year-old unwed mother living under her roof, a teen son with hormones raging like wildfire, and a parakeet that hadn't seen the inside of its cage in days.

"Mom!" A boy's cracking voice broke into her brittle assessment of her life. *Life* had returned in that one word, and she knew her son. Whatever he wanted wouldn't be pleasant or easy. At fifteen, everything in her household followed in the wake of his emotional, hormone-driven, roller coaster days.

She looked to see him boil into the living room and sling himself into a chair. The backpack in his hands crashed to the floor at his side, and his face scowled at his knees and the holes in his brand new jeans.

"Dylan, what happened to your clothes?" They'd been to the mall just the weekend before. Her son had insisted on one certain brand, and they'd been very difficult to find. Expensive, too. Now they were destroyed.

When he looked up at her was when she saw the black eyes. Two of them, left and right.

"Oh, baby! What happened to you this time?" She was concerned about his injuries, but as importantly, she was relieved that this distraction had come along at just the right time to hide her own elevated interest in the man working outside.

When she stepped toward him, he let out a disgusted

breath of air. "Same as always, Mom. Everybody's bigger than I am." He turned his head away, but not before moisture had begun to build in his eyes.

She immediately knew what this was about, and even though the black eyes always concerned her, they were routine by now. At least he wouldn't face the same problem as his sister. Lissie had matured early, and that had attracted the attention of all the boys in her school. One in particular had been especially convincing, and now Karen had a grandchild. At least the baby had come in winter, and Lissie had only been homebound one semester. Karen had insisted she return to school for her senior year. Now all the girl had to do was graduate . . . and get a job, and married, and out on her own . . . and Karen could not think about Lissie's problems just then.

That man was still outside her window.

"DYLAN, WE'RE never going to get this cleaned up if you don't sit still." She had made the fifteen-year-old strip off his pants as she filled a large bowl with cold water. Now he sat on the washing machine. His pants had been torn, but the shirt was bloodied. Looking at the pants wadded up to the side, she knew the most she could hope to salvage from them was to cut the legs off. A good hem and he could wear them for shorts all summer. The shirt, though, might still be saved. She worked it with a sponge, hoping for the best.

"Mom, just take it." He yanked it over his head, thrusting it out to her. "I'm not bleeding anymore, anyway. I'm fine."

She looked him in the face, and her eyes found the

9

features that so reminded her of Brad, that fink who had abandoned her for the secretary he was with in that Mexican villa down in Baja. This face should make her angry, especially since the boy was so much like his father, even to chasing every girl he came in contact with. He was barely more than a child, though, and the girls didn't seem as attracted to him as he was to them. She glanced up at the ceiling. Thank you, God, for that.

"Did she already have a boyfriend?" Placing her hand on the bare skin of his leg, she looked directly into her son's blackened eyes. The sudden flush in his face told her the answer she needed. These torn knees and blacked eyes *were* from a girl, or at least from the boyfriend who hadn't wanted Dylan to claim her.

"Mom!" He looked at her, and his eyes had already started to well up again. "Why do you always think they have boyfriends?"

"Is she pretty?" She smiled at him, her heart softened.

His face shifted with her question, and he began to grin. "She has two earrings, and she's a cheerleader, too."

Love for this fifteen-year-old made her laugh out loud. His response was so pure and open. He saw earrings and status. That was very different than what she had admired just outside her window a few minutes before. Even now she couldn't get the memory of that strong, suntanned back and those rugged jeans out of her mind. She had closed the blinds too quickly to see his face clearly, but she'd certainly gotten an eyeful of his bare shoulders with that sweaty sheen, and she wouldn't have known if he had been wearing earrings anyway. Her heart had been pounding too hard.

"Mom, what's funny?" Dylan grabbed a clean shirt from the basket on the dryer and pulled it on. "Did I say something I shouldn't have?"

"No, baby. Stand up so I can give you a hug." She did love this boy who was barely taller than she was, even if he happened to look so much like his father. As she wrapped her arms around him, he stood still for a moment, and then he tried to pull away.

"Enough, Mom. If you want to hug on someone, go out in the backyard. I bet that man would let you hug on him as much as you want." He grinned.

She pushed him away, feeling warmth rising up her neck. "Dylan, that's enough. I cannot believe you said that." Turning, she knew her face must be growing red.

He laughed. "I was just teasing. I need clean jeans, too. I didn't see any in the basket."

She stepped away to look out the window. "Look in the dryer. I haven't pulled them out yet." As he knelt to dig inside for his jeans, she noticed something she'd never been aware of before. In the five years since she and Brad had built this house, she had never really paid attention to the fact that she could see directly into the backyard from the laundry room window. She was dimly aware of Dylan pulling on his jeans, and she only faintly heard the sounds as he zipped and buttoned the fly. All she could think of were the muscles she saw flashing in the sun and those well-worn jeans.

A streak of yellow outside the window did manage to shift her attention to a more immediate matter—and one of vital importance.

"Oh, my word, Dylan! Junie's out again."

A door slammed in another part of the house, and she realized she was alone in the room. "Dylan!" She called louder with no response.

This was to be up to her, and that bird was her grandson Chipper's most treasured possession. It had to be recovered. The new pool and the man working on it were gone from her thoughts, and all she could imagine was the last time that yellow parakeet had gone out the door. It had flown from tree to tree, and only by luck had Dylan been able to whistle it to his finger. She didn't even know how to whistle!

Grabbing a lightweight summer slip from the clothes basket to toss over the bird when she made her capture, she opened the back door and tried her best to purse her lips into a whistle. What came out was more of a sputter than a tweet, though. Groaning, she looked up and searched for the flash of yellow that would tell her where the bird was.

"Junie," she called softly. "Junie, boy. Come here."

Stepping past the birdbath Brad had insisted on for Texas' hot summer climate, she splashed the water with her fingers. It was possible the bird might be thirsty. She guessed birds got thirsty in the daytime, and it was already heating up.

"Water, Junie. Cool water."

She found him arrogantly perched high in a tall tree, and he just looked at her.

Glancing down, she stepped onto the dirt. The soil was cool against her bare feet, and that meant it was moist. It was also soft in places. There had been so much rain that the pool installation had been started and delayed over and over during the winter, and now that warm weather was here, they were scrambling just to make up lost time. She didn't know if that was good or bad. With Brad gone, this hole in her backyard seemed either like a pre-divorce decision gone bad, that or a wonderful distraction to buoy her into a new life.

Right now it was an obstacle preventing her from chasing one irritating yellow parakeet. The bird had flown completely across the yard, directly to the other side of the dirt hole yawning in front of her.

"Bad bird," she called. "Bad, bad bird. Come to Karen, sweetie." She held up her hand and put one finger out, making a perch. She tried to whistle again, and it was no surprise when the sound came out as a dull honk.

A sudden, clear whistle from across the pool dig startled her, and she glanced around. To her horror she realized she had forgotten all about the man on whom she had been spying earlier. With embarrassment she looked away, needing to show she was not interested in him at all, that she was in fact out here simply to catch her wild little bird.

It was true, too.

Yes, she'd been peering through the blinds at him, and then she'd taken further opportunity from her vantage point at the laundry room window. However, to step directly outdoors to interact with this man was certainly outside the bounds of anything she would consider doing. Why, what would her church fellowship say if they knew she was fraternizing with a half-naked man in her own very private backyard? There'd be a prayer chain a mile wide just for praying her back to proper, upstanding Christian morality.

"You gonna catch that little-bitty bird with that negligee?"

Karen's breath caught. This man's voice, so familiar, as if she should know him. It was deep and melodious, and there was a hint of amusement there. Yet, he was just a construction worker, and this was not funny at all. A shadow of irritation made her press her lips firmly together, as she prepared a retort. She had never met this man, and she intended to tell him her bird was none of his business.

Then the final word of his question jumped into her mind. *Negligee.* All her bravado bled from her like warm butter in the Texas heat.

"Negligee?" She repeated his word with as much aplomb as she could muster, all the while keeping her gaze in the trees, attempting to track the bird as it hopped from branch to branch. At least she hoped her response came across with an appearance of self-confidence. Inside, her stomach fluttered with rising anxiety.

Negligee?

Then she reached to shade her eyes, and she remembered the summer slip. It was white and very sheer, and she supposed it could look like sleepwear. To a man it might, especially if he were single and unfamiliar with women's intimate apparel. She tried to wad it under her arm, keeping the expression on her face as nonchalant as possible.

Even so, her heart pounded in her chest.

"I'm sorry. I was folding clothes, and then somehow my bird got out. I have to catch him for the baby. Little Chipper loves Junie and would be devastated if his little pet got away. Bye-bye, birdie, and all that. There's no bye-bye birdie allowed in this house." She knew she sounded corny, but she had no idea how to shut up. Her nerves had her all a jitter. She called out brightly, hoping to cover her bumbling, "This is just a slip I wear under my summer dresses."

She cringed. That only made it worse. This man—she certainly couldn't call him a boy—was just someone working in her yard, and he was probably tired and ready to go home. He was only here because he needed his paycheck. Wasn't that the way it was with most people? Even if he did have broad, muscular shoulders and nicely scuffed jeans, that didn't mean he would be interested in her. She was practically an older woman. Also, she had two children—plus a grandbaby, heaven forbid!

What would he ever see in her?

JOHN SPRINGFIELD chuckled. This woman hadn't so much as looked at him since she'd stepped from the door. He had seen her peering at him earlier through the window, and he'd wondered if she'd needed to speak with him. However, when he'd turned to wave, she'd closed the blinds before he could even raise his arm. Now here she was outside with him, and it seemed as if she were afraid of him.

He remembered meeting Mrs. Wycliff several months before. Karen, he recalled from the paperwork. The day had been cold and business slow. He'd been looking at real estate brochures at his desk, determined to finally get out of his cramped apartment, and he had seen this gorgeous brunette step from a low-slung sports car. He wasn't much of a low-slung car type, as four-wheel-drive vehicles were more his preference, but he was sure this one was expensive.

She exited the passenger side, so he knew she wasn't alone. A leather coat and snug jeans topped hand-tooled boots. There was style in her clothing, and as she moved, he could see her style went even further. It was in her walk and the way she carried herself.

He had been entranced.

Then an older man had stepped from the driver's side. He motioned to the woman, and immediately John smelled trouble in paradise. The man didn't even wait for the beauty he was with to catch up to him, just strode heedlessly ahead.

In that moment he hoped they weren't coming into his offices. He had felt an immediate attraction to this stylish, graceful woman, and she obviously had a man in her life. The man with her might appear brusque and uncaring to him, but that wasn't his concern. He didn't know these people, and if they just walked on by, he never would. This stunning woman would be a vision that could haunt his dreams that night, and if he enjoyed the dreams, perhaps a second night, also. Then she would be forgotten. However, if he heard her voice—

He had coughed, turning back to his brochures, pushing that thought aside. Then, to his horror—and heart-pounding anticipation—the door had chimed. He looked up as the older man stepped through and released the handle, leaving the woman to catch it and let herself in on her own. Before they'd left, they'd picked a pool design and written a deposit. Rather, John remembered, the man picked, and the woman went along with whatever was suggested, seeming totally distracted and less than really interested. She never once looked his way or spoke to him.

Mr. Wycliff—he'd introduced himself that way, even after John had given his first name—was content to have the site plans done up later, saying he would sign off on them when necessary.

The next day, when he was out to the house, there had been no one there. In the upscale Austin neighborhood where they lived, he knew the homeowner's association would need to be consulted, and there would be special permits for the pool construction. However, the extreme slope of the lot would make for a challenging build, and he'd liked that. He might even want to get his own hands dirty on this job.

He had only seen her that one time. Frankie, his secretary, informed him several weeks later there was a situation of sorts, perhaps an impending divorce, and he needed to check on things before the backhoes tore into the yard. By then, the yard prep was well underway, and he had six other projects going at the same time. Before he could get out there, the wife, and he remembered Frankie's word exactly, the *wife* had called to say the pool installation was still on, and did she need to sign a new contract?

He usually didn't concern himself about family situations of people for whom he built his pools. His job was to build the best pool his family business could effectively install, and it was the clients' job to work out their personal issues. However, when Frankie had told him about the call, he remembered feeling a sense of relief, almost as if he had some sort of personal interest in this woman's life.

Now, here she was out in her yard chasing a little yellow bird, and she couldn't even whistle. He smiled at that. She was prettier today than she had been that night at his office. He felt the connection building again, or at least he felt something.

Finally, he felt sorry for her. He'd grown up whistling to wild birds to get them to come to him, and he thought he could get this one to come to him, too.

"Here, I'm glad to help. Your bird didn't come the first time, but I bet I can whistle a different tune and get him down. I know a pretty good parakeet song."

She coughed, looking everywhere but at him. "I don't think I could ask. Besides, you're here to work, not to help me chase a bird. What would your boss say?" She lifted her finger into the air and called brightly, "Junie, baby. Come to Mommy."

He was amused. He was the boss. Besides, if he could help, he wanted to. And he did want to.

He dropped his shovel and wiped his hands on his jeans. Not that it'd do much good. He'd been in and out of the muddy dig all morning, and he was pretty covered. He reached to remove his sunglasses, and his hand brushed against dried mud caked on his face. He chuckled, pulling the brim of his old Stetson lower over his eyes and leaving the glasses in place. He didn't even have a shirt pocket for them. He'd used it to wipe them off earlier and then thrown it on the tailgate of his truck.

At least the bird wouldn't care.

Ducking his head, he used his shoulder to brush some of the mud off one side of his face. Raising a hand, he

18

whistled a second time. The sound was lilting, and then the high-pitched melody from his lips skipped and chittered.

With a flash of yellow, the bird was soon sitting on his finger, pretty as you please.

KAREN WAS amazed as she watched the capture. In a quick glance, she could see this man's hat was askew, and his face was streaked almost black with soil. Dark glasses made his eyes invisible. Yet, in only a few notes, he had commanded this small terror of a bird to land on his finger.

"How did you do that?" she whispered.

He chuckled, almost as if sharing a very important secret with a novice. "I've had practice. Now, your underwear, if you please." A grin creased one side of his mouth.

Her heart stopped, even as she bristled. Her underwear? This half-naked man wanted her underwear? They were in her backyard, and while it was relatively private, they weren't completely invisible to the neighbors. Besides, she was a faithful attendee at Wayside Christian Fellowship. He could not have her underwear, even if Brad had left her and was vamping it up with that hussy in Mexico.

He repeated his request with a slight modification. "Your slip, the one in your hand. I'd like to wrap your bird in it so you can carry him safely inside."

She felt her arrogance fade away, and in that moment she knew the affront she had felt had not been righteous indignation, although that's what she would have claimed if he'd actually been serious. Her arrogance had been a moment of false hope, one driven by the loneliness brought on by a husband who had abandoned her. It had been a sudden desire for him to step to her, and, well, for other things she wouldn't admit even to herself.

With her knees weak, she handed him her slip, and she watched him gently wrap the small bird inside. He placed the package in her hands, and as she thanked him, he tipped his hat and turned to walk away. She watched him for a minute as he went back to work.

As she stepped back into the house, she realized something.

She didn't even know his name.

Chapter 2

"JUNIE! JUNIE! Hold Junie!"

The cry pierced the video segment running over and over in Karen's thoughts, and she remembered the struggling animal she held wrapped in her slip. It was chirping away, and she hadn't even heard it.

Walking in the door, she'd been in a shell-shocked daze. That man, that *creature* in her backyard, had stolen her breath away. He had been dirty and sweaty and half clothed, and he was just an employee of the company that was putting in this pool that she wasn't sure she could afford anymore. He wasn't someone she could be attracted to, for heaven's sake. After all, she had simply opened the living room blinds, and there he had been.

Her heart pounded as she tried to transition from that *man* out there, but she knew what the problem was. The last three months had been very hard. Her emotions had been dragged through the coals, and inside her soul, she had been left burned and blackened. Even her social group at Wayside Christian hadn't been able to alleviate the loneliness that had been her constant unwelcome companion. Getting back in church the past year and rededicating her life to Christ hadn't been the solve-all she'd wanted it to be. Just ask Brad—oh, she couldn't. He was in Mexico.

She knelt and motioned to the toddler making his way her direction. As she reached one hand to her face, she realized she was perspiring profusely. The house was certainly cool, and she'd been outside for only minutes. The child must have left a door open somewhere. It couldn't be her pulse, she knew, her racing pulse making her overly warm despite the air conditioner she could hear running. She would not let it be that man outside that was doing this to her, not with her daughter and grandson home.

And certainly not with her Bible study group later that evening. Dear lands, how could she face those women feeling like this?

"Junie?" the baby called. "Eat Junie?"

"Hey, sweetheart. Junie's right here. And no, you cannot eat Junie." She forced a smile at his excited little face, and she didn't think he would be able to tell her enthusiastic greeting was less than real. He wasn't even two years old, and he was only interested in holding his bird. However, she didn't want the animal out in the house for an additional three days, so she unfolded the slip slowly, reaching her hand inside to wrap careful fingers around the delicate, feathered creature. It struggled for a moment and then relaxed in her grasp.

Chipper grabbed for the bird's yellow feathers, and Karen laughed gently as she moved the animal away. The baby wasn't always easy, and she wanted the fragile creature to live to see another day.

"Easy, Chipper. One finger. Junie likes you, but you must be easy." She saw Chipper's mother Lissie walk through the doorway on the far side of the room, and she winked at her daughter, glad to feel an additional distraction from that *man* outside, and even gladder to feel her pulse slowing to something nearing normal.

"Mom! You caught Junie. How did you do that? You can't even whistle." Lissie giggled in disbelief, making an astonished face. "You, climbing on top of the dining room table to retrieve him from inside the chandelier. How funny!"

That had become the animal's roosting spot over the past few days, and it wasn't a problem, except at meal times. Then falling feathers and occasional discarded seed pieces had to be picked from the family's lasagna, scrambled eggs, or hamburgers. It was good entertainment for the baby, though, and they enjoyed the parakeet's chirrupy songs.

As Karen stood, Chipper jumped for the bird in her hand. She held it carefully aloft and quieted a twinge of guilt. She hadn't caught the parakeet at all. Someone else had brought this bird down out of a tree, and just the memory of standing close to him and having him hold her underwear, her *slip*, and then handing it back to her, made her heart pound all over again.

"Mom, I simply can't see you climbing on the table.

You'd be afraid you'd fall down. Did Junie get trapped in the window again?" Lissie made her way towards the wall of windows stretching across the back of the living room. "I caught him there once. I think he wanted outside. I bet he made a mess on the sill again."

Karen panicked. All she could think was how she felt when she looked out the blinds not so very many minutes before, and then she had run into the yard to chase the bird, and there her construction worker was, with those brown, muscular shoulders and that deep, melodious voice. The sheen of the sun on his sweat-covered skin was as crisp in her memory as her grandson jumping at her feet.

"Lissie, no!" She jumped forward to get her daughter's attention, only to feel the baby holding onto her leg. Looking down, she brushed at his small fingers with her free hand while holding onto the yellow parakeet with the other. "Lissie, wait!"

"Junie! Junie!" Chipper jumped up and down, toppling to the floor and wailing, "Eat Junie!"

Lissie glared at her mother with a frown. "Mom! Chipper needs you! Aren't you paying attention? The babysitter said he's been needy all day. He's your grandson. You have to pay attention to him, you know. You can start by telling him he can't eat Junie." She took the wand beside the window. "Junie was in this one? What do you know about that? You think the light'd hurt his eyes or something."

Karen was beside herself at this point. As long as that man remained hidden, then he wasn't real. She was the only one who had seen him, and if her heart had tried to beat its way out of her chest, what of it? No one else knew, and no one else would, either. That man and his strong arms and melodious voice would disappear forever. She would teach her Sunday school class this weekend, and she wouldn't dream of that man rescuing her from the morass of a life that had dragged her down the past three months. She wouldn't. She couldn't, no matter how the thought of him made her heart pound.

She had to stop her daughter from opening that blind.

"The bird, Lissie! If you open the blind, he'll try to fly through the window. He can't get outside again!" She was babbling now, and she didn't care. All she knew was that no one could be allowed to see that man who had pulled such strong emotions from deep inside her soul and forced her to feel sensations that no married woman should feel about a strange, sweaty man working in her backyard.

Then she remembered. She wasn't married anymore. Divorced, that's who she was, poor divorced Karen with a new pool going into her backyard. Hope surged through her chest. She could be attracted to any man she wanted.

Then her heart sank, and she wilted with despair. *Grandmother* Karen. Sure. She could be attracted to him all she wanted. He just wouldn't be attracted to her. Suddenly drained, she stopped and relaxed her hands. In that moment, the parakeet took advantage of the opportunity for continued freedom, and it flung itself across the room.

Startled into action, Karen grabbed for the bird, and as she did, Chipper stepped right into her path, bringing her down in a shambles onto the floor.

"Mom!" Lissie barked a laugh, tapping the blinds with the tips of her fingers. "Seriously? Junie was outside? I bet that stupid brother of mine left his window open again. You know that's how he sneaks out to see his girlfriend. You should lock that window with a padlock. That's the only way to keep him inside."

Then she twisted the wand, and the view outside came tumbling into the room. The trees were green, the sky was blue, and the hillside rose up to enclose the space that was becoming the family pool. On the other side, halfway up the terraced yard, were the knees of a man. That's all that could be seen beneath the paper blueprints hiding the upper part of his body.

"Yuck." Lissie turned away. "People. I want our yard back again." Then she laughed with inspiration. "Mom, you need to get a life. I'll go ask that guy out there for you, if you want. You know, for a date. He probably scrubs up pretty good." Glancing towards her mother, she laughed and put her hands on her hips. "Chipper, did you get in Mimi's way and cause her to fall?"

A flash of yellow streaked through the room, and Chipper yelled, "Junie! Want birdie! Mommy, Junie!"

Karen scrambled to her feet, appalled at the mess that was unfolding around her. Life? She had all the life she could handle. That man sitting out there was the wrong kind of life, and she wanted the blinds closed.

"Lissie, please close the blinds." Karen forced herself under control, her heart and her emotions. Even so, she could feel the room becoming hot again, and she knew the opened blinds must be letting in the summer heat once more. Seeing that man across the yard with his brown arms holding those papers and his muscular legs tight in his jeans wasn't affecting her. No, it was those blinds Lissie had just opened. They were letting the glare from the concrete porch in. That's why she suddenly felt so hot. "Please, Lissie. The blinds."

"Mom, what's the deal? It's just the yard." She called to the baby, "Chipper, come let Mimi alone for a minute. I think you overwhelmed her."

"Lissie. The blinds, please? I can handle the baby. I really want the window closed." She heard it in her voice, the way her words edged on ragged, nearing to desperation. That man was still out there, and surely Lissie could tell what he did to her. She had to control this situation now.

"Mom!" Lissie turned back to the window and glared at the man sitting there.

Karen could just see him. He had dropped the paper to his knees, and the perspiration on his browned, bare shoulders glistened in the midday sun. His sunglasses were shadowed under the brim of his western hat, and he seemed to be looking over the damage that had been done to the yard all around him.

"Close the blinds. Now, Lissie!" A stronger note of desperation crept into her voice.

"Mom! You're so funny today. Is that man out there the problem?" She grabbed the wand and laughed. "He's just a construction worker. He probably smells, too. Look, he's all sweaty." With a swift motion, she flipped the blinds shut and turned around, winking. "It's not like he's going to come in here and ask you for a date or anything, although with a nice suit and a tie, he might even be okay." An inspired look came over her. "Would you like me to see if he'd like something to eat?"

Karen's face turned white. "You better not dare!" Breathing hard, hoping she could carry off anger instead of embarrassment, she turned to stomp from the room, only to find Chipper still holding tightly to her leg.

"Chipper!" Her word was short, but she managed to keep her tone soft. He wasn't even two. She knelt to put her arms around him, giving him a hug, unable to speak another word out loud. She would cry if she did.

A hand squeezed her shoulder, and her daughter's voice was surprisingly tender. "Mom, it's just a worker with the pool company. Dad's gone, and although you wanted to believe in him, he was gone from us a long time before he walked out. I love him, Mom, but Dad left us. We didn't leave him. We have to move on."

Karen knew that. She had wanted to make her marriage work. While she might admit she had been too optimistic, she had known the marriage was failing for a long time before Brad served her the divorce papers. But, a dirty construction worker? Why did she have to be attracted to a tanned, muscular man covered in sweat? Why did he have to hide behind those mysterious sunglasses and that cowboy hat? Why did he have to whistle so perfectly and help her catch that stupid yellow parakeet?

She knew one other thing. Her daughter hadn't been looking, but Karen had seen him lower that blueprint, and bless her soul if that bare-chested man hadn't looked straight at the house, nodded his head, and grinned just as if he could see right there inside where she had tumbled to the floor.

Would she like Lissie to go out there and ask him if he'd like a bite to eat? Her thoughts were in a jumble. *Dear God in heaven, no, and dear God in heaven, yes. Yes, Lissie, yes, and don't you dare, daughter. I might just take him up on it, and that wouldn't do at all.*

KAREN CRANKED Dylan's window shut. That's how the bird had gotten out. It had to have been.

She let her eyes rove the backyard. All day she'd refused to open the downstairs blinds again, knowing what she would see out there, and she wasn't entirely sure she would be able to resist offering him some water, or perhaps a glass of lemonade. Then, of course, it would have been inconsiderate to come directly back inside. The gracious thing would have been to stay outside to visit with him for a few moments, perhaps to discuss the taste of the water or the sweetness of the lemonade. Then, if he were interested, and he would be, they would talk of the progress on the pool and of the benefits of tweaking this minor part of the design, or just what the view might be if they walked to the far corner of the yard that was totally hidden from the houses around them. She might even slip in the soft dirt where the plumbing lines had been run, and if she grabbed at his bare, muscled arm, she would have no choice but to hold on tightly as he helped her to her feet.

No one would see any harm in that, would they? Not even God would disapprove of this man helping her out of a predicament. After all, she wasn't asking him to remove his shirt. She hadn't seen him with his shirt on and then waited until he pulled it off before stepping outside. No, it had been off when she first looked through the blinds. No one could fault her there.

Her gut tightened with the butterflies she felt inside. He was gone from her yard. In the final fingers of the early evening sun, she could see that. She could certainly look, however, to make sure, even if she knew he wasn't there. In fact, she should, for security purposes. Everyone should check their yard through their windows to ensure there were no strange men lurking about. Hadn't Lissie said she needed to check this window, that Dylan had been sneaking out? That's all she was doing, what her daughter had suggested. She wasn't *looking* for that man, that horrible man who had taken his shirt off in her backyard right where she could see him and admire that strong back and his muscled chest. If she were to happen to see him, it certainly wouldn't be because she wanted to see him again, and certainly not because she had found him attractive or her pulse had throbbed in her temples at the sight of his bare skin.

No, she knew, this man was the type who probably went to Town Lake and intentionally roamed the shore wearing only swim trunks and flip flops, just to be admired by all the women who happened to pass him by. She was certain he had an apartment somewhere, a loft, perhaps, and there were neon lights underneath his bed. Every weekend he had a party, probably two, and his glass-walled loft was filled with twenty-somethings who partied hard and needed the next day to recover. That was not the kind of man a thirty-eight-year-old *grandmother* needed at all.

However, she could see her backyard was as empty as the hole in her heart. No cowboy-hatted man was waiting on her to bring him lemonade, and her parakeet was not outside. She knew, because the bird was roaming her house again.

With a suddenly quickened pulse, she realized she could have asked that man in for that. Rescuing the bird again would have been an acceptable excuse. Even Lissie would have understood. Karen could tell her daughter how he had charmed the bird with his whistle, and Lissie would see that her mother was not interested in that sweaty construction worker. Her interest lay solely in the rescue of this bird that was once again living in the dining room chandelier.

However, it would not be polite to ask this man-with-no-name to come inside to whistle for her bird without offering him a soda or some of that oversweet lemonade. Then, when she asked him if it was too sweet, he would laugh and tell her it was fine. In that moment she would offer to fix another batch. When he made to drink it anyway, she would have to place her hand on his arm to stop him. She would laugh and tell him he was just being nice, and then he would smile and tell her he was always nice. They would laugh and look into each other eyes. At least, he would look into her eyes, and then she would reach to him and slowly remove his sunglasses. In that moment, she would see his brown pupils, and they would be the creamy color of German chocolate frosting.

"Junie!" The toddler's voice intruded into Karen's thoughts, and Karen turned to see a yellow flash burst through the door and to the window. When the bird discovered it was closed, it immediately shot back out the door and was gone. Chipper's laughter followed the feathered missile down the hall.

She sighed and closed the blinds. At least the tanned cowboy with the glasses was gone from her yard, even if that bird was still loose in her house. It would have been nice to have that man whistle Junie back to its cage, even if she never got to offer him her lemonade. She chuckled sourly. She didn't even have any lemonade mix in the house. A lot of good it would have done to offer him a glass.

She headed down the stairs, shutting the safety gate before moving to the landing. "Lissie? Are you still upstairs?" She could hear music from the upstairs hall, but the baby couldn't be left alone if his mother wasn't upstairs with him.

The music quieted, and Lissie's voice called out, "Mom? You need something?"

"I'm headed downstairs, Lissie. Chipper's with you upstairs."

"Sure, Mom. I'll keep an eye out." The music increased in volume once again.

Karen sighed. Seventeen was far too young to have a child, and she had raised her two. Now it seemed she was raising another. At least that man was gone from her yard. That *boy* was gone from her yard. He was a boy, too. He might be twenty-five or thirty, but compared to her, he was a boy. She was a grandmother and soon to be almost forty. No matter that Brad had left her, *divorced* her, leaving her free to chase any eligible man she wanted, she was far too old for this boy who had magically whistled her bird onto his finger today.

Anyway, the weekend started tomorrow, and next week

her vacation would be over. Even if that sweaty man returned to her yard, she would be at work, and her respectability would be safe. So would his, as far as his involvement with her was concerned. If he wanted to waste it on his wild parties with his twenty-something girlfriends, then that was none of her business. She didn't even know where his glassed-in loft was, anyway, and there was no way she intended to try to find out.

Reaching the darkening living room, she touched the switch to turn on soft, ambient lighting around the edges of the walls. A movie might be nice tonight. A romance about a woman who falls for a construction worker.

Sure, she thought. Like I've got a dozen of those.

At least she'd insisted Brad install the home theater in here and not in the den upstairs. She liked being able to watch in the main part of the house where life was centered, not up in some remote hideaway where no one could find her. Now that the house was hers, she appreciated having it the way she wanted it.

Picking up an oversized remote, she pressed a button, and a screen dropped from the ceiling.

Then she remembered. Garbage pickup was in the morning, and the pool crew always left paper cups and such around. She tried to make the rounds of the yard twice a week just to keep things under control. She would need to hurry to take care of that before dark, too. The light was fading fast.

She grabbed a flashlight, certain she had almost waited too long. Perhaps the white of the cups would catch in the light, and she could get this done quickly.

Stepping outside, she flicked her fingers in the bird-bath, remembering how strong her response to that man had been earlier. The sound of a helicopter overhead caught her attention, and she looked up to see its running lights over-head. However, it was far away, and she dismissed it from her thoughts. Looking at the dark pit of her pool, she was reminded of how her stomach had turned over at the sight of that unknown construction worker, and she chuckled. Sure, his presence had done a number on her, but now, somehow, it was almost funny. At least it wouldn't happen again.

She stepped to the edge of what sidewalk still remained, and looking to where her sweaty construction worker had been sitting earlier, she sighed. Her weekend was perhaps not so safe after all. Just across the open space where the pool would eventually be were the blueprints and a pair of sunglasses. Now she would have to be sure to keep the blinds closed all day tomorrow, either that or make a point to be gone for the day. Her unknown man would miss his things in the morning, and surely he would stop by for them. She did not want to be here when he did, either.

Stepping to the edge of the pool excavation, she paused when the automatic lights in the trees flickered on. Then she squinted in the gathering shadows at a glint next to the sunglasses. Did she see a set of truck keys there, also? Surely he was not still around. In a sudden panic, she pivoted her foot in the dirt to return to the house, and with an unplanned loss of balance, the damp earth gave way underneath her.

She sat down roughly, scrambling to keep from going

inside the hole. Then, her feet lost their grip, and with a gasp of desperation, she felt the edge of the pool become a dirt slide. However, instead of landing on the floor of the excavation, she had an unexpected surprise. When she reached the bottom, someone was there to catch her, and it was the very man she had so desperately hoped to avoid.

Chapter 3

"SO, WE finally meet again."

"Meet?" This was hardly a *meeting*. It was more a catastrophe. Her arms had flailed the air, and she had expected to hit the bottom of the excavation hard. Even after seeing the sunglasses and keys, she had not had time to truly understand that she was not alone in her yard. After all, it was almost dark. She had looked from the upstairs window, and the yard had been empty.

Yet, even with all her assurances of safety, she had not been safe at all. She was certainly not safe now. It was dark, and she had fallen into this hole in her yard, and she had been rescued—after a sort. However safe she might be from physical injury, though, her heart was not safe at all, not with those tanned arms around her and this hole providing a level of privacy that as good as complete.

"You are in my arms, are you not?" There was a lilt of amusement in those deep, reverberating words, and intertwined in the statement was something else.

God forbid, Karen thought. It could not be *attraction*. This man could not be *attracted* to her. What would her Sunday school class think? However, his arms were strong, and he had not put her down. God help her, he had not put her down, and she felt stirrings she had not known since her children were small, and Brad had at least pretended he still desired her.

"How long do you intend to hold me? Long enough for a Beatles reunion concert?" Her voice shook and came out in a squeak. Her words were sharp—sharper than she intended. It was simply embarrassment, she allowed, not the rising warmth around her neck, nor the throbbing of her heart.

Shifting, suddenly afraid of falling, and even more afraid of what she'd be tempted to do if this man continued to hold her so closely, her hands reached for purchase, and the only thing she found to grab onto was the man who held her. One of her hands went on top of his shoulder, and the other landed directly on his chest. Touching his bare skin, she was intensely aware of two things. He was firmly muscled, just as she had imagined he would be. That thought alone caused the heat of the evening to engulf her with an intensity she could not imagine. In addition, she could feel the grittiness of the soil she must have showered on him as she fell. She moved her thumb across the rise of his pectoral muscle, aware that the dirt only made his skin more sensual.

She coughed a nervous laugh into the darkness, and her voice was barely a whisper. "I've gotten you all dirty. I'm sorry. I thought I was alone."

That brought a chuckle from deep within his chest, and she could feel his torso move against her as he spoke.

"So, that was why you were diving into your pool when it doesn't have any water inside? You were alone? Have you made a regular practice of swimming in the dirt out here? We could leave the pool like this if you enjoy it so much."

That irritated her. This was the same man she had been intensely attracted to earlier, and as she had rubbed her hand across his skin, those feelings had flooded back across her nerve endings, engulfing her with overwhelming sensations. She was barely in control of herself at this point, and now he was making fun of her.

Impulsively, without thinking of how it would feel to him, she drew her hand back and slapped his chest with the flat of her palm. "That is silly. I do not swim in the dirt. Who ever heard of such a thing?" Even she could hear the quavering in her voice as adrenalin surged through her. She was thirty-eight, and she felt just like a fifteen-year-old. God help her, this must be what Dylan felt like all the time. How horrible!

Yet, she knew it was not horrible at all. This man was everything her daughter had said. He was a construction worker, and he was filthy and sweaty. However, there was much more to him than that. Her nerve endings were on fire with the way this man held her.

Perhaps it was the darkness that made the attraction so

intense, or perhaps it was the unexpected situation she found herself in. It could even be that she had seen him earlier and then pushed him aside. She also allowed it might have to do with being held, really held, for the first time in the better part of a year. The soft purring of the house's air conditioning unit and the gentle *whup-whup* of the helicopter still overhead masked their voices, giving a feeling of privacy to the moment.

Whatever it was, she gave in to it, and in that moment, she did not want him to put her down. She needed what she felt in him. He was firm and strong, and underneath the smell of the day's heat, there was a muskiness about this man that she could not define. Surely it was not cologne that he was wearing. She would recognize that, she would think, and yet . . . it was very masculine, as if she were close enough here in his arms to draw in the very essence of this man.

His voice, even in its chiding, caressed her.

"Do you always painfully abuse those who rescue you from impending death? It is near dark down here, you know, and if you feel the need to continue venting your frustration physically, it will only be your word against mine. I'm not sure I'll complain." Then he chuckled again, and she could feel it from deep within his chest.

Her voice was stronger this time as she overturned his chiding. "You are laughing at me, sir. What will your girl-friends think of you holding a strange woman in this deep hole, and in the dark, as well? They will be waiting on you to start tonight's party in your glass-walled loft." She froze for a moment at those words. His glass-walled loft was in her imagination only. What if he really lived in such a place? He would think her a peeping Tom, er, Tomette.

To her dismay, he simply laughed. "I guess I could drop you, but there's something you don't know. The soil up top might be nicely dry, but underneath my feet, it is still very muddy. I think all my girlfriends would find me very chivalrous, indeed, to have rescued a beautiful woman from an impending mud bath."

"Beautiful!" She snorted the word. "I might be a vengeful Amazon, for all you know, out to rid the world of crazy husbands who run away with uncouth floozies. How would you like to be holding one of those?"

She felt his chuckle rise within his body once again, and when he spoke, his words caught her off guard. "No Amazon I know would come out of her house to rescue a frightened parakeet with the slinkiest piece of under-clothing she could lay her hands on—and with a whisper, too. No, I'm not holding a vengeful Amazon. Sorry. That's just not you."

She gently brushed the soil off his chest. "Then, chivalrous knight, who am I?" She held her breath, not entirely sure she wanted to hear his answer. This situation was reaching a bit far into her soul, and she could easily become entangled in this emotional moment.

She was also becoming intensely aware that untangling herself from her current predicament might be just a bit more difficult than simply leaping from this man's arms.

JOHN DIDN'T have a quick comeback for her question. He remembered the woman who had walked into his office those months ago. He had seen her with her husband in the parking lot, and he had liked what he had seen. Then, she had come inside, and he had become entangled with her after a fashion. No, there had been nothing romantic, and there had been no additional contact between the two of them. None. Yet, there had been an entanglement, at least on his part.

Entrancement. That had been the entanglement. He had been entranced, and then he had set it aside. Now it was back again, and he was holding entranced in his arms. Here, in this hole in the ground, he was speaking with her, and she was speaking back, and there wasn't even a parakeet flying around to distract their attention.

He had to admit, this definitely seemed like progress to him.

A BRIGHT light flashed into the excavation and illuminated the far wall. "Mom? Are you out here? The TVs on, and you're not inside." A second light flashed on, mirroring the first, as Dylan called out, "Hey, Mom's flash-light is out here. Mom?"

Karen pictured where she was, as well as who was holding her. No one could be allowed to see her down here like this. She reached her hands to the man's shoulders for purchase to try to at least stand, only to have him pull her tighter.

"My heavens," she hissed. "It's my son. Put me down. He can't see us here like this." She could feel the panic in her voice as she watched the two beams crisscross the bottom of the pool excavation, growing ever closer.

He whispered conspiratorially, "Like what? Like a man rescuing a beautiful woman from a desperate situation?"

"No," she hissed back. "Like a divorcée in the arms of a sweaty construction worker. My son will see us. You must put me down."

"Are you sure that's what you want?" The whispered words seemed to dance in the dark.

There was a quick flash of light from directly overhead that made her blink, one that seemed much brighter than those of the flashlights' beams. It was gone almost as soon as it had appeared, leaving her momentarily blinded. It increased her level of panic, and in the aftermath, she slapped his chest again. "He has the flashlight. Of course he'll see us. He may have already done so. Quick, down!"

The whispered words came again, "Are you really sure?"

Her words bit the air. "Are you deaf as well as sweaty? Now!" With a chuckle that was sharp and clear in the night air, he did just as she asked, and her limbs flailed the air. However, this time, there were no arms to soften her fall. There was only mud, and she hit the bottom just as the light roaming the pool found what it was looking for.

Dylan's voice called from eight feet overhead, "Mom? Did you see that flash? What are you doing down there? It's dark out here. I saw the movie screen down, but there wasn't anything playing yet. I came looking for you." He let the lights rove over her prone body, and then one of them caught the man standing next to her. "Mom? Who's that?"

She put her hands on the ground beside her to attempt to sit up, only to have them sink into the mud. Looking at the figure beside her, she was very aware of his mud-caked boots at her eye level. Her eyes followed his dirt-encrusted jeans to the large, shiny buckle just below his navel. Then came his flat abdomen and the chest she had just brushed her hand across. His arms hung to his side, his palms forward where he had just been holding her. She looked to see his face, but the light her son was shining into the pool hit the brim of his cowboy hat and created a dark pool of shadows where his face should be.

She called to her son, "I have no idea, Dylan. Feel free to ask him." At that moment, she watched the man drop his hands and step back.

"I can't do much more tonight. I probably should get going." The words sparkled with humor.

"Are you a thief?" The fifteen-year-old voice from above seemed excited with the possibility. "Should I call the police, Mom?"

The hat tilted upwards as Karen's companion replied to the question, "No, son. I'm not a thief. Your mother's safe down here."

She could just see his stubbled chin in the glare from the flashlight. However, the rest of his face remained shadowed. Then he turned to her.

"That *is* your son, you said. Right?"

She sighed, and it was big and dramatic. "He is, but I don't know that I'm exactly safe. I did just get dropped on my derrière, thank you very much."

He chuckled softly. "I did ask you. Twice."

"And you knew better." Her reply was very pointed. She was embarrassed at how she had fallen, but she was even

43

more embarrassed at her son having found them, as if she had been caught doing something very sensual and very wrong. This whole situation reminded her of when she was fifteen. At a high school football game, she had sneaked under the bleachers with one of the "cool" jocks. In retrospect, he had been a member of the football team who had been kicked off for failure to perform in the game. That night, he'd decided he had to prove himself, and since he couldn't manage it on the field, he'd give it a shot under the bleachers. She liked to think she hadn't known what he wanted, and perhaps she hadn't really, but she hadn't resisted much, either.

Thank goodness her big brother Eddy had come looking for her during halftime. If he'd waited much longer, she might have been in Lissie's position. As it was, she'd been mortified to have her brother pulling that jock off her, and she'd felt even worse when she'd had to tell her father why the police had picked up Eddy for fighting under the bleachers. It eventually became a point of pride that her older brother had stuck up for her, and after that, she'd never been approached again. However, the moment when he'd discovered what she was letting that boy do had been horrifying.

She hadn't resisted with this man, either. At least she felt that way. She had fallen on him, showered him with her presence, so to speak, and then she had let him hold her as she had enjoyed the touch of his skin. Now Dylan knew, or he almost knew. If he'd been quicker with his search, he'd have seen her in this man's arms for sure. Then everyone would have known.

Finally, in the glare of the light, she saw a hand reach out to her. An amused voice filled the darkness.

"I can at least help you up, and yes, I knew better. However, there was no way I could resist. I've been watching you skitter around me all day, and for the life of me, I cannot figure out just why. I guess maybe I'm too hot for you to handle, and you need to keep running to safety to keep cooled off."

Karen's heart throbbed. This man was playing with her. First he had pulled her to him and drawn her into the clutches of his sweaty skin and musky aroma, and then he insulted her with his saucy words. She didn't know whether to enjoy his presence, or to get angry and yell at him. However, she did want to see his face. She couldn't very well do that from the ground.

She held out her arm. "I'm muddy, but thank you. Are you sure you want to touch me?" She saw him glance up to where Dylan was still holding the light, and then he knelt to take her hand.

Leaning in close, he whispered, "Well, maybe your son shouldn't hear this, but yes, ma'am, very much indeed." Then, in the shadow cast by the brim of his rugged cowboy hat, she saw him flash her a grin with the whitest teeth she had ever seen.

She groaned and grasped the proffered hand. It didn't feel quite so alluring with a layer of mud insulating them from each other, but one thing stuck in her mind. That smile. It was just like his smooth, melodious voice. She should know it. She knew that was impossible, however, because she'd never met this man before.

Then they were standing, and Dylan's light led them to the steps. She had to watch carefully to avoid tripping, and several times, even though she cringed to know her son was watching, she was forced to grasp the man's arm to keep from taking another tumble. At least the higher they climbed, the drier the dirt was.

At the top, Dylan helped his mother, and he couldn't resist making several pointed gibes about her new, muddy fashion look. With excitement in his voice, he used the light to show her how far she had fallen.

She mumbled agreement to him, hiding her irritation when his light had intruded into the pool, finally admitting part of her annoyance had been exasperation with herself for nearly being caught in a situation that had felt distinctly compromising. After a moment she turned to thank the man who had helped her when she fell, only to realize his glasses and keys were gone.

"Dylan, that man. How did he get away so fast?"

Her son snickered. "Mom. Did you want him to stick around? He's a construction worker, if you'd bothered to notice. How'd you fall in the pool, anyway? Were you checking him out?"

She snorted her disgust. "Don't be crude. You know I don't make a practice of 'checking out' strange construction workers."

She had, though, and she had done it as she stood in the laundry room, with her son right there. She would have from Dylan's window, too, except this man had been hiding deep in the excavation, and she hadn't been able to find him. She had no idea what he'd been doing down there, either.

Waiting to catch her, she supposed. Well, if that was what he was waiting on, then he got what he wanted, plus some. That was just fine with her.

Then, before walking into the house, she froze. By all that's good in heaven, she still didn't know this man's name, and she didn't even see his face.

Ooh, she thought. If I'm going to wallow in the mud to get close to a man, I should at least find out what he looks like. That and his name would be nice, too. Stupid me. I can't chase someone if I don't know his name or what he looks like.

Dylan called from the porch, "Mom, I got mud all over my shoes. Can I use the hose to clean them?"

"Sure, I suppose so. I might need to join you."

There was a pause, then he laughed. "I'll have to squirt you all over to get you clean." The sudden anticipation in his voice was palpable.

She gave in with a sodden sense of inevitability. "You'd better get the sprayer, then. I don't have any shoes on to kick off."

The sound of his laughter caused her to turn, and she could see him already turning on the water. She might as well get ready. At least someone would have fun tonight.

JOHN STARTED his truck and chuckled. As soon as he'd gotten her to the top of the pool excavation, he had turned her over to the boy and stepped around to grab his keys, glasses, and the blueprints. Then he'd hightailed it out the gate. However, as he'd pulled his boots off to toss them in the back, he'd caught the conversation just over the fence.

Her words made him smile. Then he'd grabbed his shirt and tossed it in the seat beside him.

From an errant parakeet to the fastest window blinds in the West, he'd found being at this pool site couldn't be beat. Then, this woman had managed to rain dirt over him and come crashing down into his arms. Talk about lucky. What other man did he know who had actually had a beautiful woman fall from the sky directly into his arms? Oh, he knew a few of his friends who had prayed for that exact thing, but none had actually had their prayers answered. If he told anyone about this, they wouldn't believe him, that was for certain.

Something that had gnawed at him finally caught his attention. Several times during the day she'd called him a construction worker. He realized she hadn't yet recognized him, and didn't remember meeting with him at his office months earlier. He had to come up with a plan to remedy that.

Just then his phone rang, and he fumbled in his shirt pocket until he located the little devil. One side of it was flashing on and off, telling him to *please pick up, please pick up.* He touched the pad and held it to his ear. In a practiced series of motions, he shifted the truck into reverse, and then flipped his lights on.

"John, here." He wasn't surprised at all to hear the voice on the other end.

"Hey, good-looking. Frankie here. Are you still out at the Wycliff dig?"

He laughed. Frankie had worked for him for years. Well, Frankie had worked for his *family* for years, and he never remembered the business without her. She had this knack of trailing his movements like he was wearing a GPS transmitter all the time. He knew she could track his phone now, but she didn't need that. She could follow his movements by instinct. She was good, too.

"Yeah. We ran short on rebar yesterday, and I was figuring up quantity before I got away. Why? Are you still at the office?"

That got a laugh from her. "Friday night, son, but I know you. You haven't eaten, and neither have I. I'm out on Bee Cave Road. Meet me somewhere? I've got your credit card. I'm paying."

"I'm paying, you mean. Frankie, I'm a mess. I don't know."

She chortled at that. "You've always been a mess, John, ever since you started coming to work with your father when you were six. I like you a mess. Otherwise I'd find me another job."

In the background, he could hear George Strait on her stereo, and he smiled.

"Food, John? It'll keep you out of that dive of an apartment you insist on staying in."

"Saving money, Frankie. I want to buy a nice place someday."

"Ten years you've been saving, and as much as some people make each of those years. Tomorrow I'm taking you looking. I've got some places in mind. I've seen those brochures on your desk. Now, as far as tonight. I've found a new place just west of here. It's sort of a bar, really, but they sell these fabulous ostrich-meat burgers, too. They also play

George when I request him, and they play him loud."

"Ostrich burgers. That sounds interesting, but I'm telling you, Frankie. I'm really a mess." She couldn't imagine. After all, he'd been showered, and that didn't include the mud on his boots.

"They've got picnic tables outside. I'll go in to order. It's called the Ostrich Bar and Grill. Now, here's how you get there . . . ."

He sighed as he noted the directions. Yeah, he could find it, he told her, and after he hung up, he laughed. That woman was the mother he'd never had. She ordered him around, and he'd be suckered if he didn't let her. He loved her, too, and if she wanted to take him looking at a place tomorrow, well then, he'd just go. That didn't mean he'd sign on any dotted lines, but he'd certainly go look.

He liked to make Frankie happy now and again. Besides, he remembered those brochures, too. Maybe looking wouldn't be too bad. Maybe it wouldn't be too bad at all.

Chapter 4

KAREN WORKED her face deeper into her pillow. Although the sun had brightened her bedroom, she wasn't ready to get up.

It was Saturday.

She brushed at something in her hair. A high-pitched voice intruded into her pleasantly drowsy morning.

"Junie! Junie!"

She sat up, and in that motion, a fluttering of feathers told her just what had awakened her. As she involuntarily brushed at her face, she was somehow aware that the bird was not flying away.

"Junie! Want Junie!"

She was growing frantic. Still half asleep, she knew the bird was somehow in her hair, and she just wanted it gone. Then, the baby's voice rang out a third time.

"Mommy! Junie stuck!" A squealing giggle rang throughout the room. "Pretty Junie!"

"Mom, what are you doing with Chipper's parakeet?"

"Lissie, help?" Karen called in a sleepy mumble to the opened door, where her daughter leaned inside. The bird fluttered wildly, its wings beating at her face.

"Stop fighting. You are such a baby. I think the bird's claws are caught in your hair." Lissie barged into the room, and she plopped on the bed by her mother's side. Her hands reached towards Karen's head, and Karen involuntarily flinched.

"Quick, Lissie, before he poops."

"Mom, hold still. He just wants out." Lissie laughed at the bird's antics. "Don't you, little bird? Junie just wants out." She said those final words in baby talk, as if for Chipper's benefit, not Karen's.

Karen was finally awake enough to speak, but she wasn't awake enough to be nice. "Get him out, then. I cannot stomach this animal in my face. Your Uncle Eddy is right. We should serve this bird up in a good soup."

"Well," Lissie snorted. "I'm just trying to help. You can do it yourself if you want." She stood, shrugging one shoulder. "Come, Chipper. We'll go find someone who'll be nice to us. Saturdays aren't made for grouchy grumps. And nobody's going to eat your little birdie, not if I can help it. Junie's safe as long as I'm around."

As Chipper began to wail his frustration at being taken away from his trapped, feathered friend, Karen sighed and called out, "Lissie, I'm sorry. Please come back and help me with Junie. He'll be in my face all day if I have to get his claws untangled by myself. And for heaven's sake, Lissie, hold onto him. I want him back in his cage for once."

Her daughter laughed at that. "Don't blame me for this, Mom. You're the one who tripped over your own two feet trying to get me to shut the blinds. Just close your eyes and let me get this." She climbed on the bed with her mother, and grasping the bird gently in her hand, she began to work its claws out of her mother's hair. Turning to the baby who was trying to get on the bed with them, she whispered loudly, "No, Chipper. Stay down. You can pet Junie when I'm finished."

"Want Junie." He grinned as he continued to crawl up the bedding, slowly sliding it off the bed and into the floor.

"In a minute, Chipper. Don't distract your mother. Mimi needs her help for a moment." Karen blindly waggled her hand at the boy.

His little laugh rang out as it raced up the scale into a range no mortal adult could possibly manage. He ended with, "Chipper want Junie."

Karen chuckled at that. "You can have him, Chipper, but only for a bit. He goes in his cage this time."

With a final scramble, he was on the bed, and in moments, he was dancing up and down. "Pet Junie. Chipper pet Junie. One finger."

It was Lissie's turn to answer. "Here, Son. Mommy has him, now. One finger, though. Easy. You don't want to hurt Junie. Let me have your hand so I can help you be easy."

However, he was through being patient, and he really wanted the bird. "No! Chipper hold Junie. Eat Junie!"

"Easy, Chipper. Let Mommy help. By the way, Mom.

You can open your eyes. I'm finished."

Karen fell back to her pillow with her eyes still closed. "Thank goodness. Lissie, don't let the baby hold that bird without your help. He probably will have it for a snack this time. It has to be back in that cage today. I can't take much more."

Lissie crawled off the bed. "I'm not irresponsible, you know. I'm not the one who leaves my window open, and I've never forgotten to close the cage. Besides, Chipper wouldn't eat Junie. He just says that. He loves him too much. Hey, I've got cheerleading practice this afternoon. You have to keep Chipper. Don't be lazy and sleep in like you have the last two weeks. After all, your vacation's over, you know."

"Cheerleading practice? What for? Football ended before Christmas. What do they need cheerleaders for in the spring?" There had been a certain amount of attitude in Lissie's words, and Karen got her message just fine. She wanted her mother to do her daughter's job, as usual.

"Mom, pay attention. I told you last week. I'm a senior, or have you forgotten? Everyone in the school gets to vote on the new cheerleaders for next year. I can't cheer then, so someone has to be elected to take my place."

"That means you have to cheer now?" Lissie had always been a social butterfly, and she liked to be in every organization the school offered—every nonacademic organization—with all her friends. Karen expected as much, but cheering because someone was taking her place?

Lissie laughed. "Mom, you are so old-school. If the senior cheerleaders don't cheer first at the assembly, who'll know how high the standards are? We can't have the ninth graders vote on just anybody. The new girls will actually have to be able to cheer, you know."

"Girls? What about that junior boy who was here for your sleepover last fall?"

Lissie giggled. "Oh, you mean Kerry. Trust me, Mom. Kerry's no boy, even if he does have all the right equipment. Remember? That's why you let him stay the night."

Karen moaned. "I thought I let him stay the night because he slept in Dylan's room."

"That, too. Be glad Dylan wasn't home, otherwise you'd have two of us. Kerry's nice, but he's only safe around us girls." She took the baby's hand. "Oh, I forgot. Even if Dylan had been here, you couldn't have gotten another me. Boys are lucky. They can't get pregnant."

"Lissie!" Karen's voice was sharp, but she laughed. Sometimes her errant, edge-walking daughter was actually funny. "Don't talk about your brother that way. He's only fifteen. Besides, Dylan might chase the girls, but Wayside Christian's been good for him. They keep him on the up and up."

"Mom, I was talking about Kerry, although Dylan tries harder to get girls than you know. It's just that the girls all run away from him. Besides, I was barely fifteen when, well, you know."

"Don't remind me, and yes, I think I will padlock your brother's window."

About that time, Chipper, who had been bouncing on the bed the entire time, lunged for the bird.

"No, Chipper!" Lissie held him high in the air.

"Lissie," Karen reprimanded, "You hold onto that bird. Don't let him loose. Pick up a paper before you come home from practice, too."

The girl shot her mother a look. "I've got the bird, Mom, and remember, I'm not the one who let him get away yesterday. You need to trust me. I'm responsible." Then, she snatched up the baby and was gone out the door.

Karen whispered to herself, "Sure, and that's why we have little Chipper around." Then she took a moment to lie in the quiet of her bedroom for a time, enjoying the peaceful Saturday morning. After a moment though, she thought she heard feet scrambling on the roof. Throwing back the covers, she walked to the bank of windows that overlooked the pool and pulled back the sheers. There on the ell where Dylan's window stood tall against the sloping roof was her son, and he was running across the shingles to where the gutters dropped down the side of the porch.

He was actually amusing, she thought, and cute in that half-grown fifteen-year-old way teen boys had to endure before they became men. She knew he hated it, but it sure made her love him to look at him like this. His hair was freshly tousled from bed, and all he had on were his tee shirt and boxers. His jeans were in one hand, and his shoes were in the other. She knew that particular pair of boxers, too. Blue with white Dallas Cowboy stars all over them. They'd been on vacation when Dylan was twelve, and he'd begged his dad for them. Brad had bought him a package of three, and the boy still wore them, even though he had just about outgrown them.

However, he couldn't be allowed to escape in his underwear, no matter where he was going. She rapped sharply on the glass, and she was relieved to see him look her direction. She cranked her window open and called to him.

"Dylan, where do you think you're going in your shorts? Put those pants on. Now."

He glanced to the gutters, and then he turned back with a sense of urgency on his face. "Mom! I'm late. I can't stop to get dressed, or Zack will leave without me."

Her eyes narrowed. "Now, young man. Just because your father's not here doesn't mean you can run all over Austin in your star-studded boxers, no matter how cute you look."

"But, Mom! Zack's in the car waiting. We've got swim practice. There's a meet next weekend, and coach says we have to put in four hours at the pool today, or we sit out."

However, she intended to be firm. "Jeans, Dylan. Now. Put them on." She would tolerate her son using his second story window for a door, but she would not endure his underwear being exposed to the world. "And next time, use the front door. You stay off the roof."

"Mom!" However, he did put his shoes down and slip his jeans on, one leg at a time. He lifted up his shirt and snapped the pants at the waist, even if she could still see white stars on a blue background protruding from his fly. "Can I go now?"

"Zack's driving? I thought he was still fifteen."

"His dad, Mom. Please? We'll be late."

She had one more question to call out across the roof. "Speedos?"

"Speedos!" His eyes grew wide, and his glance flicked

toward his window. She heard the urgency in his voice as he scrambled back to his dormer. Reaching inside, he withdrew his hand holding a bright yellow bundle of cloth. He looked back to his mother and grinned. "Thanks! Come watch us practice."

He was already to the edge of the roof by the time she got her question out, "Gregory Gym at U.T.?"

He grinned and waved, "It's a natatorium, not a gym!" Then, in a flash of blue, white, and tousled hair, he was gone over the fence.

She closed her window, and she smiled. There on the roof were his shoes. She guessed he would have to do without those. However, it was better to have bare feet than a bare bottom when he was in that pool today. She was certain Zack would appreciate that. Zack's dad, too, if he went in to watch, and if she knew Zack's family at all, the man would.

She ran her eyes across the pool excavation that had destroyed her perfectly landscaped yard. There would probably be a crew here even on the weekend, and to avoid them, she thought she might take Chipper down to Town Lake. Lakeshore Park would be nice. At least with Dylan gone, nobody would be out on the roof, and the crew could have peace and quiet.

Then, she changed her mind. Town Lake, yes, but Town Lake Park would be even better than Lakeshore. It was smaller, and that would be better for the baby. They would have to park and walk under the rail bridge, but she could take the stroller for that.

Then her eyes caught the ragged edge of the excavation

that had caved in on her the evening before, and in that look, being held by that construction worker was as sharp and clear in her memory as if he were with her in her own bedroom. He had been sweaty and covered in dirt, and his cowboy hat had shadowed his face. His arms had been strong, though, and the muskiness she had inhaled underneath it all made her knees go weak even this morning.

Thank goodness that after her excursion in the yard, her son had sprayed her with the water hose to get the mud off. She had needed a distraction. With all the good-natured ridicule her son had forced on her, she had been so embarrassed that she had let that man slip from her for a time.

However, now he was back, and with a vengeance, too. All she could picture was climbing out Dylan's window to retrieve the boy's shoes and waving to that sweaty man at the bottom of her pool. *"Hey, there! I see you're back again today!"*

She threw the sheers in place, and she turned from the window. "Ooh! Everybody needs to just stay off the roof!"

"Mom? Is everything okay?" Lissie's voice was shaky, and that got Karen's attention.

"Lissie? What is it?"

The girl appeared at the door, and Chipper was in her arms. He was holding one yellow feather. Her eyes were red with frustration.

"It's Junie, Mom. He got away again. I'm sorry. Chipper grabbed at him, and when I tried to stop him, the bird just slipped away."

Karen felt the tension of the man who had been in her pool break, and she laughed, suddenly magnanimous.

"That's all right, Lissie. Where is he?"

She actually smiled. "He flew towards Dylan's room. At least he can't get outside."

Karen froze. Then, with a quickness she no longer knew she possessed, she was at the window again just in time to see a yellow bird flash from the boy's open window. She turned to her daughter with despair in her eyes.

"Mom, what?"

Karen motioned for Lissie to come to the window. Holding the sheers aside, she pointed so they both could see the flash of yellow flitting from tree to tree.

"Junie! Want Junie!"

Chipper had seen, too.

JOHN HELD a box of stuffed croissants under his arm as he pressed the button on his truck's remote. His truck door made a noise somewhere inside, and the horn beeped once. Through the window, he watched the lock pop up. Then he pulled the handle and leaned in to set the box down.

At that moment his phone rang.

He slipped it out of his back pocket and laughed to see a chicken running back and forth across the screen. Its head was cut off, and comical little splatters of blood were flying to and fro. He knew to whom that avatar belonged. He keyed it to answer.

"I have your croissants, Frankie. Do you have the coffee on?" He knew she did. He'd never been to her place near Brentwood without finding a pot ready to drink. He'd spent a lot of time up there in the past few years, too.

He liked Frankie's setup. Her house was small, the area

around it well established. Some would say the neighbor-hood was past its better days, but they couldn't say that about Frankie's house. No, she'd lived there before her hus-band died and then raised three girls alone in the only house she'd ever owned. Over the years, she'd taken landscaping bits and pieces left over from pool installations, and she'd done a bit here and a bit there. Now, she had one of the prettiest little places in all North Austin, homey, comfort-able, and easy to take care of, all on a corner lot. It was just what John was looking for, and he'd told Frankie that. *"Let's buy you a condo, Frankie. I'll move into your place."*

However, she'd just laughed and pointed out that she worked really hard to maintain her "easy-care landscaping" so that it looked like it took no time at all. She'd be glad to show him someday how much time and effort were in-volved. He might find he'd never be able to keep up, not and maintain the family business.

However, she'd assured him, he could consider it his home, too, whether she was in residence or not. There was even a key on his ring that went to her back door. She had made sure of that. The more she could get him out of that apartment he insisted staying in, the happier she was.

John swung the front of his truck around the curb and into Frankie's drive. His vehicle was tall, and with four-wheel-drive, it was easy to run over people's landscaping and not even know it. Since they were heading into town, he hoped Frankie'd want to take her car. It was small, and although to ride in it too far made him claustrophobic, she was right about it being great in traffic. She'd even let him drive it once. He'd laughed at her when she'd offered, but he hadn't laughed when he'd gotten out. It was a city car through and through, and it had been quite useful in its element.

Stepping to the back porch, he looked through the screen to see the door open. He sniffed, and the aroma of coffee filled his lungs. Frankie's was home to him, like his father's had never been.

"Frankie?" He called just once, and then he checked the screen. It was unlatched as he expected. "I'm letting myself in. Pouring coffee, too. Breakfast is on the table." He reached for the pot as he set the croissants on the counter.

"John, you better wipe the table first." Her voice filtered in from down the hall. "I was potting some flowers last night, and I think I spilled a little fertilizer. I'm drying my hair."

He chuckled. He knew Frankie, and he knew he could eat off the floor if he wanted, and without a plate, too. However, he would wipe the table. There might be an errant microbe or two to tweak their digestive systems, and he wouldn't want Frankie to ask if he'd done it, only to have to lie to her. He didn't think he could, anyway. She continually inserted opportune bits of her life at Wayside Christian Fellowship into their conversations, and he knew enough to understand her penchant for honesty. Over the years, it had rubbed off on him, too.

He pulled a paper towel from the roll, wet it in the sink, and ran it back and forth across the kitchen table. Pouring a second cup of coffee for Frankie, he carried both cups outside to the table on the patio. Stepping back inside and leaning into the hall, he called out, "I brought two ham, two egg, and one bacon. Which two do you want?"

She appeared in the hallway rubbing her hair with a towel. "You brought both egg and bacon? I do love you, John. You and George Strait both. When God made you two, he said, 'I've made all the real men the world can handle. Now I'm breaking the mold.'" She grinned in anticipation. "Give me those two—egg and bacon."

He kissed her on the forehead. "I love you, too, Frankie. That's why I brought bacon, just for you. You want to eat inside or outside?" He knew her answer, though. The coffee cups were already there.

"Outside. Get the melamine plates down, the ones with the yellow flowers. They're perfect for the yard. Those flyers behind the canisters, take those, too. I want to talk about which ones we're going to see today. I've got some nice ones lined up."

He reached to rifle the edge of the stack of flyers. "Frankie, this is a lot of condos. You wasting your printer ink on this?"

He turned and she was already gone, but her voice came back to him. "I'm wasting *your* printer ink. I did all those at work yesterday while you were out on that job. You know we pay people to dig those pools. You don't have to go out there."

"I like it. I miss being out during the process. Somehow it's not real when all I see is the landscaped yard before we dig it up, and then the finished pool afterwards. This one's gonna be challenging. I'm looking forward to being out there while this job goes forward."

She walked back in tying her hair in a loose knot at the

nape of her neck. "That's what I thought you'd say. Well, I've got the office covered. You go play in your little sand pile, and when you get your fill, come back to the grown-up world. You'll still be welcome."

He chuckled. "Thanks. I appreciate that."

Then, as she picked up a plate and chose her croissants, she led him into the yard to find their coffee steaming and waiting for them.

John watched her smile. He'd known what she'd choose all along.

Chapter 5

KAREN PULLED her Campmobile up to the Gregory Gym natatorium and put it in park. Looking behind her, she called out to Chipper, "Hey, little guy. Are you ready to go see your uncle swim? I hear he's got a mean backstroke on him."

She chuckled as she set the emergency brake. She knew Dylan loved the swimming, but she also knew he loved to show off in his Speedos. He thought he was a man already, and he didn't understand why the girls didn't see that in him.

Walking around the van, she opened the side to unbuckle the baby from his seat. This vehicle was one of the things she'd wanted that had driven Brad nuts. Maybe it was why he'd run off with that mud-sucking low-life of a secretary. He had to drive his little Jaguar, and nothing else would do. He'd been tempted by a Rolls, but when he went to drive one, he'd laughed at how boxy it was. Sleek was what he wanted.

Not Karen. She'd found this old VW on eBay, and she'd bought it without telling her husband. It'd been one just like her parents had owned when she was growing up, and she had fallen in love with it from day one. It had been rough, though, upwards of forty years old, and it had embarrassed her husband to have it in the drive. When Karen had set her foot down, he'd given in, but only on one condition. He'd sent it off, and it had come back to her better than new. Now it had an automatic and air, quite necessary for driving around in the Texas Hill Country. He'd had a larger engine put in, too, and an all-new interior. She had loved it before, and now she refused to drive anything else. At least Brad had done this one good thing for her, fixed up her little Campmobile.

In addition to her automatic transmission and air conditioning, there was something else she loved about her Campmobile. She smiled at the thought, with Chipper at her side. It was great for hauling an almost two-year-old grandson around.

"Chipper, do you want to go see Dylan swim?" She set his stroller on the ground and adjusted the straps to fasten him in.

The baby pulled his pacifier out of his mouth and cried, "Dilly swim? Go see Dilly swim?"

She smiled at him and stroked the side of his face. "Yes, Baby. See Dilly swim." Dylan hated that name, but it was the best poor little Chipper could do. Enunciation was not his strong point. "Uncle Dylan will be all wet. We can call him a soggy rat when he climbs out of the water."

"Soggy w-at? Uncle Dilly soggy w-at?" Moving towards the building, Chipper kicked his arms and legs, and seeing a yellow flower, he laughed and pointed, "Junie. See Junie. Junie soggy w-at."

Karen rubbed his head as she opened the natatorium door. "No, Baby. Uncle Dylan is the soggy rat. Let's go say hello to our little rat." Pushing fast to get past the closing door, she smiled at the echoing sounds that always came with swim meets. Dylan's "natatorium" sounded like her son.

"Mom!" The word rang loud and clear as Karen stepped inside. She watched a boy, one not quite as tall or developed as most of those inside the natatorium, as he sprang from the leisure pool in a sudden fountain of water. One hand waved from inside the flying spray as the boy's youthful legs leaped her direction. "You brought Chipper. Hi, little boy."

Dylan leaned over to pat the baby's head.

"Soggy w-at. Dilly soggy w-at." Then Chipper squealed with excitement.

At the high-pitched words, Dylan froze, and he stood immobilized, a frozen statue in his yellow Speedos, his hair plastered to his head. His chest still heaved with exhaustion from his recent practice, and his skin sparkled with moisture. To Karen he looked adorable, but dismay filled his eyes.

"Mom! Did you teach him to say that, *soggy rat?*" He glanced at the boys sitting on the steps going up one side of the natatorium, and several of them were turned his way, clearly paying attention. Near the far end were Zack and his father. "You want me to have that for a new nickname? Because of Chipper, the guys already call me Dilly Bar. Now you want me to go by Rat? Oh, that's right. Not just Rat. *Soggy* Rat." His eyes were red, too. It was clear he found the idea seriously distressing.

Then, with a change in his tone as well as in his stance, he became very serious. "Mom. Don't look. Behind you is the person I wanted you to see." When Karen began to turn anyway, he grabbed her arm. "No, Mom. Play with the baby or something. You can't turn around."

She looked at her son. "Dilly Bar, I cannot see who this is if I don't turn around. You can't have it both ways." She instinctively knew this was about a girl, and with her words, she remembered the previous evening. She had wanted it both ways. That man had grabbed her in his arms, and she had wanted him. She had also wanted no one else to know. Dylan could not be told that, though.

"Mom!" He stepped to her side and put his arm across her shoulder. "Please, Mom. Just don't look until I tell you." He glanced down as Chipper grabbed his wet leg.

"Soggy w-at, Dilly. Hold soggy w-at."

"Yes, Chipper. You're holding a soggy rat." Dylan patted his head. Then he grimaced. "Mom, you even have me saying it. I bet I'm labeled Soggy Rat when the yearbook comes out."

His mom put her arm around his waist. "I like soggy rats, Son. Who do you want me to see? Can I even peek? What's her name?"

His face brightened. "That's why I hoped you'd come today. The girl's team is practicing right after the boys, and there's this new member they had join several weeks ago." When he saw his mother start to turn her head, he tightened his arm around her neck. "You can't look, yet. She'll know I'm talking about her. Besides, her dad's with her. He always comes to all the practices."

Karen took a deep breath. "Can I at least kneel down and take Chipper out of the stroller?"

"Sure, you can. Don't be silly. Chipper already knows you're here. He came with you, so he expects you to know him."

When she knelt, Dylan squatted beside her. Once she began unbuckling the straps, Chipper put his arms up and yelled loudly, echoing his words all over the natatorium.

"Dilly! Hold me, Dilly!"

Dylan took him in his arms and pointed to an empty seat with his head. "There, Mom. Let's sit. Act natural."

"I thought I was. You're the one running around in a Speedo that reveals more of your level of maturity than if you were wearing your underwear."

He made a face at her. "Mom, these are swim trunks. Competition rules say we have to wear them. They always fit like this. Now about that girl—" There was a grin on his face. "They show I'm grown up, huh?"

That wasn't exactly what she'd meant. "Does she have a name?"

"Of course, Mom. Don't be ridiculous. Everyone's got a name."

"Okay. What is it? I can't call her *that girl* all day."

He looked pained. "Mom, that's where you come in. You know Dad's been gone three months—"

She held up her hand. "Stop right there. I don't know where this is going, but I can already see my day headed downhill—"

His voice interrupted her. "Mom! Grow up. I was there last night, and you were down in the pool with that man. I'm a big boy. I like girls and all that. I know all about the birds and the bees." He grinned at her impishly before continuing. "Anyway—"

"Dylan!" Her voice was suddenly stern. "You'd better not know too much about the birds and the bees. Lissie already found out enough for both of you together."

He snickered. "You could've gotten Kerry for a son. You know, Lissie's cheerleader friend. He keeps asking to come stay the night with me. I could always invite him over, you know." He grinned mischievously and began to play with Chipper's ear.

The baby laughed and grabbed at his uncle's hand.

"Yeah, right. He can come spend the night. You'll be at Uncle Eddy's that night, too. I've heard about that Kerry." Karen slapped his leg.

Dylan laughed. "He's not so bad. Everybody at school likes him. A lot. He wants me to be his friend. His real friend. Lissie says so. She says that's why he came to the sleepover."

Karen's eyes narrowed as she looked at him. She knew what he was doing, and she could get back at him. "If you like Kerry so much, my charming Dilly Bar, then you won't mind me looking right at that girl I'm not supposed to see.

After all, anyone who likes Kerry won't be interested in dating her."

"Mom!" He grabbed her arm, this time blurting everything out. "See, her dad isn't married. Her mom died or something, only it was like a really long time ago. Anyway, after last night, I figure you're over Dad and ready to move on."

She chortled. "You want me to date the father of a girl you don't even know?" Chipper was reaching for her, and she pulled him into her lap. She winked at his little face, and it lit up in a smile. She looked at her son to see his expression of anticipation had melted into disappointment. "What, Dylan?"

"Well, Mom, I thought that if you did date him, then I could get to know her. Then if you married him, I'd have a built-in girlfriend. She'd even live in our house with us." His face brightened at that idea.

She prodded him with a pointed barb. "What happened to Kerry? What if he falls in love with this girl? Then he'd be over our house all the time, too."

"Mom!" The exasperation was evident in his voice. "Kerry can't fall in love with my girl. He's already in love with me."

Karen looked at her son with raised eyebrows. "And, my precious soggy rat, how do you know that?" His face flushed, and then he looked up with relief as his coach called his name in a gruff, no nonsense voice.

"Dilly Bar, quit lollygagging and get over here. You're up for laps. You want to compete or sit out at the tournament?"

"Sorry, Mom. Can't answer now." He got up to run to the other side of the room, talking the steps down the bleachers two at a time.

Karen wasn't finished, though, and she called to him, rather more loudly than she intended. "Dylan, how do you know Kerry's in love with you?" The sound echoed throughout the water-filled natatorium, and the entire room froze. All eyes were on Dylan as he turned to his mom.

"Gosh, Mom! Why'd you have to tell the entire team Kerry's in love with me? That's worse than Dilly Bar."

Just then a high-pitched voice piped up, "Dilly soggy w-at! Dilly soggy w-at!"

"YOU DON'T worry about moving your truck out of my way, John. I can maneuver my little car out just fine." Frankie winked at him. "See that nice wide sidewalk across the front of the house? When you drive a very small car, it also makes a very nice driveway."

He laughed. "And I thought this was all just for the sake of pretty. Now I know the real story. I've got a secretary who's all practical and useful inside that warm and fuzzy exterior."

She raised one finger and waggled it at him. "And that's exactly why you're still in business after all these years. I keep your finances in line. You'd better be glad, boy."

"You have no idea. Can I stand outside and spot you?"

"Spot me? Does that mean to stand around to see whether I'm going to hit that pretty truck you love so much? Only if you want to insult me. Make sure you have those brochures your printer so nicely printed for me, and then get in the car. We'll visit the one on the top of the stack first."

Sure, he thought. They could visit the one on top. However, in spite of what he'd thought last night about not being interested, he now had an outside motivation for agreeing to look at these today. He'd never been able to decide just what he was looking for in a place of his own, but there was something in what Karen Wycliff had said to him. *"Your glass-walled loft."* That was a silly way to establish criteria for purchasing something that could easily set him back well over half a million, but something in the way she'd said it appealed to him, as if he'd have her approval, and as if that mattered.

He climbed in the car and closed the door. He shuffled through the top few sheets. In the pictures, the first one was a box in a tall building, but the second caught his attention, and he drew it out. There was lots of glass. When Frankie cleared her throat and tapped the stack, he slipped the sheet back behind the first. He'd barely caught the name. Bridges . . . *Something* over on Lee Barton Drive. In one of the pictures, it looked like it fronted a park. Trees. Grass. A place to get outside whenever he wanted.

He knew Lee Barton well, at least where it intersected Riverside near South Lamar, but he didn't recall this set of condos. He'd been to Town Lake Park numerous times growing up in and around Austin. He'd always liked the feel of the people who frequented it, so maybe he'd get lucky and find it was nearby.

He glanced at Frankie as she twisted her head this way and that, making sure she turned the car around without damaging anything with her bumpers or her tires. He rubbed the side of his nose, slightly embarrassed. His reasons for wanting a glass-walled loft were wrapped around Karen Wycliff, and for no other reason. However, it was more than just her references that had gotten his attention. It was a leather coat and hand-tooled boots, and it was relief at hearing she was no longer encumbered by a man who had seemed to treat her callously. It was a caring person who couldn't whistle for a small bird, yet still gave it her best attempt anyway, just because it was important to a small child. It was a woman who had fallen in his arms in the dark of night, one who hadn't been in a hurry to get away, and yet had panicked when she thought her son might see them.

He also remembered the way she had brushed the dirt from his chest. He sighed aloud, and Frankie chuckled. She glanced at him, and he forced his thoughts away from Karen.

"Okay, woman. I admit it. You are really good in this car. I feared for my truck there at one point, yet you were stupendous." He made a face as she pulled to the edge of the yard and then dropped off the curb. The car jerked suddenly and sharply. "Ouch, I take it all back."

"You are a piece of glass, John." She reached over and tapped him on the head. "You assume just because you think something in your noggin, none of it comes out on your face. Well, I know you, and I can see through you. Who is she?"

He frowned. "Who is who?"

"Twenty-five years I've watched that face, and I've loved it the whole time. I remember your first girlfriend and how she broke your heart. You cried, John, even though you told everyone you didn't. I saw the tears, though. I'm watching you now, and I know you're doing this today because of a girl. Is she the one from last night?"

He chuckled and looked out the window, not wanting Frankie to see she'd just hit a home run. "You see love in the air everywhere you look. You are a helpless romantic. All I'm doing today is looking at a condo, and at your insistence, I'll remind you."

As she stopped at a light, she reached a hand to his collar and pulled it away to expose his collarbone. She wrapped her hand around his neck and rubbed the skin with her thumb.

"Hmm. Flushed skin. Goose pimples. Won't look at me. Feels like love if anyone cares to ask." She smiled gleefully. "I know you, John, and don't you try to hide from me. You want to claim you're just looking today because I asked, then I'll let you tell that lie. However, you and I both know the truth."

He pulled the top flyer off the stack. "Davis Street. You like this one, Frankie? It's got a terrace, and it's on the north shore of Town Lake. A river, actually, it looks like in this picture. How creative! It's even called The Shore." He looked at her with a bright grin on his face. "This might be the one."

He knew, though, that it wasn't the one with the glass walls. That was the second one in the stack, and it was on the south shore of the lake, right across from a park. He glanced idly at the paperwork and noted that the name of the park was actually listed halfway down the page. Town Lake Park. Perfect. He looked up as the light turned green.

Pleased, he grinned.

Frankie lifted her head and looked out at the Austin traffic already filling the streets as the morning started to warm. She sighed and spoke softly, but she also made sure the man next to her could hear her plainly.

"Gonna be hot today. Hot, hot, hot. Some pretty woman's gonna wish she had her pool finished, and I know just who she is. Hot, hot, hot."

John barked out a laugh, and he slouched down in his seat. He did love Frankie, and she knew it. He was just glad she loved him back. She could be a tough old cookie, even if she was all mush once you got inside.

"Let's go shopping, Frankie. I just might buy me a condo today."

She looked ahead as she changed lanes. "Sure, boy. I still say it's gonna be hot, hot, hot, even if you're not telling me who she is."

John didn't plan to, either. Frankie would have to ferret that out on her own. The thing was, he was pretty sure she already had.

Chapter 6

"I LIKE this," Frankie said. "You would enjoy having some outdoor space, and this terrace has a good view of the river. Unobstructed, they call it. What do you think, John?"

He wanted glass walls everyone could see in and where he could see everyone outside. Then, when he had a party, everyone could see the goings on. He had to chuckle at that idea. He'd never thrown a party in his life.

Yet, he had to agree with Frankie. The terrace was nice, but he would have to keep it swept. He'd use it probably two months of the year. April. October. Winter would be too cold, and summer would be too hot. Besides, the terrace walls blocked the view of the river. He wanted glass walls with unimpeded views.

Then there was Town Lake Park. He wanted that park. Why, he wasn't sure. Green, he guessed. Trees. Anyway, he would probably go to a park more often than he would go out on a balcony. He just couldn't let Frankie know why he wanted glass walls, even if she acted like she already did.

She gently took his arm and pulled him back into the condo's air-conditioned space. The realtor looked up at the sound of the door opening, and he began very smoothly, "There is over twelve hundred feet of space here, all built of the very finest of materials. Although the building is three years old, this unit has never been lived in. The price is two hundred thousand under the initial pre-construction price. You won't find better quality anywhere." He smiled at Frankie and John. "Would the two of you care to write up an offer?"

Frankie laughed. "I would not. However, the boy here just might if you continue to sweet talk him."

The realtor turned his full attention to John. "Sir, you do realize your condo fees cover all outside maintenance as well as insurance on the building itself? When you factor in the lower utility costs in a place such as this, the monthly outlay no longer seems prohibitive. Having the second bed-room for your mother would be quite convenient, I'm sure."

John winked at Frankie. "I would think so. She does love working in her yard, though. I doubt I could get her to use it very often."

The realtor had his comeback ready. "It is always wise to be prepared. Life circumstances can change unexpect-edly."

Walking back to the windows, John looked at the view. He pointed across the river. "The south shore. You have a building there by a park. Town Lake Park, I believe. Is there something at that location I can see?"

"Bridges? On the Park? Yes, I have units there we can see. I think that's one of the developments already on my list today. Units there are actually a bit larger than this. If you are interested in parks, though, Lakeshore Park farther east might be a better bet. Town Lake Park is comparatively much smaller. I may have something quite near Lakeshore if you would like me to check."

John really didn't like the looking part of buying a condo all that much, though. Buildings were buildings to him. An extra piece of crown molding or a different color of granite didn't make much difference in his mind. Being able to see outside did, and he wanted glass walls.

He also remembered what Karen had said to him, as if she had somehow seen it in him, predicted it in the man who held her in his arms. *"In your glass-walled loft."* She had seen him there, and he almost felt that if he looked at a loft with glass walls, then maybe the tenuous connection that had snagged them the previous night could somehow be made more solid. Later he would return to her pool site, and he imagined telling her that yes, he had looked out of his glass-walled loft, but there had been no girlfriends. All he could see was Town Lake Park, and would she like to walk there with him sometime?

He caught Frankie's eyes, and she tapped her fingertips against themselves. As she did, a sizzling sound came from her lips. He grinned at her subtle reminder.

"Hot, hot, hot."

He began to smile. He calculated the years in his head, and Karen could easily be his age, thirty-one, nearly thirty-two. Sure, even with a thirteen-year-old son and the Chipper kiddo with the bird. John wouldn't really mind children. He was sure he could do that, raise two kids. He might need three bedrooms, though. Maybe there would be one at Bridges on the Park. He'd have to look and see.

The realtor spoke up, "Sir? Ma'am? If you'll let me lock up here, we can head over to Bridges."

"Frankie?" John help out his arm.

"Yes, Son." She winked.

"Time's a wasting." He smiled as he led her out the door.

THE CAMPMOBILE purred to life.

Karen loved her son, but she was a little put out by him. That she should date a strange man just so her fifteen-year-old could have a built-in girlfriend?

Then this romance thing with the male cheerleader. She was pretty sure there was nothing to that, but if Wayside Christian would hold a prayer vigil for her just for being in the pool with that construction worker, what would they do if they even thought Dylan might be in a tryst with a male cheerleader?

"Cookie?" Chipper's voice called to her from the back of the van. "Chipper want cookie?"

"In a bit, Chipper. Let me get to the park. I'll give you a cookie when we can be outside." Karen looked in the mirror at the baby strapped in his seat behind her.

Then, more brusquely, she mumbled another list of reasons for heading to the park as quickly as possible. "We won't meet any sweaty construction workers there, either.

No muscular men without their shirts hiding in deep holes in the dark. There'll be no smooth-talking Romeos who tell me they'd like to touch me. No, Chipper. We won't see any of that. All we'll see are mommies and babies and jogger nuts. That's what I want to see at the park."

When she turned and drove down Riverside, she was very pleased to see her predictions were true to form. There were joggers and lots of mommies with strollers. However, there was something she did not see, and that was an empty parking place just west of the railroad bridge.

"We've got a problem, Chipper." Her words over the back of her seat were bright, but the situation was also very frustrating. Riverside could be very busy, and parking elsewhere could easily mean a very long walk. She didn't mind. However, walking while pushing a baby stroller could be another thing entirely.

"Prah-lem. Mimi prah-lem." The childish words rang out in the baby's high-pitched vocals, and Karen looked in her mirror to see him happily swinging his legs as he pulled his pacifier out of his mouth and repeatedly slipped it back inside. "Prah-lem, Mimi."

Talking more to herself than to the baby, she answered in a monologue. "Yeah, Chipper. Mimi has no place to park. I'll circle the block and see what's available. You just sit back there and play with your paci, and I'll find us a place to leave Mimi's van. Then we'll walk to the park." Seeing a familiar turnoff, she slowed. "Yes, we'll turn right here at this street. Now if I'm right, this should be Lee Barton Drive." She flipped on her blinker, and as she pulled up to turn, she hooted and slapped the steering wheel with the palm of her hand. "I'm good! I know my streets. Good heavens, though, Chipper! Look at these glassed-in condos. They must be brand new."

"Con-oes," his voice sang as he picked up small pieces of her conversation. "Con-oes, Mimi. Gwass con-oes."

She called to him, "That's right, Chipper. Glass condos. Lofts, maybe? They look like they could be." Then, as she pulled onto Lee Barton, she looked up at the building's shimmering glass façade and caught the name. "You know, Chipper, I bet that pool man from last night could live here. Bridges on the Park. I think I remember being by here when this was under construction."

Then she laughed as she remembered the rest of her imagined story from the day before, the supposed parties filled with girls. She chuckled, talking to herself more than to her grandson, murmuring, "So, my pool man lives in Bridges on the Park. Let's think why he'd want to live here. He'd want to be able to see the park from his glass-walled loft, and he'd hope for a beautiful woman to be out walking her dog. Then because he's right here, he'd be able to swoop down at a moment's notice and catch her in his arms. At night, people would be able to see in his loft. How else could they tell he was throwing a party for sexy twenty-somethings? He could stand in the window and motion for them to come on up." Louder, she called, "So, Chipper, which unit does he own?"

"Oonit? Own oonit?"

"That's right, Chipper. Which unit does he own?" She pulled into the parking lot, even though she couldn't leave her van there. She turned to look across Riverside at the view of the park, and she tried to imagine that sweaty construction worker from her pool living here. Somehow it just didn't fit. These units looked very polished and horrifically expensive. How much could a construction worker make, anyway? Surely not enough to afford this.

Sighing, she backed up and began to pull out of the lot. Then, just across Lee Barton, the backup lights on a sports car flicked on.

"Chipper, we're saved!" She laughed.

"Save? Save?"

"Yes, Baby. As long as I can parallel park, Town Lake is right there." She did not like to parallel park, though. Brad had offered to get her a Lexus that would do that for her automatically, and just a bit at times like this, she wished she had taken him up on that offer. Still, she could do this, even if she knew it would take much gear-changing, braking, and head turning.

Finally in, she put on her emergency brake and unfastened her seatbelt. Turning, she called, "Chipper? Are you ready to go to the park?"

He began to bounce. "See Junie. Junie in park."

She laughed. "Maybe not. Grass is in the park. Trees are in the park. Shade will be in the park." She looked forward to that, too. Spring in Texas was not like spring up north. Spring in Texas meant biting sunshine, wearing shorts, and lots of shade. Oh, and air conditioning. Lots and lots of air conditioning. "Let's go, pumpkin." She reached and opened her door.

"Umpkin! Et's go, umpkin!"

"That's right. Let's go, pumpkin."

Karen loved her grandson, even if she wished she could have waited another ten years for this particular blessing. However, love came to a person when God chose to send it, and she had been forced to learn that with Lissie and Chipper. Even if he had been unexpected, love was still there, and that was all that counted.

FRANKIE'S SMALL car followed the realtor's as the man's SUV crossed Town Lake and turned on Riverside. The realtor had offered to let them ride with him, but Frankie hadn't wanted to leave her car behind. Also, John had privately told her that he was along to look, not to carry on animated conversations with realtors he didn't even know.

"A park, John." Frankie pointed to a green space that had lots of people walking kids, dogs, and strollers. "We might find you a woman there."

He chuckled. "A man, Frankie. You find you a man in that park, and I'll let you have the condo. I'll move into your place."

She grinned. "You will not. I've raised three daughters there. They wouldn't be able to find me for Sunday dinners if I lived in a fancy place like this. Besides, I'm in a neighborhood of old people like me. How are you going to fall in love if you live there? I just can't see you with an older woman."

He leaned his shoulder against the window, and he put one hand on the dash. The other he put on the back of Frankie's seat. He looked at her and grinned as he shook his head.

She tapped him on the knee with her hand. "What are you looking at me for?"

"I see me with you. Besides, I might be standing and minding my own business someday, and a beautiful woman might fall right into my arms. How about those potatoes?" When she glanced at him, he chuckled.

"Potatoes? I thought we were talking about you falling in love."

"Frankie, I am in love." She looked at him with raised eyebrows, and he just grinned. He was remembering a beautiful woman who *had* fallen into his arms. As impossible as he knew it was, it had happened to him. He even knew where she lived and that she might be available. She had snagged his emotions, and he was hooked. He wasn't about to say that, though.

"With who?" She glanced at him skeptically.

"With you. If anyone else wants me, well, I don't guess anyone is waiting around to fall into my arms." *Like last night.* "Until then, I'm single for as long as necessary. After all, what would you do without me for company? Your house would get mighty lonely with you there all by yourself."

She snorted. "I've got daughters."

He grinned and looked out at the park as she slowed for the turn into Bridges on the Park. "None of them live in Austin, though."

Through pursed lips, she retorted, "Pflugerville's Austin. Almost Austin, anyway."

He chuckled as she turned onto Lee Barton. "San Antonio's not. Neither is Marble Falls. I come visit during the week. You love that, and you know it." He ran the backs of his fingers down her cheek. "Tell me you love me, Frankie. I need to hear it, or I cannot bear another minute of life."

She slapped his hand away. "I don't have to say it for you to know it. Besides, with the boring life you lead, I'm not surprised to hear you can't bear another minute of it. That's why you need a woman." She put the car in park. "We're here. Get out, John." She stared straight ahead and refused to look at him.

"Coming in?"

"In a minute. Get out. The realtor is waiting. I want to move the car." After he did, she sat for a moment before switching the vehicle to the street. Finally, parked and grabbing the door latch, she whispered her next words, the ones she hadn't said while he was in the car. "I do love you, John, and that's why I'm willing to give you up."

Then, she opened the door, but she brushed her hands along her face before she turned to face the two men waiting on her. Her fingertips came away wet, but when she walked to the building, she had a smile on her face.

"GLASS WALLS!" John was very pleased. He could even see the park and Town Lake beyond that. He turned as Frankie walked in, and he called her over to the window. Pointing to the street, he laughed, "There's a Campmobile down there. You parked right next to it. I want to buy me one of those."

"Buy one? You'd better drive one, first. You might not like it." She stepped up to look at the reddish colored van.

"You might have a key to my house, but not even you know everything about me. I know Campmobiles."

He grinned as he winked at her. "Go on vacation with me, then. Did you know there's a place in Atlanta that rents them for people to camp in? They buy old ones and refit them. I saw it in a magazine. That one down there looks brand new, though."

"Pretty much," she said. "There's a baby seat in it, too. They probably live in this building, and that van is too tall to fit in the parking garage." She turned from the window and looked at him knowingly. "Believe me, John. Drive one first. I know Campmobiles."

The realtor stepped up to look out the window. "I'm fairly certain the owner of that van doesn't live in this building. No parking sticker on the windshield, see? Mostly adults live in this complex, so don't worry that you'll be bothered by children." He turned away from the window. "In fact, the parking garage offers plenty of headroom for anything except a raised-top van, that and over-sized four-wheel drive trucks. You don't drive one of those by any chance?"

John chuckled and took a deep breath. "Not today. As long as my *mother's* tiny car can go in and out, we will have no problem touring the parking garage."

"In any case, there is limited outside parking available on a first come, first served basis." The realtor smiled, changing tactics. "Would you care to see the pool area?"

"Did I install it?" John looked at Frankie and smirked. When the realtor gave him a puzzled look, he just waved his hand at him. "Never mind. No, thank you. I see them all day long."

Tapping the window, Frankie called to John. "Your Campmobile is leaving. Some woman with a stroller is unloading her baby inside. Admire it now or forever hold your peace."

He stepped to the glass, hoping to watch it drive away. Then, as he looked, the woman stood with the baby in her arms. In that moment, his heart caught, and the tenuous bond that had hooked him while he was down in the Wycliff pool the evening before snapped tight. He had come to this condo only because Karen had seen him behind walls of glass. Now, mysteriously, just below, she was here.

It was kismet.

Without thinking, he rapped the glass sharply several times in a row. His heart began to race. She could not simply get in that van and drive away. She must look up and see him. This was exactly how she had described him, looking out of his glass-walled condo. She had to see that he was really here. This was a chance that might never come again.

"Sir," the realtor chuckled, misunderstanding his actions. "The glass has a very high tensile strength. You can trust it not to break."

However, John had seen Karen look up, and she was even more beautiful today than she had been that night she had gotten out of her husband's low-slung sports car. She searched up and down the building, as if trying to place the noise, then shrugging, she turned to open the van door. John rapidly knocked again, this time much harder.

"Sir, even high-strength windows will break. Do be careful." The realtor was not chuckling the second time.

"Sure, sure," he replied with a smile. "I understand." This time Karen had found the window, and her eyes paused a moment before she raised her hand to wave. Then, she flashed him a smile and turned to place her child inside the van. With movements he couldn't have planned if he'd wanted, John turned and vaulted toward the door, stumbling over his feet as he did so.

"John," Frankie called. "My car is fine."

At the door, he stopped and grabbed the frame before disappearing. "It's not that, Frankie. It's *her*." Then he laughed and was gone.

Chapter 7

"DID CHIPPER get a boo-boo?" Karen kissed her finger and touched it to the boy's knee. She knew Lissie would probably complain. Her daughter hated that baby word, but boo-boos were what toddlers got, and Karen didn't plan to let Lissie's misguided compunctions stress her out. After the kiss, it seemed Chipper was okay with his boo-boo, proving Karen right.

"Mimi kissed. Owie gone." He reached to pull a flower from one of the park's flowerbeds.

"Owie gone," Karen repeated, pulling his hand away, and hoping to move to a shadier location. The sun had shifted, and it was too warm where she was. She glanced at the empty stroller. "Chipper, let's go for a walk, then we can get another cookie."

"Cookie?" His head shot up as he looked for one nearby.

"At the bakery. We have to go to the van, first."

He made a face, and then he stood. "Owie, Mimi."

"It's not bleeding anymore. Remember, Mimi kissed your owie."

"New owie, Mimi." The boy pulled at his diaper, and the smell hit her.

"Oh, Chipper. We have to take care of that." She would prefer to go to the van to change him, but she also didn't want to risk mussing the stroller fabric. That meant it would have to be done here.

Pulling a diaper and changing blanket from the stroller, she deftly whipped him down on the ground and removed the offending package. With practiced hands, she did her one-two-three, and the deed was accomplished. However, it had taken her enthusiasm for the park away. Even her pool crew would be preferable to this.

Pulling his shorts back on, she looked him in the eyes. "Chipper, let's go see if Mommy's back from practice. Home, Chipper."

He squealed, and his face lit up. "Home. Junie. Chipper want Junie. Eat Junie!"

She smiled. "Into your stroller, then. Up, Chipper." Buckles flew into each other, and soon they were back at the van.

The knocking from the glass-walled building as she was putting Chipper inside the van surprised her. It was sharp and brittle, and she looked around to see who it was intended for. There was no one else, and except for one very small car right next to hers, the vehicles seemed to be the same ones that had been there when she arrived.

As she turned back to her car, the knocking came again, and louder. Her eyes searched, and she finally located a man standing in one of the windows. She was confused at first, and then she realized he was probably admiring her restored VW. She waved, and as an afterthought, she flashed him a smile, even though she really couldn't see him well through the tinted glass. He was inside the building, though, and she was safely here on the ground. It didn't hurt her to be friendly.

Then, as she pulled from the parking spot, there was a loud noise from the back of her Campmobile.

"Chipper," she called out, horrified, stomping the brakes. "Surely I missed that tiny car." She was a very good driver, even in traffic. "Oh, I hope I haven't done any damage to the Campmobile."

Looking in her mirror, she caught a glimpse of a man in the street just at the back of the van. He called to her, his words muffled by the glass in the van. His chin and the shape of his shoulders felt familiar, and unexpected butter-flies opened tiny wings in Karen's stomach. She replied for him to wait a moment before she realized he hadn't heard her. Chipper let out a hungry wail at just that time, and she turned and snapped her fingers to distract him. Glancing behind her, she was puzzled. She was nowhere near the cars parked around her. She couldn't have hit anything.

As she reached to roll her window down, another car coming down Lee Barton appeared out of nowhere and honked at her. Startled, she hit the gas hard, her too-big engine squealing the tires, and she took off, leaving the man standing in the street.

When she managed to make it around the block, he was gone, and she had no idea who he was.

FRANKIE'S CHEST was tight, her expectations pressuring her to watch out the window. She had heard John's words, and she had seen the excitement on his face. *Her.* The woman he'd fallen for. She stepped to the glass, watching the van. There was a baby in that van, and thinking of John changing a baby's diaper amused her, in spite of her anticipation. She'd done that for three daughters, and John was better digging in other types of dirt, the natural earthy kind.

"Hot, hot, hot," she murmured to herself. "Are you sure, John?"

"Ma'am?" the realtor questioned.

She just waved him away. She wanted to watch the story unfolding outside.

The van's backup lights came on, and as it began to work its way out of the parking space, Frankie was reminded of her husband. He'd driven a Campmobile years ago, a yellow one she still treasured, and he'd never been able to see what was behind him, nearly backing over her one time. She had refused to back it up, ever.

She smiled, tears coming into her eyes, when she saw John burst into the parking lot and run across the street. He had a bright expression on his face, and before the old van could get away, he slapped his hand on the side. As the woman inside began to roll her window down, another car whipped down the street and honked. Without warning, the

Campmobile squealed its tires and was gone.

That was something Frankie never remembered her husband's van doing. It couldn't have, not with its tiny VW engine.

What brought real tears to her eyes was when John returned to the condo. There was no life left in him, and he told Frankie and the realtor he was ready to go. He didn't even walk through the rest of the unit.

The event made for a very quiet drive home, and he wouldn't talk at all. Frankie believed him, then. This was the woman he was attracted to. Nothing else would have torn him open wide like this, nothing else at all.

"THAT WAS strange, Chipper. I wonder what that man wanted?" Karen looked again in the mirror to see what the baby was doing. She could see his head rolling to one side, and she knew he was already falling asleep. She really should call to him to keep him awake, but there was something else going on inside her heart right then, or perhaps something going on with those butterflies she thought she felt a few minutes earlier, and the peace and quiet of a sleeping baby would be nice.

A yellow car pulled past her, flashing its lights, and she was reminded of Junie. For no reason, she tried to whistle the song the man had used to help her capture the small bird the day before. It came out dull and flat, even though the sound was fresh and crisp in Karen's memory.

She muttered, "I can't stay married, and I can't whistle. I can't even pull out of a parking space without nearly getting run over. Chipper, you need another grandmother, one who's good at something." She glanced in the mirror, only to see his eyes closed and drool already running down his chin.

She tried to imagine why she felt so disquieted. She had been to the park numerous times, even walked down the sidewalk next to that building on occasion. She certainly knew no one who lived there. Yet, someone had clearly wanted her attention . . . *a man* had wanted her attention.

Then she laughed. Now, that was silly. How could she know a man she happened to meet on the street? He was probably a panhandler or a con artist. She didn't need any of either, and that was that. She already had that man in her pool, and she knew she didn't *really* have him, even if he had felt strong and smelled good to boot.

She sighed and pushed her hair back from her forehead. Sometimes she wished *life* would give her a break. Enough was enough already.

However, the drive home with the baby asleep was restful, and it gave her time to think. The only thing was, the image in her mirror kept returning to her over and over, as if she should be able to place why he had seemed so familiar. She never could, though, and that bothered her. It bothered her a lot.

"MOM, I'M home." Lissie's voice filtered through the empty house. "Here's the paper. And I caught Junie."

She threw her cheerleading bag in a chair and walked up to Junie's cage. She didn't know why her mother had so much trouble getting the bird to come to her when he was outside. All Lissie had to do was whistle.

"Good Junie. Stay in your cage, boy. Else you'll be lunch, if Mom finds you out again." She poked a seed covered chew stick inside and grabbed the paper. Someone at practice had said there was a story on the cheerleading squad. If so, she hoped her senior squad photo would be there. That would be so cool.

Pulling an orange soda from the fridge, she plopped down at the kitchen table. It frustrated her that her mom never realized how busy life was for a high school senior. She couldn't be a *parent* all the time and do school things, too. After all, Chipper was her mother's *grandchild,* and grandmothers were supposed to babysit their grandchildren.

Laying the paper flat, her eyes flicked over the headlines as she looked for the index. At the top was the big news story, and the headline read, *New Police Copter Takes Suspicious Photos.* There were several pictures underneath it, and one of them showed two people in a muddy hole. They were lit by a flashlight held by a boy, and underneath it was a caption: *Suspicious Rendezvous. Should We Feel Safe or Scared?* It was trailed with the following blurb: *This photograph at an undisclosed location was taken with the force's new night-capable, minimal-flash RealImage camera. Is this you?*

Lissie laughed before looking down the page to find the index. She whispered to herself, "So, two people hide in the mud. They're probably just making out. That's funny." Then, seeing Local Events in the index, she flipped to Section D and scanned down the headlines.

Her squeal split the air. "That's us! Oh, my goodness!

My picture's in the paper! I've got to call all my friends!"
Jumping up, she began to dance with Section D in her hand.
When the rest of the paper was knocked to the floor, she
grabbed it and tossed it back to the table, before running upstairs with her section to cut her picture out for her scrapbook wall.

She didn't even notice that she'd knocked the birdcage
door open.

Back on the table was that picture on the front page, one
of the people wearing a cowboy hat, and the other person
looking suspiciously like a thirty-eight-year-old divorcée.
The place they were standing looked very much like a
backyard pool under construction.

What were the odds of that?

KAREN PUSHED the button to open the garage door, and
she was relieved to pull inside. Chipper had been asleep for
a while, but his bodily systems certainly had not. The odor
of gas filled the inside of the van, and she suspected there
were solids in his diaper, also.

Then, in the rearview mirror, she saw Zack's father pull
up, and her son crawled out of the back window feet first
wearing nothing except his Speedos. She watched as his
shirt and pants were flipped to him one item at a time, and
he balled them up to toss them through the basketball hoop.
The final item was blue with white stars, and Karen covered
her eyes. After a moment, the door to her van opened, and
a fifteen-year-old voice let her know just how bad Chipper
really smelled.

"Mom! Did you feed him onions? It smells awful in

here. Are you sure we can ride in this to church tomorrow?" He climbed in anyway. "It is the baby, right? This smells so bad."

Karen looked in the mirror to see him grinning. However, the smell was no teasing matter.

"Yes, sir, and you get to take him in. I'm exhausted. Be careful. He might leak. Is your sister home?"

He looked at her as if she were a dinosaur. "Mom, don't you pay attention? I just got here when you did. How would I know if Lissie's home? Besides, even if she is, she isn't. She's an airhead. That's why she goes to airhead practice."

With a sigh, she grabbed her purse. "She was at cheerleader practice, for your information."

He grinned broadly at that. "Like I said, airhead practice." Then, with the quick motions of a boy of fifteen, he snapped the baby loose and was out of the van. "I'll see if she's here. If so, she can change him." He cackled laughter all the way into the house, leaving the door into the kitchen standing wide open.

Karen sat for a moment in the silence and was glad the air in the van had begun to clear. The smell had grown gradually, and she hadn't been truly aware of just how bad it had gotten. There were other things that had preoccupied her on the drive home, like the events of yesterday. Now, everything reminded her of that construction worker, from the yellow car that had passed her to that man she'd nearly backed into at the park.

Then, in a flash she remembered where she had seen that chin and those shoulders. Her pool. Her face felt suddenly warm. Surely it was not his brother! It would be a coincidence too unlikely to believe that she would almost back her van into the brother of the very man who had caught her as she fell into her own partially constructed pool.

She shook her head to clear her thoughts. She knew better than that. She was simply seeing what she wanted to see.

With no warning, a flash of yellow caught her attention, and in that moment, there was no room for either of her two unknown brothers any longer. She had a bird on the loose, and it was flying past her window right here in the garage. Reaching desperately, she punched the button to close the door, and she prayed to God that the bird would be too stupid to fly out before the door reached the floor.

However, either God enjoyed creating smart birds, or he was punishing her for her tryst in the pool the previous night. She watched in frustration as the door got almost to the floor, and then a flash of yellow caught in the final rays of sun filtering in just at the bottom. In that one moment, and with a degree of certainly she would bet her eldest child on, she knew either the bird had escaped, or the garage door had cut it in half. She didn't know which would be worse, either. They both made her want to cry.

"TAKE A big-boy pill, John. Come to services with me tomorrow. You've been dragging like a sick puppy since seeing that condo." Frankie flicked a leaf off the patio table with her middle finger, and she watched it flutter erratically to the ground.

"Services?" He laughed sourly. "I haven't been to

Wayside with you since I was seventeen." He reached to pour himself another cup of coffee. "Do you remember why?"

She chuckled as she picked up the coffee pot and shook it. "I sure do, boy. It was that Tammie Brubaker. She was all you could think about that summer, and when she dumped you, you were too embarrassed to come back, no matter how many times I asked you."

"Here," he said, reaching for the empty pot. "I drank the last of it. Let me start a new batch."

She stood and snatched the container from him. "Not on your life. I like my coffee drinkable. I'll start the new pot, thank you very much. I'll be back outside in a minute."

He jumped up to follow her. "Hey. You drank some I fixed last weekend. Why the change today?" He caught the screen just as she let it go, stopping it from slamming. Stepping through after her, he paused to slow the light-weight wooden frame, making sure it landed gently.

Her words floated back over her shoulder. "Because I drank the coffee you fixed last weekend. That's why. I know better now." As she flipped on the water to fill the pot, she pressed him for an answer. "Services, John? You don't have to come for Sunday school. Just services. One. Morning only. Ten-thirty."

He sighed, and he sat at the kitchen table. He really didn't want to go. Sometimes he enjoyed the tidbits Frankie shared with him about her beliefs, and as a teenager, he remembered enjoying Wayside, even begging his dad sometimes. However, the way he recalled the services now, it seemed to him they took twenty minutes of meat and tried to make an hour and a half meal from it. He got bored easily, and he had no way to fill the time when he was trapped at church.

"I don't know, Frankie."

She put her hand on his and sat beside him. "For me. For when you went with me as a boy. I'd enjoy your company." A look of longing settled on her face.

"Okay. Ten-thirty. We sit in the balcony, though. Will you do that?"

She slapped the tabletop. "Done! Now, boy, go outside and pick up the paper. I don't want the neighborhood dogs to get it." When he didn't move, she pushed on his shoulder. "Go, John. There might be something interesting to read inside. I want to see."

He stood, but as he did, he gave her his unfiltered opinion. "There never is, Frankie. All the news happens on the other side of the world. It's never from your own backyard, even when they say it is."

She dumped an extra scoop of coffee grounds in the pot, and she chided him, "You never know. You might open it and find yourself on the front page someday. You just might."

He moaned at the idea of that. "God help me if I ever do. That'd mean I was in trouble for sure."

"Maybe," she said. "Still, you never know."

"Trust me, Frankie. I don't ever want on the front page of the paper." He grinned as he exited the door.

Once he was out of sight, she smiled as she called after him, "It might be a good thing, John. You just never know."

"LISSIE! POOPIE-britches needs you!"

His sister's bag was dumped in a chair, so she must be home. Chipper was her responsibility, and Dylan called again, "Lissie!" Then he saw the paper on the table. "Cool! A police helicopter's catching criminals. I want to read that before Chipper tears it up."

Stepping to the stairs, he called again, "Lissie!"

She showed up on the landing wearing headphones. When he motioned for her to take them off, she pulled the cords and let them pop from her ears.

"What, shrimp-in-yellow-tights?"

He frowned. "Chipper needs changed. Mom said for you to do it."

Turning to return to her room, she said, "I can't. I'm busy. You'll have to do it. Besides, if Chipper's back, then Mom must be here. She can do it." She grinned, calling out in an excited voice, "I got my picture in the paper."

"In the wanted section?" He laughed and felt the baby shift in his arms. "He's yours, Lissie. Mom said."

"Okay, but you have to play with him afterwards. I need to put my picture on my wall before any of my friends come over."

"Sure. I'll be glad to loan you my darts, too."

She smiled, stepping down the stairs, pleased by his generosity, even if she didn't understand it. "Darts?"

He grinned wickedly, "For target practice. Your picture, of course."

"Ooh!" Her eyes narrowed as she snatched Chipper from him. "He stinks!"

"Tell me!" Shaken and jostled, the toddler was finally

awake and had taken enough. A wail of disgruntled frustration filled the air.

Lissie shifted personas with the sound, and the petulant teenager disappeared to make room for the caring mother that she could be. She hefted her son gently as she moved towards the top of the stairs.

"Ahh, Chipper. Did you get a dirty?" She kissed his forehead, and his wail softened to a whimpering sob. "Yes, now that you're away from that meanie brother of mine, we'll get you all fixed up. Then you can go play with him. You like Dilly Bar, don't you?"

Dylan called up the stairs, "Dylan, Lissie. Not Dilly Bar. My name is Dylan."

However, Chipper's face brightened. "Dilly? Play Dilly?"

Lissie turned to glare at her brother from the top of the stair landing. Her eyes narrowed, and a mischievous smile toyed with her lips.

"That's right, Chipper. You can play with Dilly Bar." Then she was gone down the hall.

A door slammed in another part of the house, and at the sound of his mother calling his name, Dylan turned to see her across the kitchen. The look on her face was not pleased, either, and he cringed. He remembered his clothes in the drive at the bottom of the basketball goal.

He could distract her, though.

"Mom, Lissie is home after all." He painted excitement all over his face, and he jumped into the kitchen in his Speedos to twirl and do an imaginary slam-dunk in a pretend hoop. "Did you see me outside? I made six points."

Then he twirled again, another slam-dunk in the process.

KAREN LOOKED at the almost-man standing in her kitchen with her. He was running around in skimpy, skin-tight briefs, and he was pleased that he had wadded his underwear and tossed it through a basketball hoop—all on a very public driveway. She did love him. However, she did not love the bird being out.

"Dylan!" She kept her voice firm. "Do you know where your little yellow birdie is right now?"

He immediately looked at his yellow Speedos and back to his mother. "My birdie?" His eyes were wide with confusion, and a flush quickly crawled up his neck. He began to stutter. "W-w-well, M-m-mom. Um—"

She turned her head and covered her mouth with her hand to hide her amusement. Although she found his boyish fixation on his developing maturity amusing, she would need to correct the misunderstanding.

"Chipper's birdie. Junie, Dylan. You left the door open. I think he might have been beheaded by the garage door. I may have killed him." In that moment, picturing the little animal pinched in two was more than she could bear, and just saying the words made her eyes burn. She huffed her irritation at her irresponsible second child.

The boy's face fell. "Junie? Chipper's Junie?"

"Do you know another Junie? Of course, Chipper's Junie. Please go check under the door. I didn't have the heart to look when I got out of the van."

About then, Lissie's voice came down the stairs,

"Somebody's let the bird out again. Look out back. Dylan? Have you been playing with him outside again?"

He gave his mother a bewildered look. "I just got home, Mom. You saw me get out of Zack's car."

She remembered, and it had been tail first, too. She also remembered his underwear underneath the basketball goal. However, she was relieved that the bird might still be alive, and that was enough for the moment.

There was a flash of yellow outside the kitchen window, and she pointed her son's attention that way.

"Dylan, is that Junie?"

The boy ran to the counter, and unable to see the entire backyard, he leaped up to kneel on the granite plant ledge extending past the sink. Leaning out, his hand caught a water tray underneath a flower and turned it over. As he tried to steady himself on the wet stone, his hand slid out from under him, and in a flurry of limbs, the boy knocked over three other plants and landed seat-first in the larger of the two sink bowls.

Karen was no longer simply smiling. Her desperate-to-be-grown fifteen-year-old was sitting in her kitchen sink wearing nothing but yellow Speedos, and it was very funny. He had even managed to shower himself with dirt from the pots he had knocked over. At the dismayed look on his face, tears of laughter filled her eyes, and she had to turn away to distract herself.

Seeing the paper on the table, she called to him, "Helicopters, Dylan. We have helicopters." Then, unable to exert her self-control any longer, she turned to him, letting her laughter out. "You should have seen yourself. If I had a video camera, you'd be number one on America's Funniest Home Videos."

He struggled to get up, finally reaching out a dirt-covered hand. "Help, please."

She offered her hand, and as she grabbed his dirty one, she remembered that gritty touch from last night. In that moment she was in the pool again, lying in the mud, and a tall, sweaty construction worker wearing a cowboy hat was standing over her, blocking the light from her son's flash-light. Then her mind skipped to the park and that man who had been there at her van. In a flash, the two somehow became interconnected, as if they were truly brothers, even though she knew they could not be.

A chill ran down her back.

Holding her son's hand, she rested her arm on one of his legs and let her eyes look to the hole in her backyard. He had been there, right there, and he had held her. For those few minutes, she had felt young and beautiful and desirable. She had also wanted that man in ways she could not admit to, and Brad had been gone a very long time, longer even than the three months he had been with that secretarial pool floozy.

She also knew she had church in the morning, and she considered herself an upstanding Christian. She was attempting to raise her rambunctious teen children as respectable Christians, also. She could not have this man and keep her virtue at the same time. She knew that, but it didn't keep her emotions her from tearing at her soul.

As she stood there and tried to hold the two halves of herself together, she felt the tears begin to flow.

"Mom?" It was Dylan. "I'm okay, and that's Junie outside. You didn't kill him with the garage door. I can get him back, or at least I can get Lissie to whistle for him. He'll be all right, Mom. You don't have to cry."

She pulled herself erect and tried to smile as she ran her hand up and down his bare leg. This boy of hers was sweet and young and innocent. She loved him, but what she remembered was that whistle from yesterday. It had skipped and chittered, and the bird had just been there. That's what she wanted, and at the moment, she wanted it desperately. That man had been magic with Junie, and he had been magic with her heart.

Then she looked at her son and smiled in earnest. That man from her pool was also a construction worker with no grandchildren, and he was little more than a boy, himself. Even if he had caught her when she fell in the pool, that didn't mean he would be interested in an older woman. It was stupid of her to wish for that. She had her own man, and he was here in her kitchen sink. He also lived in her house with her, even if he was a boy who slept in his own bedroom.

"What, Mom?"

"Dylan, your mother is just having a moment. Nothing's wrong. It's just that seeing you here like this reminds me how much I love you. You are the man of the house with your father gone. You're doing a good job, too. Here, let me help you up."

His face lit up with her words, and with a strong tug, they managed to work him out of the sink.

Once free he said, "Mom, I'll get Lissie. We'll get Junie

back. Then we'll make sure he doesn't get out of his cage ever again." He even leaned in and gave her a peck on the cheek.

She smiled as she watched her Speedo-suited son run from the kitchen to commandeer his sister. He had two bright-red whelps across the back of his thighs, and she suspected he would suffer some bruising from his fall. She might need to buy him tights to cover those legs at the swim meet. It wouldn't do for someone to heap charges of child abuse on her after all that had happened this weekend.

Then she remembered tights were for ballet. She supposed they made something similar for swimming too, and as she walked to the table to glance at the paper, she wondered how much swim tights would cost. As she absently picked up the front section, she decided she could just call his coach. Surely he would know.

Then her eyes caught exactly what the headlines in the paper said. *Suspicious Photos.* She glanced at the four pictures casually, and then with a strange sense of deja vu, she studied them closely. One looked strangely interesting, *familiar*, in fact. It was a picture of someone in a hat holding a woman who looked very much like the reflection she saw in her mirror every morning, and they seemed to be standing in a pit of dirt. Someone else could be seen holding a flashlight.

Her eyes glanced out the window to the hole in her yard. She blinked, and in her mind it was dark again. Dylan was shining the flashlight on the opposite edge of the pool, and then there had been a brief flash of light.

Her stomach turned over as she laid the paper aside.

That flash of light. The helicopter she had seen as she had walked outside. In her desperation for the man to put her down, she had assumed the burst of light had come from Dylan's flashlight. Now she suspected differently, and this she couldn't hide. It was on the front page of the Austin American-Statesman, and everyone in Austin took the Statesman.

Then one more thought flashed through her mind. Sunday school. Wayside Christian Fellowship. She didn't want to have a prayer chain set up to pray her back to Christian respectability. Oh, dear God, how could this be happening?

She looked out the window to see Lissie and Dylan whistling for the bird. She drew in a deep and torturous breath as she struggled for self-control, and then she heard a voice filter down the stairs.

"Junie? Mommy get Junie?" The baby! Lissie had left him alone in the house! Karen dashed to the stairs to see him trying to unlatch the gate at the top step.

"No, Chipper! Wait right there. Mimi is on her way up."

As she began to climb, deep in her heart, Karen knew one thing for certain. There was no room in her life for a construction worker, sweaty or otherwise. There was too much *life* in her life already, and she had no room for more, especially not if it was on the front page of the largest newspaper in the city.

She was doing good keeping Chipper from eating the parakeet.

Chapter 8

JOHN OPENED his eyes, and the sun filtered through the window beside his bed. He blinked hard. The blinds were never open in his bedroom. He didn't like people seeing in, and he never could remember to close them when they were open. Besides, his underwear felt really tight.

Then the powder blue walls inside and the green trees outside jarred his memory. He was at Frankie's, and he never did get a chance to look at the Saturday paper. He'd unrolled it, and then Frankie had pulled an ice cream cake from the freezer. He had poured them another cup of coffee, and the evening had melted away in good conversation.

He didn't care about the Saturday edition, anyway. It was the Sunday paper he liked to read. Frankie could shred the one from yesterday for mulch around her roses, and that would be fine with him. He just wished he had shut those blinds before crawling into bed.

Then three sharp raps came at the door.

"John, church services at ten-thirty, remember. I have your things from yesterday washed and pressed." After a moment, the raps came again. "John, are you awake?"

"I'm awake, Frankie."

She reminded him, "You promised. Don't be a weasel."

"I'm up, *Mother*. Let me at least open my eyes." He heard her laugh.

"I'm leaving the clothes on the door. I'll be back in fifteen minutes. I'm coming in next time. Leave Herbert's underwear in the bathroom."

John groaned. Tightie-whities. He never wore support briefs on purpose, but he had last night. Herbert's. He guessed he should be glad Frankie hadn't cleared the house of all her husband's things after he passed on. His boxer briefs would be hanging on the door with his shirt and pants, and he threw the covers back. Stepping to the door, he opened it to see if the hall was clear. At one point, the hinges creaked, and he grinned.

"You're safe, John. I know the squeak of those hinges. I've been listening and keeping out of your way, so you just head on to the bathroom. I want to get that bed made."

He shook his head. However, he had expected it. This was the way she was at work, aware of every nuance and detail around her. Nothing slipped past Frankie.

Relieved to find his boxer briefs and socks along with his other things, he quick-stepped into the bathroom. Looking in the mirror, he decided his face would have to do. Washing up, he slipped his clothes on and opened the bathroom door to find Frankie standing there looking at him.

"Just like I thought. Can't go to church scruffy. Here." She held out an electric razor. "It gets used for everything, but it works on faces, too. I cleaned it up this morning. Shave those whiskers." She smiled as she reached to pat his face, but she insisted he take the razor before she turned and walked away.

"Thanks, Frankie," he called after her.

Then she turned and looked at him with discerning eyes. "I think I saw your cowboy hat last night."

"What cowboy hat? I didn't know I had one here." He hadn't worn one yesterday, and he hadn't been home since then.

"You don't. That's why I'm not absolutely sure. It looked like your old Stetson, though. You insist on wearing that silly Hooters pin on it, and when I saw that, I was pretty suspicious."

"That hat's at my apartment, I think, unless I threw it behind the seat in the truck Friday night. I can go look for it if you want."

"No," she replied with a stern look. "I'll just show you the picture. You can tell me if it's your hat." When he looked at her with a puzzled expression, she chided him. "Go on, now. Shave. Come see my picture when you're finished. Then it'll be time for breakfast. I want to head off to church in plenty of time not to be late. Get busy, now."

He saluted and made to close the bathroom door when she called to him one last time.

"I'm missing Sunday school for you, you know. That's because I love you. I'll be getting breakfast now." Then she turned away, and taking several quick steps, the hall was empty as before.

He hefted the razor, and then he closed the bathroom door. As he looked in the mirror, he chuckled.

"Why would Frankie have a picture of my hat?"

However, he had no easy answer to that, so he plugged in the razor and pressed it to his face. He wasn't sure just what she meant when she said the razor shaved everything, but it sure worked well on his chin. If it weren't pink, he'd sure consider getting one just like it for his own. He didn't mind using it at all.

KAREN'S ALARM jarred her from sleep, and as she slapped at it to quiet the buzzing, it toppled condescendingly to the floor. It laughed at her, becoming more obnoxious than ever, vibrating roughly against the hardwood. She groaned and decided that since she now had to climb out of bed to turn it off, she might as well just get up.

Stumbling into the bathroom, she flipped on the cold water and splashed her face.

"Oh, that's freezing!" She shivered and grabbed a towel. After patting the water off her skin, she looked in the mirror and studied her face appraisingly. Her jawline had thinned a bit since high school, but she had always been a bit full in the cheeks, anyway. She actually liked her looks better now than she had back then. As a teenager, she'd sometimes been called chipmunk cheeks. What a name! Well, no longer.

With a quick pat to her neck, she turned to wake the household. Sunday school started at nine, and she wasn't about to allow her kids to make her late after missing the past two weeks.

Stepping to Dylan's door, she knocked. "Dylan, baby. Church in one hour. Say something to me so I know you're awake." She waited a moment, and then she tried the door. Stepping into the darkened room, she saw the computer on and her son sprawled on his back across the bed. Only one leg was under the covers, and she could see he was wearing the de rigueur blue boxers with white stars.

She yanked his blanket over him and stepped to his computer. When he'd turned fourteen, they'd had trouble with inappropriate Internet browsing. Now he knew she checked up on him. Moving the mouse, she opened the history window and laughed to see he'd been exploring Transformer websites. She looked at him with a smile. He was still her little boy, even as hard as he was working to appear grown up.

"Dylan." She shook his foot. "Pumpkin, you have to get up." She smiled again as he twisted sideways away from her. Even as a small boy he'd done just that when she tried to wake him. "No, Son. You can't get away that easily. I'm bringing Chipper in here to play if I don't see your eyes open now."

He moaned as he lifted a hand. "Okay, Mom. I'm up."

"No, you are not." She reached a hand to run her finger-nails along his ribcage. "When you stand is when you're up. Chipper! Come play!" Her final words were called with gusto.

"No, Mom. I really will get up. Please." He groaned, working himself farther into the bedding. It was clear he had no intention of doing so.

"Eyes, Dylan." She pulled at his arm to force him to his back. "Now, Dylan. I have to wake your sister, too."

"Wake her first, Mom. She takes forever to get ready."

"That's why I want you in the bathroom first. You get in and get out, and then you can back the van from the garage this morning."

That got his attention, and he immediately sat up, rubbing his eyes. "You mean that?"

She laughed and rubbed his hair. "Are you kidding? I don't let your sister drive it, and she has her license. You're awake now, and that's what counts."

"Mom. That was cheating." He grimaced, and his eyes closed for a moment. Then he sighed defeatedly.

"I know. Whatever it takes, Dylan. You have other underwear, you know. You don't have to wear your Cowboys every day."

"I don't wear them every day, Mom."

She grabbed his chin in her hand and looked in his eyes. "I never see any others in the wash."

He grinned, scooting away from her on his bed. "Sometimes I don't wear any at all."

She made a face as she stood. "I can't even think about that. You just make sure you have on underwear at church today."

"Cowboys?"

She covered her eyes. "Yes, Son. Cowboys. Any, just as long as it's between your pants and your body. Please. I'm heading to get your sister up. I hope she plans to wear underwear today."

He sprang from his bed and down the hall to catch the bathroom. At the bathroom door, he turned and laughed, "Good luck there, Mom. I don't think she has any clean ones." Then he shut the door with a sound loud enough that she was sure she wouldn't need to wake her daughter at all.

She was surprised to hear voices from the bedroom as she walked to her daughter's door. Both Lissie and Chipper seemed to be fully awake and having a conversation, and that pleased her. At least one child finally seemed to be growing up.

Opening the door, however, she was startled by a flurry of yellow feathers in her face. Caught off guard and throwing the door wide, she batted at her head, only to hear Chipper cry out, "Junie! Junie gone!"

Karen looked at her daughter and grandson sitting on the bed together. With dismay, she called to them, "That was Junie? Does this mean he's out again?"

"Only because you *let* him out, Mom." Lissie let out an exaggerated sigh.

Karen raised her eyebrows. "I let him out? All I did was open the door."

"Junie gone!" Chipper's repeated cry reflected the distress on his face. "Junie!"

"See, Mom? You did this. He was happy watching the bird fly to the ceiling fan to land and ride around before flying off again, and then you had to upset him. I hope you have fun catching poor little Junie. I helped Dylan-dork do it yesterday. It's not my turn this time." She picked up a toy to try to distract the baby.

"You were letting him fly loose in your room?"

"Of course, Mom. Chipper likes it. I had the door closed, and he was safe until you let him out."

Karen knew it was hopeless to argue with her daughter. The girl was a master at flipping anything her mother might say into an attack against Karen. She had better stick to arguments at which she could win.

"Church is in an hour, Lissie. Remember, Chipper goes to the nursery today. Don't forget to pack his diaper bag."

Suddenly the girl was all sweets and smiles. "Mom, you know I had cheerleading practice yesterday. Do you have any idea how tiring that was? Then I had my friends over last night to see my new picture on my scrapbook wall."

Her mother interrupted her. "Your friends were over? When?" Karen had gone to bed early, and there were no friends present at nine o'clock. "What about Chipper? What time did he get to bed?"

Lissie shrugged. "It was late when they came by. They went to see a movie first, and they came over after. Don't worry about the baby. He was already asleep. You know nothing wakes him."

"Still, Lissie. You had friends over in the middle of the night, and you didn't let me know."

She waved her mother's concerns away. "Oh, Mom. They didn't stay *all* night. Besides, I still beat you up."

"One hour, Lissie. Be ready." Karen sighed in resignation. She knew she was giving in too easily, but it was Sunday morning, and she did want to be on time.

"Mom?" It was Lissie's best little-girl voice. "You'll fix the diaper bag?"

She frowned at her daughter, but with another sigh, an

exaggerated one this time, she agreed. "You be ready, though. Okay?" Maybe this way Lissie would have time to actually get dressed *before* they climbed in the van.

Running down the steps, she looked at the dining room chandelier and was satisfied to see Junie comfortably ensconced in his preferred roost. He would have to be dealt with later. Right then it was time to prepare breakfast, and maybe the smell of bacon would draw her two lazy children downstairs.

Reaching in the refrigerator, she murmured aloud, "Six eggs, six slices of bacon, and three slices of toast." When a yellow flash made her look up, she sighed. "Plus one steamed bird, freshly plucked." That made her smile. Just to imagine it was very satisfying, indeed.

She hadn't yet remembered the paper on the kitchen table, and maybe that was just as well. The morning was going very badly already, and she didn't need to be reminded it could soon get much worse.

"FRANKIE, WHAT about aftershave?" John hung out of the bathroom door. His question was accompanied by a grin of anticipation. She seemed to have everything else. Why not that, too?

"Under the sink, John."

He laughed, "Why do you have aftershave?"

Her reply was very matter-of-fact. "I have a razor, John. What do you think I do with it?" She looked around the corner at him with her eyebrows raised.

Chagrined, he let the smile fade from his face and closed the door. As he reached under the counter, he muttered, "I should have known she'd have an answer for that."

After he splashed his skin with the pungent lotion, he stepped out and called to her, "You keep Old Spice?"

She walked up to him and smelled his face. "Umm. Herbert." She smiled and told him she always used it on her legs, and then she washed it off afterwards. It was a little reminder of Herbert in the mornings, one that she enjoyed experiencing.

"Well," he remarked, "I like Old Spice well enough, but there are other aromas I like even better. I smell some of them right now. Bacon and biscuits. That makes two of my favorite smells. Frankie, I should marry you."

She patted his face. "I've got daughters older than you, John. You just want to marry my biscuits."

"And that's so bad?" He grinned.

With a snort, she led him to the table. "There are other things to marry besides biscuits, young man. I've still got my picture to show you. You tell me this isn't you—or at least your hat." She opened the paper, and she held it out to him.

IIc glanced at it, not really paying attention, and then he turned to Frankie with a chuckle. "They can take pictures this clear at night?"

"Read the headline. They took that from a helicopter. Is that your hat?"

He frowned at the four pictures for a quick moment, then pushing his hand through his hair, he laid the paper on the table. "Might be someone's hat, but no one's taken my picture recently, and not in that old Stetson at all."

"Might? John, it either is, or it isn't. Did you even look

at the person next to the hat?" She reached a weathered finger and pointed.

"Can I do this after coffee? I focus better then." He pushed the paper across the table.

She pushed him towards a chair, and turning, she placed a cup of steaming coffee in front of him. Her own chair came out, and sitting, she pulled the paper his direction to point to the picture again.

"That's a woman, John. I think that's the one in the van."

Now she had his attention. He turned his eyes back to the paper, and he remembered. He'd been wearing his hat out at the Wycliff job, and Karen had fallen into his arms. There had been no photographs, though. Only the son with the flashlight had been out in the yard with them. And . . . that helicopter he'd heard flying overhead.

He looked up as he felt his heart catch. "She slipped on the side of the pool, and I was inside figuring up rebar shortages. I happened to catch her. Her son is the one in the picture with the flashlight." He looked back at the paper. "I remember a flash, but I thought the boy jerked the light at us. You don't think the helicopter . . . ."

She pointed to the caption. *This photograph at an undisclosed location was taken with the force's new night-capable, minimal-flash RealImage camera.*

"Did you see a minimal flash?"

"Maybe. I was holding Karen—" He coughed.

"Karen?"

"Mrs. Wycliff. I spent all day on the Wycliff site. I had seen her earlier, so I recognized who she was. When she slipped into the pool, I was about to make my exit, and I guess I was thrown off guard. I wasn't thinking of much except that she had fallen in my arms." He touched her face in the picture. "RealImage, huh? We're not safe anywhere."

Frankie lightly slapped his arm. "It's supposed to *make* us safe. That was a construction zone. People vandalize construction zones."

"We weren't vandalizing, Frankie." He knew, however, they had been indeed vandalizing, after a fashion, except it was not property. It was Karen's reputation. In the photo, while small, her face was perfectly clear, and it was a picture of a very pretty woman. Of him, only his hat and his arms could be seen. No one would know he was in the image. Was that good or was it bad? And for him or for her?

Frankie cleared her throat. "What's going on there looks very compromising, John. You do realize that. I guess you should be glad your face is covered. What about this Karen? Anyone who knows her will recognize her."

He was torn with that question. The sincere and overwhelming attraction he had felt for this woman was surging through him once again, and yet, he knew neither of them had done anything wrong. He had been at the end of a very hot workday, and she had simply fallen. If he hadn't caught her, she might have been injured. Once they had gone topside, he had left with no fanfare, and he hadn't seen her since, except at Bridges, and that didn't really count. He was certain she hadn't even recognized him that day. He hoped not, anyway, not with the way she'd squealed her tires and taken off.

"You want to know the truth, Frankie?" He shoved the

121

paper away, suddenly irritated that the photograph should even be there at all. "That picture being in the paper is not fair."

She stood abruptly and turned to place several covered platters on the table. Just as swiftly, she placed two plates and glasses of orange juice alongside, and she paused and looked at her boss.

"I already know the truth of that. I have just spent the night with an honest, charming, and if I may have an opinion, extremely good-looking man. I trust you, John. I feel pretty sure you are attracted to this woman, and very strongly, even though I don't understand all of it. That presents us with another question." She stopped for a moment and uncovered the bacon. "Have some cholesterol?"

He sighed and took several pieces. "What other question?"

"Does she like you, too? Does she know if she can trust you? Also, John, if she does like you, can your relationship withstand what this picture appears to show?"

"That's actually three questions, and the answers are all no, except maybe the last one. I don't think there's a relationship, yet. I'd have to know if she really likes me to answer that one. I think she might, though."

"What are your reasons for thinking that?"

He chuckled and looked out the door. "She brushed dirt off my chest."

"Your bare chest? Like in the picture?"

"Yes, Frankie. She did it right before that mysterious flash when this picture was undoubtedly taken. I guess I could sue the paper for invasion of privacy."

"And make it worse for her. Not only does she have this photograph to deal with, but then it would go to court, and from there to the tabloids. No, John. You cannot sue and make it better." She took the paper from him and tapped it with her finger. "I know how I would feel if I wiped dirt off a strange man's chest. You were sweaty, too, weren't you?"

He looked at her, unsure of the reason for that particular bit of probing. He nodded, remembering the feel of Karen's hand on his chest. It had stirred him, and afterwards he thought it was put aside. Now he realized the feelings had only been banked.

"John, I know if I wiped the dirt off a strange man's chest, especially if he were sweaty, I would only be feeling one thing." She pressed her lips together, and she looked at him hard.

"Nauseous?" He smiled sourly.

"Sort of, if you consider butterflies in a woman's stomach as nauseous. I would be feeling attraction in the strongest manner possible."

"Is that bad?" Her words almost gave him hope. That this woman might find him attractive was something he wanted to be true.

She turned the paper around for him to see the picture again. "It's only bad if you're caught doing it, and it's plastered on the front page of the Statesman. I imagine she will be very embarrassed."

It took a while for him to respond. This was a wrench in plans he didn't even know he wanted to have two days ago, and from this point he didn't know just how to proceed.

"So, Frankie. Do you have any advice for an old

friend?"

She pursed her lips. "I see two possibilities. You can leave it alone. After all, your picture is not there, not really. That would be cruel though, and that's just not you."

"Thank you. The second?"

"Find her before she tries to wash her hands of the humiliation. Otherwise, you will become the whipping boy. If you really like this woman, do not allow that to happen. Fix it."

He looked at her face, and he could see the truth there. Yet, the actions behind her words might be difficult to carry out. The woman in the picture was recently divorced, and there were children to consider. One was even a baby. He was also contracted to do business with her. Surely he couldn't just walk up to the door, ring the doorbell, and announce, "I would like a date to discuss our tryst in the pool."

"It will be hard, John, but you can fix this."

"Can I?" His eyes remained on the picture in the paper.

"I'll be glad to help if I can."

That was all he needed. Frankie was his bastion of strength, and if she were on his side, then the game was already won.

Now, though, they needed food.

"Biscuits, first. I didn't know just how hungry I really am." He smiled.

She returned the smile, and her pleasure was written all over her face. With no more prompting, she picked up his plate, held it out to him, and told him to help himself.

Chapter 9

"MOM! YOU promised!" Dylan had his hand out for the keys, and he had his face twisted to look as sad as possible. He'd cry, if he thought he could get the tears out.

"If you insist, Dylan, you can back the van out." Karen handed him the keys, rolling her eyes.

He sat in the driver's seat already, and a look of excitement brightened his features as he smirked triumphantly at his sister.

"Mom," Lissie wailed. "No. You've never even let me drive it."

"He won't be driving it, Lissie, just backing it out of the garage. Besides, I sort of promised him this morning." She had, too, except it had only been a ploy. He was fifteen, she told herself, and he had to learn sometime. What could it hurt for him to back it up twenty feet? "I'll be right back.

Don't move this van until I return, Dylan," and she stepped into the house for her purse.

He chirped to his toddler nephew, "Uncle Dilly's going to drive, Chipper. Do you want to go for a ride with Uncle Dilly?"

Lissie glared at him, a smirk on her face. "Uncle Dilly?"

"Sure. Why not?" He reached to adjust the rearview mirror. Nothing mattered to him now. He was in control of the van, even if it was only for twenty feet. In his mind, that seemed forever. The end of that twenty feet was the other side of the world. "He calls me that anyway."

Lissie was in a sulk by then. "Uncle Silly would be better. Silly Dilly."

Chipper piped up, "Silly Dilly. Silly Dilly."

Dylan pulled the mirror down to shoot daggers at his sister and the baby. He called, "Mom! Lissie's being a pain!"

Karen's face appeared in the kitchen door. "And you're not used to it?" Adjusting the things in her hands, she muttered, "At least at church, we'll be in four different Sunday school classes. I'll get an hour and a half of peace. Dear God, please."

Climbing in, she put her hand on her son's arm. "Dylan, slowly. Your father put a big engine in this van, and it has more power than you think."

He snickered. "Mom, I ride with you. It never goes fast."

"Slowly, Son."

With the assuredness of teen invincibility, his hand slipped the gearshift into reverse, and he grinned in the rearview mirror. He saw his sister glaring at him and the baby tugging his pacifier in and out of his mouth.

"Okay, Dylan-brat." Lissie's sneer was clear in her words. "Any time, now. Back it up."

KAREN WAS just about to caution him once again when the wheels squealed. The van jerked backwards, then the engine revved and the tires skated as if on something slippery. In a neck-snapping jerk, the vehicle jumped backwards and slammed into the basketball goal, setting it to rocking back and forth on its water-filled stand. Karen glanced out her window just in time to see a pair of underwear fly past her window. She noted the white stars and the blue background with some chagrin.

As the van idled in place, she asked, "Dylan, did you ever come out and pick up your clothes last night?"

"Clothes?" His drive to the far ends of the world had come to a very unbecoming end, and his self-inflated ego could be seen fading in his eyes.

"Clothes, Dylan. You heard me. I think the van just flung your underwear onto the air conditioning unit. They will need to come off before we drive away."

Lissie snorted, "Underwear? We ran over Dylan's underwear? Gross, Mom. I told you he shouldn't drive."

A high-pitched chant started up from beside her, "Dilly drive? Dilly drive?"

Lissie patted his head. "No, Chipper. Dilly can't drive, and that's the whole problem."

Dylan grimaced. "Sorry, Mom. I didn't know the van would do that, slip on my underwear, I mean."

He looked contrite enough. Still, she was irritated.

"Your foot slipped on my accelerator, you mean. I told you slowly, Son. Now, go get your underwear and throw them in the garage. I'm taking over the driver's seat."

"Mom," Lissie called out. "Do you want me to see how badly he wrecked the back?"

Karen caught the grin on her face, and that wasn't somewhere she wanted to go at this point. She wanted to be at church on time for once, and everything else had to wait, even her back bumper.

"Dylan, underwear. Lissie, quiet. Campmobile, I am so sorry. No teenager will ever drive you again."

As Dylan climbed out to retrieve his errant boxers, Lissie whined, "But Mom, now that Dylan's driven it, you have to let me drive at least once. Otherwise I'll never hear the end of it."

Karen slid into the driver's seat and turned to look at her daughter. "Lissie, quiet." Then she turned to face the front.

When Dylan got to the passenger's door, he opened it and asked, "Are you sure you don't want me to check the back of the van?" He had a guilty look on his face.

Karen just looked to the front and kept her voice very steady. "It can't be fixed this morning, and for that reason, I don't need to know. We'll start driving, and if it breaks down, we'll call a tow truck. Until then, we're going to church. Get in."

Chipper chimed in with his version of instructions. "In, Dilly. In, Dilly."

Lissie patted his head. "You tell him, Chipper."

Karen pushed the garage door control, and her voice

was iron as she looked in the mirror. "Quiet, Lissie, or else."
Then she shifted into gear, and the Campmobile drove
away.

"Mom," Dylan's voice was very subdued.

"What, Dylan?"

"I'm sorry."

"Thank you, Dylan. Now, quiet."

Chipper chimed, "Dylan ki-et. Dylan ki-et."

Dylan sat for a moment brooding, and then he twisted
around in his seat and stared at the baby. He grabbed his
mother's arm and shook it.

"Did you hear that, Mom?"

"What?" She put her hand to the side of her face and let
out an exasperated sigh. Her children never listened to her,
not even when she was stern, and this morning was already
in the toilet. She had no idea what he was talking about, and
if it were a noise caused by the accident, she would just
drive until the van stopped of its own accord.

"Mom, he called me Dylan." He reached to the baby and
called excitedly, "What's my name, Chipper?"

"Dilly? Dilly 'rash?"

Lissie laughed. "He's asking if Dylan crashed, and I
didn't even say that to him. I have the smartest son in the
world."

Her brother turned around, snorting in derision. "At
least we know he didn't get it from his mother."

"Mom," Lissie cried.

Right then, Karen knew one thing. She intended to start
a prayer chain. It would be the largest prayer chain in the
world, and it would plead for relief from two decidedly

obnoxious children.

Then she sighed. It might also pray for a father who was actually interested in being here to help raise them. That might be just what she needed. If she had someone to help her, if only for a few hours each day, she could have a little peace and quiet. That's all she would ask for, just a little peace and quiet.

"Mom," Lissie called once again.

INSTEAD OF help with raising her children, what Karen should have asked for was a local newspaper that checked for identities of people photographed and published on the front page. Then she could have refused her permission, or at the very least she could have prepared for the onslaught that was to come.

After all, she was on her way to Sunday school, and everyone there knew just what she looked like. Most of them took the Statesman, too, and in another twenty minutes, it would seem that everyone would want to ask her just what was going on when her photograph was snapped by that new city helicopter and its RealImage camera.

If she had known, she might have devised a pat answer to ward off curiosity seekers. As it was, she was distracted by the events of the morning, and to her credit, she was not thinking of that night at all.

"WE'RE IN no rush, John. I'm always up early to head to Sunday school, and I'm forgetting we're not going. I could have let you sleep an extra hour." The look on her face told him she wouldn't have, though. "Come see my hummingbirds. Mornings are when they like to come out, and I have several feeders around the patio."

It was a good time to be out, too. The Austin air was just starting to warm, but the moisture from the early morning sprinklers had Frankie's patio pleasant and cool. Later it would be muggy, but not yet. As they stepped through the door, the tree leaves let dappled sunshine dribble across the porch.

"Look, John." She pointed across the patio that stretched the width of the lower yard to a bush planted on the far side. "I have a feeder there with a bird at it. Follow me, slowly though. They spook easily." Just past the patio was another building, a garage that didn't match the design of Frankie's home. A brightly colored door above a low stoop opened directly onto her yard, and it was closed and padlocked. However, with the odds and ends she had used from the pool company, not much around the yard matched. Several of the bird feeders were hung from its eaves.

"Frankie, I suppose you asked permission to hang your feeders from Herbert's garage," he teased. It was the one place on Frankie's property he'd never prowled. It was her husband's, filled with all the things he'd left when he was no longer around, a giant memory box full of Herbert, and off limits to boyhood exploration.

She looked hard at him for a moment, then snorted. "Don't have to ask. Now, follow me."

He nodded with a grin and tucked along after her. Frankie pointed around the yard, focused on one of the true joys in her life.

"They are beautiful, aren't they? Sometimes I even cry

131

when I watch them fly around. Hummingbirds are some of God's most special creatures." The whir of their shimmering wings whispered their appreciation of Frankie's feeders to the morning.

He whispered, not wishing to disturb the moment, "I guess God loves hummingbirds."

Frankie took his arm, hearing the tone of his voice. "He does, John. However, if I don't feed my hummingbirds, they will die. God loves them, but he expects me to take care of them. It doesn't happen without work on my part."

"Then I guess I have some work to do." He pressed his lips together and tried to blink gathering tears away. He got her point, and it hit him hard. "I have to save Karen, or at least her reputation."

"I guess we do, John."

"Thanks, Frankie. You are the mother I never had, and I love you more than anyone I know."

She nodded, crossed her arms, and watched her hummingbirds, but her eyes grew moist. John wrapped his arm around her, and they let the small, beautiful birds swirl around them as they darted in and out, taking sustenance where they could.

KAREN BREATHED a sigh of relief as her last child slipped from her van and into the church. Lissie and the baby had disappeared through the stained glass Jesus door, and Dylan had dragged himself through a back entrance to the upstairs youth hall.

Turning the air up a notch, she let it blow across her face. On the way to the front of the church to park, she was surprised to see so many people carrying newspapers with them. Several of her friends saw her van and waved their papers at her. Wide grins greeted her, and she strained to remember what was planned for class this morning. Glancing at her watch, she tried to decide if she had time to run down and pick up a paper of her own.

No, she decided. Someone surely would be willing to share. It had taken too much effort to be on time, and she would not waste that by running to get a newspaper. Parking would be a better option, and being on time meant she could park right at the door.

"I'm here," she said aloud to her empty van. "Sunday school and peace and quiet for one hour at least."

However, there was an unexpected voice from the back seat.

"Dilly go?"

She turned, and she closed her eyes in exasperation. Lissie was supposed to drop Chipper off at the nursery just inside the Jesus door. Now she would have to lose her parking space or walk to the far side of the building to drop off the baby. She had no stroller with her, and that meant he would have to be carried.

"Lissie," she hissed, venting her frustration at her daughter's careless attitude.

"Issie? Issie mommy?" Chipper swung his pacifier back and forth, and then he flung it into the floorboard.

"Yes, Chipper. Lissie is your mommy." She opened her door and walked around. While she unbuckled him, she talked to him. "We have to get you to the Jesus door, Chipper. You get to go to the nursery today. They do all sorts of fun things in there."

"Issie there?"

"No, Chipper. Lissie won't be there. Other babies will be, though."

"Dilly there?"

She patted his face and looked for the diaper bag. She knew she had packed it back at the house. It wasn't in the van, though. With mounting tension, she hoped her daughter hadn't forgotten to bring it, yet it was obvious she had.

Holding her grandson, she sat on the van's step and looked at the church. The steeple was tall and white, and the grass was beautiful and green. There were even flowers everywhere. She should be here, and she should have the opportunity to enjoy this. No, she had a daughter who was terribly irresponsible, and that meant a grandson without a diaper bag. Now she would have to miss Sunday school to go back home to get it.

She smiled resolutely at Chipper. "Home, Chipper. Mimi needs to go home for a minute. Can you say home?"

"Ome." He laughed in his high-pitched little boy squeal.

"That's right, Chipper. Home. Home sweet home." Standing, she buckled him back into his seat.

What she said to the baby wasn't what she was thinking, though. Home nightmare home was more her line of thought. At least she wouldn't need that newspaper. It would be twenty minutes home and twenty minutes back, and that was if all the lights cooperated. She couldn't go to class for just twenty minutes, and that was a fact. Instead, she would just be a little early for the main service, and that would be better than nothing. Besides, it would give her a little more time with the most enjoyable member of her household, baby Chipper.

She called to him as she started up the van, "Music, Chipper? Would you like some music?"

He clapped his hands, and the music that came out of the speakers was Creedence Clearwater Revival. She had hoped for the Beatles. That was her favorite group ever. She made a face, but when she looked in the mirror, Chipper was laughing and clapping his hands to the oddly structured beat of the song.

"I guess this is what we'll listen to, Chipper. I'm glad you like it." More quietly, and to herself, she said, "At least I think I'm glad."

Chipper just chirped, "Oo-sic. Oo-sic." Then he clapped his hands one more time.

THE GARAGE door slowly lifted, and Karen could see Dylan's underwear sitting just where she normally parked the van. She breathed deeply, gratefully aware that the house would be empty for a change. One moment of silence, and she felt that she would be able to deal with this small glitch in her morning.

She shifted into park and killed the engine. She glanced in the mirror, wondering if Chipper could just sit in the drive for five minutes. All she needed to do was grab the diaper bag.

She decided he could.

"Chipper, Mimi's heading inside the house for a minute. Sit still. Your diaper bag is just in the kitchen, and you'll be able to see me the entire time."

"Kis-hen?" The small voice echoed her adult one.

"That's right. I'll be back in just a sec."

"Sec."

"In a sec." She opened the door and took the keys. "Sit tight, Chipper."

"Tight." He squealed and threw his hands into the air.

Running to the house, she threw the door open and keyed the house alarm. Then she reached for the bag in the chair where she had set it just before they loaded the van to head to church. However, there was no bag there.

"Bag, bag. Where would Lissie have moved it?" She glanced into the driveway to make sure Chipper was fine, and then she dashed across the room to peer in the laundry. When she didn't see it there, she opened the pantry, and finally she leaned into the dining room.

"The van," she groaned. "I bet she put it in one of the van's cabinets, and I drove home for nothing." Setting the alarm, she stepped back to the van and opened the door.

"Mimi find kis-hen?"

Smiling in a preoccupied way as she climbed inside and began opening doors, she replied, "Mimi found the kitchen. Mimi didn't find your diaper bag." Nothing.

Her heart starting to increase in speed, she knew she could try one other space, but she didn't think she would find the bag there. However, she was leaving no stone unturned, so to speak, and she climbed back out and went to the rear. Opening the door there, she glanced behind the sofa bed and stood, breathing hard in frustration. No diaper bag.

Glancing at her watch, she knew it was time to give up.

136

She had spent much longer than five minutes at home, and the main service started in twenty-five. She had to get back. Reaching and slamming the door, she glanced down and smiled. Kneeling, she rubbed a marred spot on the bumper and glanced at the basketball goal. Only the bumper had hit, and there was no real damage.

In that moment of revelation, a sense of relief flooded her. Two good things had happened. First, her van was undamaged, and second, she had a very good excuse to keep the keys out of Dylan's hands. Maybe things would start to look up the rest of the morning. God knew, she needed things to look up. They had to. Certainly nothing worse could happen to her day.

Grabbing two emergency diapers from a warehouse package on an open garage shelf, she climbed back into the van. "Let's go, Chipper. We can still make church, and I didn't even have to buy a newspaper. What was it that the pastor preached on last week? *'All things work together for the good of those that love the Lord.'* That's us, Chipper. Even the bad things are going to turn out just fine. You wait and see."

She looked up as his small voice cried, "Oo-sic. Oo-sic." He stretched to where the radio controls were, even though he was half a van away. "Oo-sic."

Karen smiled and flipped it on. "There you go, pumpkin."

"Umpkin."

His repeated words were entertaining to her, and she enjoyed hearing them. When hard-driving music came on, she froze.

"AC/DC? No way!" She knew this group, and she was uninterested.

She reached up and punched the button, and the radio immediately changed to a Spanish station. She rolled her eyes. She didn't know any Spanish. However, when she looked up, Chipper was nodding to the music, and his legs and arms were bouncing. With resignation in the face of the inevitable, she knew then that she would be listening to Spanish all the way to church.

As she pushed the button and waited for the garage door to close, she felt a rush of dismay. A flash of yellow zipped from under the closing door, and away it flitted to land in a tree just beyond her unfinished pool. She let her forehead drop to the steering wheel, and the horn began to honk.

From the back seat came the words, "Honk, Mimi? Honk?"

Karen had no energy to answer.

FRANKIE PUT her hand to John's smoothly shaven face, and she drew in the aroma of his aftershave. Closing her eyes, she smiled.

"You are a wonderful man, John. If we can pull your sweet-smelling face out of the fire, that woman in that picture is going to be very lucky."

"Lucky? So far, cursed is more like it." He chuckled. "Her picture is on the cover of the paper. Everyone she knows will see it."

"Well, we'll deal with that when we get there. Last Sunday the pastor taught on a scripture that's very applicable here. He told us that all things work together for the good, and so on. Have you ever heard that one?"

"Yeah, but it seems to be a cop-out for people who can't seem to find any light at the end of the tunnel. Like me right now." He smiled at his words.

"Well," Frankie said. "I want you to do something for me, something just for church this morning. If you don't want to, you don't have to, but I would sure like you to consider it. Wait right here."

He looked at the clock and called after her, "It's almost ten, Frankie. Didn't you say we need to leave at ten after?"

She called back, "I didn't, but I can see you remember just fine from fifteen years ago." Then she stepped back with a slender box in her hand and held it out to him. "Wear this, John. You are such a handsome man, and handsome men should dress to show it off. I want everyone to notice when I walk in with you. Everyone." She smiled as he opened the box.

"A tie?" It was matte black with red pinstripes running diagonally.

She laughed. "Oh, I see. You don't want to admit you can't tie one. Is that it?" She took it out of the box and held it to his chest. "It's your shirt that made me think of it. You have that red thread in the fabric, and it's perfect with this tie. Herbert never wore it. It was his last Christmas, and he was gone before he could open the box." She turned, and her voice broke. "It's just an old woman's connection with the past. You're a youngster, John. A bolo, maybe. You probably like bolos."

"No!" He reached over her shoulder and snatched it out of her hand. "I like black with red pinstripes, and I can too

139

tie my own. Watch." He swung it around his neck, and flipping his collar up, he adjusted the black strip of cloth, flipped one end over, and with a pull and a tuck, laid his collar back down. "Like that. Was I convincing?"

She reached to smooth the tie, and her eyes were moist. "Very convincing. I have one more thing. You wait right here, and I'll be right back."

When she returned with a black, sixties' style fedora turned upside down, he chuckled.

"A hat? This is church, you know. Let me see that." He reached for it.

She pushed his hand away. "It's not the hat. What I want is inside." She dug for a moment, then she pulled out a small chain triumphantly. "This."

"A chain? What for?"

She reached to his tie. "No one will see the chain. It's what's at the other end that counts. It's Herbert's tie tac. I bought it to go with the tie. He wore it at the funeral. I intended to let it be buried with him, but my eldest daughter, the one in Marble Falls, took it off at the last. She returned it to me a few months back. I never knew. She was just a girl when Herbert died." She worked it through the tie fabric, and reaching behind, she pushed the end of the chain into a buttonhole.

John turned it to where he could see it better. "Diamond?"

She nodded. "Over two carats, brilliant cut. Eighteen carat gold, too."

He was impressed. "You were going to let this go to the grave? Two carats must have been expensive."

She patted his tie down again. "I loved him, John. After all these years, I still do. Now, you're wearing it." She smiled, and then she turned her head, pausing for a moment to compose herself. She took a deep breath and rubbed the fabric of the tie once again.

He whispered, "Is there anything breakable in the fedora?" She shook her head and watched as he dumped the contents out on the table. She smiled when he flipped it in the air, and he made her laugh when he tugged on the brim to snug it over his forehead. "Can I wear this, too?"

She put her hand to her mouth, blinking her eyes to clear the moisture that had gathered there. "Oh, John. My Herbert used to don that hat just that way. You are so handsome."

He leaned to kiss her on the forehead. "So you've told me. Now let's see if we can convince the pool lady."

"Well, if you wear this the next time she falls on you in the bottom of her unfinished pool, then I think you will have accomplished your goal." She reached to touch her finger gently against the brim of the fedora.

"Done!" He grinned and held out his hand. "Ma'am, are you ready to ride my four-wheel-drive steed to your church? Then she'll know us if she sees us coming. After all, the company name is displayed proudly on the doors. Surely we'll cross paths somewhere in this great city, and I can just jump out and ready my arms to catch her as she swoons."

She slapped him on the chest. "It's your church, too, John, whether you have your name on your doors or not. You just haven't been in fifteen years. Welcome back. You'll get another welcome from Wayside Christian when we get there."

141

"From Wayside Christian? What do you mean?"

"It has been a long time, John. They'll want you to stand so everyone can see you."

He tugged the fedora down on his forehead. "Can I hide behind this?"

Once again she brushed her fingertips along the brim of her husband's old felt hat. Then she smiled. "The velvet matches the tie. They look good together."

"We look good together. Can I hide behind the hat?"

"Sure. You try. However, I want to warn you. It just makes you look dapper. For young'uns like you, that means something very alluring to woman. I might need to drive my car. If some female sees you do that, I may have to find my own way home."

He put his arms around her and said, "Frankie, you're my date today. No other woman is allowed to come within five feet of me." As he stepped to the door, he looked outside and remarked, "I guess we'd better take your car anyway. You have me blocked in."

She held up her keys. "I knew that, and I'm prepared. Let's git."

He laughed at her word. "No, Frankie, we'll just mosey along."

She slapped his shoulder. "You'll git out that door, or we'll be late."

"If we are, then we'll mosey into the church together, and everyone'll see I have the most beautiful woman in the house on my arm."

She slapped him on the arm again, but as she locked the door, she had a smile on her face.

Chapter 10

KAREN PULLED into the parking lot and wasn't surprised to see her spot from earlier gone. However, one of the pastors' spots was empty. Glancing at her watch, she mumbled, "Service starts in ten minutes. If they're not here by now, then they're not coming."

She whipped into the parking space.

"Chipper, we're at church. Let's go in." When she got no response, she turned to see him asleep in his seat. "Lucky you. Just go to sleep, and the world's troubles fade away. Well, we're headed inside, my little one. Get ready."

When she stepped to the building with him, his head resting on her shoulder, she was surprised to see no greeters to open the doors. That told her she must be really late. She attempted to check her watch, but with the baby in her arms, she couldn't. It must be off by twenty minutes at least, as she had thought she was on time. Hurrying, she stepped through the second set of doors that led directly into the sanctuary.

What she saw caught her off guard. The entire congregation ringed the auditorium, and they were engaged in an enormous prayer circle. It looped onto one end of the platform and down the other side. Her heart lurched when she saw Lissie and Dylan standing right in the center of the platform being anointed with holy oil by the pastor, himself.

Then she heard him start to pray.

"Dear Father in heaven." There were murmurs of agreement all around the auditorium. "We do not know what demonic forces have attacked the life of our dear sister in Christ, but we know when your finger has given us divine intervention."

There were murmurs of amen at sporadic intervals around the ring of people.

Karen stood very quiet, wondering what her children had done now, because whatever it was, they were right in the big middle of it. At least little Chipper was asleep. If she couldn't get him to the nursery before he woke, he would scream for Lissie and have the entire church service in an uproar.

The pastor continued his prayer, "Father, we don't know what has caused these children's mother to abandon her two precious lambs at your house, but we pray she realizes her errors and returns for them. In the meantime, Father, we thank you she at least had the sense to give them to your people, ones who can love and care for them. The church's arms are open to welcome abandoned children, no matter their ages."

Karen frowned, looking around. Those were her children up there, and while she hadn't heard the pastor mention any names, it sure sounded like he was talking about Dylan and Lissie. They weren't abandoned. She was right here in the auditorium with everyone else. Then things began to make sense when the pastor went on.

"Father, we hold up your divine finger." Almost everyone in the prayer chain raised a copy of a newspaper. "Thank you, Father, for the Austin Statesman and its willingness to open our eyes with the truth. Our sweet sister Karen has been caught up in a compromising position, and we send our prayers heavenward for her salvation. We know she would not have gone down this road if you could not lead her home. For her children's sake, we pray for her redemption."

Karen was frozen with shock. In the rush of the morning, she had forgotten all about yesterday's paper. Now it was here to haunt her in all its indignity.

Then a voice rang out loudly in the quiet of the auditorium, "Pastor, the Lord has already answered our prayer. It's our wayward sister, Karen."

Those around her turned, and with faces filled with layers of excitement and gratitude, they swept around her, welcoming her back into the fold.

"Dear, your children need you."

"That man in the picture is no good, my child. I have a cousin . . . ."

"Pray, Karen. Three times a day will keep you pure."

Her mind was numb after the first three comments, and

the admonitions seemed to be endless. Then there was one that caught her attention, and she turned to find Lissie at her side.

"Mom! I cannot believe you didn't take Chipper to the nursery. When I went to pick him up, they said he must have been abducted. There was panic all over the church. They went to get you, and you weren't anywhere. Even Dylan helped look for you." She narrowed her eyes at her mother. "How could you, Mom? Everyone knew something must be terribly wrong. That's why I asked the pastor for a prayer chain."

"Something? What did you think had gone wrong?" Karen felt near to tears. "I just ran home for a second."

"Mom, are you as dense as you seem? Good heavens! How would you survive without me? You and that man in the paper. What were you thinking? Now all of Austin knows. Why'd you steal Chipper, anyway?"

"Steal Chipper? I went to look for his diaper bag, except I didn't find it. I have two diapers, though." She pulled them from her purse and held them out to her daughter.

Lissie turned up her nose as she shifted her position, readying to walk away. "No thanks, Mom. I have the diaper bag at my seat. It was in the nursery all along, right where it was supposed to be. I thought it was all I would ever see of my baby ever again."

"His diaper bag was in the nursery? How did it get there?"

Lissie snorted, "I dropped it off. You just never brought my baby." She sniffed as if about to cry. "Goodness, Mom. Start to pay attention to the world around you!"

By this time the crowd of church members had made it back to their seats, and the pastor called from the platform, "If everyone will stand, it's about time for our service to begin."

Karen slipped into the nearest seat, hoping to become as invisible as possible. She would have felt better if she hadn't noticed so many people glancing at her and then to the newspapers at their sides. That made her very uncomfortable, indeed.

"ISN'T THIS a red light, Frankie? I don't remember it blinking repeatedly like this before." The signal flashed mournfully off and on again as John pulled up and stopped. The street was facing up the hill, and all he had to do was let off the brake to stop.

"Sunday morning, John. Not much traffic, and it's set to blink on Sundays." She laughed as she patted his hand. "You don't get out on Sunday mornings, I imagine."

"Not much. I guess I can go if the light's just going to blink at me." He accelerated and tried to be patient with the slow uphill progress from the small car.

Frankie laughed at the look of exasperation on his face. "Small engines mean good gas mileage, John. Be patient. It will drive better on flatter surfaces. Besides, the church is just ahead. Your blinker. Be safe."

"Safe or saved, Frankie? I remember my Sunday school lessons from all those years ago. We were always getting saved." His eyes roved the façade of the building that was still just as he remembered it. As he paused, readying to turn, he remembered other things, too, and the frustrations he'd wrestled with fifteen years earlier flooded through him. "It's been a long time. I knew I got saved, but I never felt safe, not here." He glanced at the woman beside him. "I only felt safe with you."

"Not safe? Now, are you sure that's not too strong?"

"What does the name Broady mean to you?" He took a deep breath as he pulled into the lot. "It means a lot to me."

"Yes, yes. I haven't forgotten. I just hoped you'd forgiven."

"Do they still attend?" He glanced at her. The sun through the windows caught her face, leaving half of it shadowed. *Mother Frankie.* He hoped she'd say no.

"Well, today, John, you will be the best looking man in the house, and I think God will be very pleased to see you. He might even have something to say to you, too."

"The Broadies?"

"Yes, John. They still attend, but we're here for God to speak to us. No other reason." She patted his arm. "The Broady boys have grown out of that meanness."

"Will God tell the music director to play George Strait?" He turned to her and winked.

Frankie sat back and laughed. "Oh, John, you don't know how much I like that question. Thank you for asking it." She chuckled as she looked at the cars passing in the church lot. "Drive up front. Sometimes there are visitors' spaces open. I think you qualify after fifteen years."

"Me, too." He smiled as he replied, but it wasn't qualifying as a visitor that had him amused. It was her response to George Strait. "Why did you like my question so much?"

"About George?" She licked her lips and drew in a deep

breath as she smiled. "God speaks in mysterious ways, you know. Divine finger and all. Well, several years ago, George Strait visited the church here—"

John stopped the car. "George Strait was here? In Austin at Wayside Christian Fellowship?"

Frankie patted his arm. "He was born just south of San Antonio, John. Poteet. Of course he came here. Now to finish my story before someone runs us down, the song director, who is a good friend of mine, by the way, asked him to sing. He did, too."

"George sang a country song in your church?" John was incredulous. Strange things were done to humor celebrities. He knew that. However, something like singing secular music from the platform could cast any church in a very bad light.

There was a twinkle in Frankie's eyes. "Sort of and not really. It was about a jailhouse, and that is very country, I must admit, but it was also about finding Jesus. I have it on CD. The church provided one for everyone who asked. Do you want to hear it?"

He sat back and tipped his fedora up in the front. "The song he sang while he was here in your church. So, Wayside is now helping promote George Strait music."

"John," Frankie chided. "This is your church. George didn't play just at Wayside. He played at your church. However, you are clearly not a country music person. That song was already a commercial success for George. Sometimes I even hear it on the radio."

"Its name?" He wanted to hear this. Did Jesus get in a fight and wind up in jail? George's songs were usually pretty gritty for Sunday mornings.

She pulled out a commercially produced CD and looked at the label. *"I Found Jesus on the Jailhouse Floor.* Listen to it, John. I might get you hooked on George, yet."

"Maybe," he mumbled. "However, we're about to be late if I don't get parked." Moving to the front of the building, he pointed to the pastors' parking section. "What about that? There's that Campmobile I saw outside the condo yesterday. You have female pastors at this church?" He felt his heart elevate at the thought she might actually be here. "Wycliff. Do you have any Wycliffs on staff?"

Frankie frowned. "I don't think we do, not senior pastors, anyway. I don't normally keep tabs on their cars, but I don't recognize that one." Then she brushed his concerns aside. "Anyway, I'm usually here early, and I visit before getting away. I don't see most people's cars."

"Well, in any case, pool lady might be here, Frankie. Keep an eye out for me this morning." He found himself breathing more rapidly than normal, and his skin was warm at the thought. This would be much better than George Strait on a Sunday morning.

"You can't call her pool lady, John."

"Karen, Frankie. Maybe Karen will be here. She'll have a baby and a son about thirteen." He had caught just a glimpse of the boy in the dark, but he knew he couldn't be any older than that. He turned up an aisle looking for a space. They had about two minutes, and then they needed to be inside.

"There, John. A parking space." Frankie pointed.

He frowned. "It says compacts. That must mean motorcycles. Nothing bigger would fit."

"It means us, John. We will fit just fine. Pull in."

"Okay. They're your fenders." He was a good driver, but in his truck, he always kept an eye out for extra-long, extra wide, and lots of swing room.

"Just pull in. Church starts now, and I want to go to the balcony. I want everyone to be able to see you."

He tipped his fedora and grinned. "Yes, ma'am. It's as good as done."

By the time he took the key out, his passenger was half out the door. They made it to the building and up the stairs just as the pastor stepped to the microphone.

"If everyone will stand, it's about time for our service to begin."

Frankie dropped her purse in the seat, and as the choir began to file in, she reached and stroked Herbert's tie. "You make me proud, John. Very proud."

He lifted one hand and tipped his fedora with a smile. He would keep it on throughout the service this morning. He would do that just for Frankie. Besides, he enjoyed being told he looked good, and if the hat helped, then the hat was a very good friend for as long as she would let him borrow it.

KAREN STUDIED the auditorium, looking for Dylan. Lissie had certainly made her presence known, but her son had disappeared in the fracas. Checking the balcony, the youth began to file in, their hands in motion as they chattered over the sounds of the praise and worship songs caressing the hearts and souls of the faithful Sunday service attendees. She scanned the faces for someone familiar, someone about fifteen, a half-grown boy who was attempting to sit among as many girls as possible.

However, what got her attention was an older woman in the balcony, very nicely dressed, vaguely familiar, escorted in by a very dapper, muscular young man wearing a fedora. After they reached their seats, she watched the woman reach to the man and flatten his tie. Then, with goose bumps running down her arms, Karen saw him tip his hat to her and smile. His eyes were shadowed by the bright floodlights sweeping from the church ceiling, yet that smile in that clean-shaven face made her stomach twist inside her Sunday best clothes.

Oh, how could this be happening, and with yet a third man? Was she really as bad as that picture had made her out to be? That man in her pool, the one at the park, and now this one in the church balcony. The church balcony, for heaven's sake!

Karen put her hand to her mouth, letting her fingers rest on her lips, and she groaned. Here was another man she could not possibly know, and yet he was wresting feelings from her that were very inappropriate for a Sunday church service. She was a grandmother shaving the fur from forty. She should be ashamed.

She jerked her eyes away, refusing to look any longer. The man in the balcony must be the woman's son, and since she didn't recognize him, she assumed he was visiting from out of town. Yet, that smile. It was as if she had seen it somewhere before. It gave her a sense of being held, of warm cajolery, and also a feeling of something else entirely.

Embarrassment? Trepidation? Magic? Not magic, she was sure. It was probably ripples of foolishness from that ridiculous prayer Lissie had requested, and all because of her daughter's teenage irresponsibility.

When the congregation had crowded around her, she had felt like a failure as a mother. Dylan's driving fiasco; the diaper bag; not making it to Sunday school; and finally, the horror of that prayer. Karen was not Chipper's mother, and yet Lissie refused to take even the slightest responsibility for him.

Even those uncharitable thoughts filled Karen with guilt. Look at all the poor thing had gone through. She was only seventeen, and it was Karen who had insisted she return to school to complete her senior year. She could have taken her GED and gotten a job, but no, Karen had insisted.

As *Jesus Saves* wound to a close, she dropped into her seat along with those standing around her. Stealing quick glances, she could just see that man in his fedora, and when an associate pastor asked all the visitors to stand, he ducked his head as if trying to hide. That charmed her. His mother prodded him up, eventually standing beside him. He tugged the fedora farther down over his eyes. Once, when he leaned over to speak to his mother, Karen was relieved to see Dylan sitting several rows behind. She was pleased to notice that from this distance, his most recent black eyes had faded to mere shadows. Of course, he was surrounded by girls who looked much older than him—although in all likelihood they were fifteen, also. All fifteen-year-old girls looked older than her son.

"Good," she whispered to herself, "I have to look that

way to keep an eye on Dylan." She realized she had spoken the words aloud when several people looked her direction. It *was* a good justification, though. She wouldn't actually be looking at that man in his hat. No, she would be looking past him at her son. She couldn't help it that the man in his fedora was sitting right in the way. If looking out for Dylan's best interests meant she had to put up with these butterflies in her stomach, then that was the price she felt she had to pay.

When the visitors were introducing themselves, it was the woman at his side who spoke for the man in the hat. She introduced him as John, telling those in the building that it had been fifteen years, but he had grown up here. Several people around Karen waved and called out greetings. It was when he smiled that the butterflies began to flutter again.

Maybe the pastor's prayers were right. Maybe the dark demon of lust had laid its encroaching fingers on her soul. One man was attraction. Three were much, much more. Not just more, worse. There he was, his hat dipped over one eye, and that charming smile flickering across his face from time to time.

Then she jerked her eyes away. She was not what her husband had left her for. She would not be a low-life floozy, no matter how strongly her emotions were being pulled towards three different men. Tears flooded her eyes, and she reached to her purse for a travel-size package of yellow tissues.

As she wiped her face, she felt others reach to her to pat her shoulder or her knee. Their voices whispered their encouragements about how God would provide her strength to change her ways. Her children would love her more for it, and God might even bring her husband back to her.

Their words only made her cry harder. Would this morning never end?

"ANY OF the old crowd here?" John chuckled as he said it. The people he'd known would be his age, not old at all.

"Old?" Frankie lifted one eyebrow.

He laughed. "You know what I mean. People I might remember. Test me." He held his hand to the brim of his hat as if shading the overhead light.

"See? Just over there you can see Katrina. I think she was Flores, then. You do remember her from when you went here? She has four girls." She pursed her lips. "One in the oven, too."

"No boys?"

"She keeps trying. Her husband is in the military, and when he comes in, well, nine months later."

John smiled at her response. He knew he would have given up by now. "I remember the Broadys always picking on everyone. There were several of them, all brothers. Do all of them still attend?"

"Yes, they do," she whispered. She very discretely pointed to a bench overburdened by three very large men. Crowded around them—rowdy and disrespectful— clustered wives and numerous large children. "With their families, like clockwork. All that stained glass?" The wall behind the choir loft sparkled with it. "In honor of their father. I think that's why they still show up. By the way, I love you very much, John, just the way you are. You are much nicer this way." She patted his slender, muscled leg. "Pool work does that for you."

"What do they do?" The glasswork was impressive and must have set them back a small fortune.

"Barbeque. Four restaurants. Very successful."

"Where's the fourth brother? There was a really short one, and I don't see him." At a spat of loud laughter, he glanced behind him at a group of giggling girls crowded around a boy who appeared several years younger, and he remembered sitting just about there a few Sunday mornings when he was about thirteen. The boy looked vaguely familiar, but he put him aside when he couldn't place him.

"Why do you ask?" Frankie fought a smile.

"I remember once when that fourth brother punched me after church one weekend, all because I talked with his girl."

"Heart disease. His funeral was here last year. He was laid out right there where the altars are." She kept her voice low and pursed her lips. "I remember that boy hitting you, and I doctored a black eye because of it. You know, a few grown church members were bullied by him after he became an adult. You didn't get the worst of it."

"Why do they bother coming? You'd think God would kick them out at some point. Or at least the pastor would."

"Shush, John. The windows. They keep them connected. I pray for their souls every day. Think how bad they would have turned out if they hadn't found a home here at Wayside. For that I thank God regularly."

His attention had shifted elsewhere, though. He was looking over the pastoral staff on the platform. Seeing that old VW Campmobile in the pastors' parking spaces, he was certain he'd find Karen here, perhaps even up there with the others on the platform.

"Where else might one of the pastors be sitting?"

"The front row, perhaps. Maybe working with the kids in back. I don't ever remember seeing the woman in that picture here on the staff, however." She looked at him and chuckled. "She doesn't work here, at least not that I've ever seen."

He sighed. "Her name is Karen. Her car is in one of the pastors' parking spaces. There certainly couldn't be two of them like that."

"You know there could. I might even own one myself."

"Yeah, right, Frankie. You're all about gas mileage."

Her eyes twinkled, but before she could respond, the pastor called for the congregation to stand for a closing prayer. He encouraged those with special needs to gather in the Living Room. The prayer team would be there to minister to them. Then, he requested them to close their eyes as he prayed.

"Frankie, ready?" John nudged her. Karen wasn't here, and his adrenalin was fading. He was ready to be away, and there was no one here he wanted to visit with, especially not and risk running into the Broadys.

She opened her eyes and smiled. "You always did like to skip out during the final prayer. I'm ready if you are."

"Lunch calls. My treat." He tipped his fedora at her with a smile.

As they moved up the steps past the whispering teenagers, she caught his arm and pulled him close.

"To have you with me this morning wearing Herbert's things is like having a bit of my own Herbert back again. I know you aren't really my husband, and that's okay. It just feels good, and I'm enjoying it while it lasts."

He grinned, and they walked arm-in-arm, reaching the door long before the pastor's legendary, detailed prayer began to wind down.

DOWN ON the auditorium floor, as the prayer ended, Karen looked up to find Dylan, and her heart sank. The man in the hat was gone. So was his mother. She thought with more than a twinge of sadness, *Always a bridesmaid, and never a bride.*

Then the pastor's words caught her attention.

"Congregation, before we dismiss today, I would like to take this opportunity to give thanks to God for his answer to our prayers. Just this morning we prayed that the good Lord would return our sister Karen to us, and many of you may have seen her contrition as she spent the morning service in tears. Those of you standing around our dear sister, please help her to the platform so we may say a prayer of thanks for the Lord's drawing spirit. It has brought her back home again."

There were several cries of *"Amen"* and *"Praise the Lord"* from around the congregation, and from the balcony, a fifteen-year-old voice hooted, "Go, Mom!" Karen was mortified, but with her yellow tissues in hand, the loving arms of her family in the Lord tugged her forward. She didn't have the strength to resist.

Finally reaching the platform, she turned to see the

church members who were gathered around the altars as they reached their hands towards her. She took a deep breath and closed her eyes. Just before the pastor anointed her with holy oil, she heard one more voice.

"Mimi? See Mimi? See Junie? Chipper want Junie!"

STEPPING OUTSIDE into the heat had taken the wind out of John's sails, well, that and not finding Karen inside the church. He was drained, and he gently placed the hat in the back seat. The young, handsome, and charming son from the balcony was just a tired pool man, one who needed lunch, if he intended to be civil much longer. Starting up Frankie's small car, he pulled it up behind the Campmobile, and he studied it. It was a deep shade of red, with black steel wheels, and darkly tinted windows. It had to be the same as the one he had seen the day before. There was a small ding on the back bumper, more of a paint smear, actually, and he memorized it, hoping he'd see it again. Karen might be on the other side of that paint smear.

"Did you want to park here and see if she walks out? I have plenty of gas. We can let it idle and run the air conditioner to keep cool." John looked to see a smirk on Frankie's face. "We might have to do this five Sundays in a row. There are five main exits to the building."

"Spoil sport. I had really hoped, Frankie. This news thing. Neither one of us did anything wrong, and I don't want her to suffer." He growled as he pulled away.

"It's too late for that, boy." He shot her a look, but she continued, "You're already suffering, and all because she might be. This sounds serious. This love is all from one meeting?"

"I don't know that it's love. How do I tell, anyway?" A boy playing in a yard several doors down let a ball go, and it rolled right into the street. John slowed and motioned for him to come get it from in front of the car.

"That's how, John."

He glanced at her as the boy waved and moved back into his yard. Pulling away, John pushed the fingers of one hand through his hair.

"What do you mean?"

"Back there. That boy stopped at the curb to wait on you, and you could have driven on past."

He shrugged, not understanding just what she was getting at. "That would have been mean. He's just a kid. Why wouldn't I wait on him?"

"See?" She grinned. "I know you just like you were my own. You thought of him before yourself. That's how you know when it's love."

He grunted his disagreement. "Not exactly, *Mom*. I don't love that kid. I don't even know him. He was just there, and I slowed down to let him get a ball that had gotten away from him."

"You don't get it yet, do you, John? Good people don't get their own goodness. They assume it's natural and the only way to behave. However, good people do love others, and it comes out in how they behave towards them. No, there's no romantic attachment between you and that boy—"

"God, I hope not!"

"—but there's love there, or you wouldn't have let him

get his ball first."

He laughed. "You're a hoot, Frankie. You think that place we went for ostrich burgers is open yet? I might head out there if it is."

"You liked those, huh? The restaurant part opens at noon on Sundays. The bar is closed all day, however."

"Good. All the little birdies had better watch out. I'm hungry." Birdies. He grinned. He thought of that yellow parakeet. He had whistled for it. It had been no big deal for him, yet she hadn't been able to get it to come to her. Love? Like the boy with the ball? He pushed that thought aside, and he snorted out a chuckle.

"What, John? I see that look on your face."

"Assuming you're right, Frankie, how have I let Karen go first?"

"Think." She reached up to tap his noggin. "Think with that head of yours. Ever since you found out about that picture in the paper, you've done nothing but worry she might be embarrassed by being found out. You haven't worried about your reputation at all."

"My reputation? You can't even see my face."

"You can see your timesheet and your phone records. You can see your name on that contract, and that woman knows who held her."

He stopped her. "Frankie, I don't think she does. She kept calling me a construction worker."

"She must. You sold them that pool, the night she and her husband signed the contract. She's seen you."

"When she fell in the pool, it was almost dark, and before we got out, it actually was dark. Her son held a

161

flashlight just to help us find our way to the top."

"You've made my point for me, John." She clapped her hands together, and she laughed. "You *know* you have nothing to suffer if you let this go. You also have nothing to gain if you pursue it."

"I do have something to gain." He slowed for a light, and he rubbed his hand across his hair again. "I have a lot to gain."

"Spell it out for me. I want to hear what you have to gain by helping this woman out."

"Well," he began slowly, and then his words picked up speed, "At first, I didn't want it to be my fault she was ridiculed, and I also felt bad that I was getting off, since my face couldn't be seen, you know. Then . . . well, I began to worry about how her son would feel. Now it's all about Karen. I don't want her to feel bad. I want to take the blame if that would help. If she likes me, that's fine. If not, then that's okay." He looked at the upcoming light as it switched to yellow then red, moved his foot to the brake, and shook his head to clear away what he'd just said. "No, it's not okay if she doesn't like me. I'd feel stomped down, but that's not why I want to make this right. At least I don't think it is. I want it to be right so she feels better."

Frankie lifted her hand and brushed the side of his face. "I'll tell you right now, John. What you just described to me? Well, in any book I know, that's love, and you've got it bad."

He grinned. "You think so?"

Instead of answering his question, she tapped his arm and pointed. "Look, over there. Take the next exit. We're almost to the restaurant."

As he pulled over and stopped, waiting to turn, he looked at her, unwilling to let his question go unanswered. "You think it's love?"

"John," she said. "You were concerned about yourself first, and then you were concerned about those around her. Now, what's important is her. If you'd said she was the very first thing you cared about, I'd know it for what it was. Lust. However, you didn't. She's growing on you."

He pulled in and parked in the shade of a tree before replying to her assessment. "She's also divorced with two kids."

She sat for a bit before answering. "What do you think about that?"

"I don't. At least not in a negative way. They're part of the package, and that's okay."

She grasped the top of his wrist with her hand and rested it gently there. "You remember all those books I told you about?"

"All the ones you know about love?"

She laughed. "Yes, those books. That's Appendix A. A person's baggage is part of the package, and we have to like it."

That set him back. "Her kids are not baggage, Frankie."

"Oh, I love you, John. What you just said? That's how I know it's love."

He breathed out heavily and chewed his upper lip. Then he whispered, "Love." However, by that time, Frankie was already out of the car, and he was hungry. His bacon from that morning was long gone, and ostrich sounded really good to his taste buds.

He was sure his stomach would enjoy it, too.

Chapter 11

"AT LEAST they cast their newspapers on the altars, Mom." Lissie looked at her fingernails, and then she put one in her mouth to chew on it. "They all forgave you."

Karen mumbled, "They cast them there to exorcise the demon on the front page. That demon was me. Plus, there was nothing to forgive, young lady." She was aware, though, that part of her irritation over the events at church had nothing to do with the newspapers, or the prayers in the sanctuary. She was jittery because of that man she had seen in the balcony. He had been number three this weekend, and with that black fedora, that steel gray shirt, and his black tie, he had impressed her. It had been his smile that had wrapped its fingers around her heart, and while the emotions of that moment were still very real to her, the reason for them was not exactly clear.

"Mom," Dylan started, "since I didn't really wreck the van, can we do something before we go home?" He sat in the back seat with Chipper, and from time to time, he reached to the floor to retrieve the baby's pacifier. "Here, Chipper. Hang on to it."

"Chipper hang it!"

"That's right. Hang on to it." Dylan pushed the pacifier in his mouth.

Karen looked in the rearview mirror. "Paintball, again?"

"I can't. Coach said we can't have paintball bruises at the meet." He slumped into the seat.

Lissie piped up, "We can go to a bar."

Karen hit the brakes and pulled onto the shoulder of the road. "What did I hear you say, young lady?" Perhaps it was her daughter the pastor should have been praying for up there. A bar?

Then Dylan leaned forward, reanimated, "Yeah, Mom. Lissie was telling me about it. It's cool. They have picnic tables to eat on, even outside, too. The coolest thing is their burgers."

Karen turned to look at him, "Dylan, you can't be serious. You are fifteen, and you want to go to a bar?"

"Lissie's stupid, Mom. It's not really a bar—" He shook his head at his mom's naivety.

"Is, too!"

"—if you go where they serve the burgers. Besides, the bar's not open on Sundays. It's safe if anyone sees us there."

Karen sighed. "Cool burgers, huh? What makes them so cool?"

"Ostrich." Lissie looked up from her finger with a

smirk, turning to her brother. "Or maybe it's Dylan meat. They just can't tell the difference."

"Mom!"

A small voice piped up from the back. "Os'rich?" Chipper banged his pacifier on the side of his seat.

Karen frowned. "Ostrich? In burgers?"

"They're good, Mom." Dylan moved up to squeeze between the two front seats. "The swim team went there after our last meet. They're really tasty."

"I thought you said your sister told you about this place." She looked at him with a frown.

"I did, Mom," Lissie said. "He wants to pretend he already knew, like he always does. It is good, though. Please?" She reached to turn up the air, and she smiled sweetly at her mother.

Karen felt her resistance melt. She needed something tasty, and something very far from all the *life* that had taken over her weekend. She wasn't exactly ready to head back to the house, not and have to chase Junie from another tree.

"Here. I'll pay." Dylan dropped two crumpled dollars in the front seat.

Karen laughed. "Okay, where's it at?"

He jumped back to his seat. "Follow Bee Cave. It'll take you right to it."

"Dylan, can I know what the place is called? I can at least know that, can't I?"

"Mom," Lissie huffed, her politeness quickly fading, now that she had her way. "I'd think you'd have figured it out by now. It's not like it's rocket science."

"Ostrich Bar and Grill, Mom. What else?" Dylan

grinned.

Karen released the brake and pulled forward. As the Campmobile moved back into traffic, she muttered, "Ostrich Bar and Grill. What else *would* it be called?"

At least they wouldn't be at home with that crazy parakeet of Chipper's. Anyway, what could happen at a restaurant out on Bee Cave Road? They'd be safe, and if it were a bar and grill, then hopefully no one from the church would be there. She needed some peace and quiet, and if this was the only way she could get it, than to a bar she would go.

JOHN FROWNED when Frankie led him inside and away from the restaurant side of the foyer. "We sat outside Friday, Frankie. Are you sure you want to be in the bar?"

She took his arm and pulled him along with an excited grin. "Only the restaurant is open on Sunday. It's the busiest day of the week, and they make the bar do double duty. You can hear George better inside, anyway. You find a seat while I go make my request for music, and by the way, I want one of those tall tables for two that have barstools to sit on."

"Do I get to hear the Jesus in jail song?" He winked at her.

"They have it here. I will make it a very special request." She tiptoed and kissed his cheek.

He laughed at that. "They actually have the Jesus song?"

"I liked it so much, I brought it to them. They'd never heard of it, but I'm spreading the love. Tell the greeter you want by the front window. George sounds best up there."

"Will do. By the front window it is."

He watched her walk off, her steps strong and assured. She was the best role model that had ever happened across his path, with her years of facing hardships and overcoming each one. He had learned some tough lessons by her example, and he was sure there were many more she would try to teach him. He suspected this weekend was one of them, too. He turned when a greeter stepped up to him.

"Sir, I'm Tricia, and I will be seating you today. Would you care to sit at a table or a booth?"

"A table, please. Do you have something by the front window?"

"In the bar? Absolutely. For one, sir?"

He chuckled, remembering George Strait. He wondered for a moment if he could get away with telling her he needed a table for three. Instead, he held up two fingers. "Just two. George will be in spirit only."

"I see. A relative?" She smiled.

"After a manner. He should be singing for us today." Her look made it clear she didn't understand, and then a familiar voice began to filter through the sound system. "Ah, George has arrived."

She laughed and pointed to one of the overhead speakers. "I understand. You mean George Strait. We have an older woman who comes in on weekends and requests him all the time. I haven't seen her today, but then I just came on at noon. Follow me and I'll show you your table."

As they moved through the high-topped tables that usually served as a bar, the brightness of the expansive front window drew John's attention. Just outside, he could see

Frankie's little car, and he was glad it would soon have shade. The afternoon was predicted to be another warm one, which was typical spring weather for Austin.

"Sir," the greeter smiled in apology as she moved a tall table closer to the glass. "Let me shift this table over to give you as much room as possible. The restrooms are right down this hall, and you may have a few people walking by. I hope the traffic won't disturb you."

"Well, being near the toilet might actually be a convenience if we have an emergency." He glanced at a neon sign above a nearby doorway that spelled out Gents and Gals. Then he laughed. "No, it's fine. That older woman you mentioned is my date today, and she tells me George sounds best right here."

"Your date, sir?" Tricia's face drained of color. "Oh, sir, I am so sorry for my tactlessness."

About that time, Frankie came walking up with a smile on her face. "John, I see you've met Tricia." She came up and put her arm in his. "Isn't he a cutie, Tricia? We want the regular, ostrich with barbeque. Bring out the biggest iced teas you have, also." She smoothed John's tie and pushed him to his seat.

Tricia cleared her throat. "Barry will be your server, today. He'll bring your burgers out for you shortly." Then she leaned in to Frankie with a whisper, "Your *date*, Miss Frankie?"

Frankie winked. "And my boss, Tricia. I even claim him for my son when he lets me."

A look of relief spread across Tricia's face. "John, I'm very glad to meet you. Miss Frankie is a favorite of ours."

Then she whispered dramatically, "Sundays are the only time she ever comes in the bar. She doesn't like the alcohol." She smiled and carried her menus away with her.

John gave her a puzzled look. "Miss Frankie?"

She climbed into the chair and patted the tabletop. "Sit, John. I eat alone so often, I want to monopolize your company."

"Miss Frankie?" He did climb in the chair, though.

"Wayside Christian, John. I teach a Sunday school class from time to time, and she was one of my students. They all know me as Miss Frankie."

He chuckled. "And she works at a bar?"

She pursed her lips and reprimanded him. "Be nice. It's not a bar on Sundays. Tricia only works on Sundays. Besides, this is a bar and grill. That translates to a restaurant. She would be mortified if you said she works in a bar." They paused as Tricia delivered their tea and placed it on the table.

After she left, John winked at Frankie. "Then I won't say it, especially as she was one of your Sunday school students." Picking up his tea, he glanced out the window, and as he took a sip, he snorted the liquid through his nose and laughed out loud.

"What, John? Are you all right?" Frankie patted him on the back.

"Sure," he said. "It's just that your three favorite men are here."

She turned to look. "The Broadys. I guess they're tired of barbeque, finally." Looking back at John, she teased him, "I thought they were your favorite people, too."

He smiled as he took another sip of tea. "That would not be my choice of words. Growing up, they taught me a lot, though." At her raised eyebrows, he clarified his statement. "How to run fast. I learned that from those brothers. I also learned to take a beating and also to look before I rounded a corner while I was at church. I learned to do that, because if a Broady brother was waiting, he'd punch me with his fist when I showed my face. I still don't know why they picked on me."

"Ever heard of envy, John?"

"Envy? Me? I was just a scrawny kid who had nothing." Truly nothing, without a real family, except Frankie. He chuckled, watching the water on the table as he moved his tea glass around. He glanced up to see her looking at him with pursed lips. "What?" He expected there was a pearl of wisdom hiding in there somewhere, either that or a barb of criticism for his lack of understanding.

"Nothing, John? To those boys, you had everything."

He looked to see Barry walk up carrying a large tray. The waiter stopped at the table, leaving two plates with huge open-faced burgers steaming in the light from the window. John pulled his closer, and he drew in the aroma.

"Smells as good as it did Friday, Frankie." He put the sandwich together and took a bite, then his attention was captured by a squirrel scampering up the trunk of a tree. It stopped halfway up and turned to the window. He watched as it seemed to look at the diners just on the other side of the glass. Then it darted into the foliage. He turned back to Frankie. "There's just one thing I'm not clear on."

Frankie finished slicing her burger in half, and she set

her knife aside and wiped one finger on her napkin. Finally, she spoke in a measured way, "What's that?" Her eyes were trained on his.

"How did I have everything? I was a kid with no mother and a father who worked all the time. What was the everything I had?"

"A successful father, John. You have to admit, he was that. You lived in a nice part of town, and the girls were all over you."

He laughed. "Yeah. They left my heart shattered, too. Every one of those girls did that to me."

"The Broadys didn't know that. They saw a bright, handsome boy, an athletic one who edged on wiry, and they knew they could only gain approval by might. They had to bring you down to their size."

He licked one finger, and winked at her. "Don't you mean up to their size?"

"You know what I mean. They were at their worst around you, and that was all you knew. They weren't cruel all the time. You came to church with me, and then you headed off to the affluent side of town. That goaded them."

He took another bite and chewed for a while. Then he swallowed and glanced outside for the squirrel again. Its tail could just be seen flicking in the leaves.

"That was all my dad's life. You know that. I would've rather lived in the city where I could have had friends. I never wanted an acre to mow or a pool to clean." Then he laughed with the irony of what he'd said. "I just build them for others. I don't even have a house. I'm in that little apartment. Surely they don't envy that."

"Maybe not your apartment, John. Your life. You saw all their kids at church sitting on that bench with their parents. They are all overweight, and they struggle with the myriad health issues weight brings. You can go and do. You have possibilities available to you they will never have, and that's part of the problem. The youngest of the Broadys is already gone and buried. You're as fit as when you were seventeen."

"Fit but not loved. How does that compare?" This conversation was taking him down a road he'd just as soon exit as quickly as possible.

"You're loved, John, and you know it. You're just in love, and that's what's got your goat."

"Frankie, look over there." A flash of taillights got his attention. "Tell me if that's not the same van from church this morning." His heart began to pound. However, he had seen that van and looked for Karen at church, and he'd been soundly disappointed. He refused to hope too strongly.

Even so, he couldn't slow his heart down.

"Careful, John. What are the chances she'd show up here while we're eating lunch? Remember what I told you about that van. It's not the only one in the world. Trust me on that. Let's enjoy this big old bird we ordered, and if she comes to you, then she does. After all, there's a lot of beach between the sharks' teeth."

He leaned back and laughed. "You just lost me there. I don't get what the beach and sharks' teeth have to do with anything we were talking about."

"Oh," she said, with a twinkle in her eyes. "You've never heard this story? I was at the beach one time when I was young, Galveston, I think, and I found a shark's tooth. I got really caught up in it, and before the day was over I had found several more. By dark, I was tired of bending over looking for them, but I just couldn't stop myself." She chuckled at the memory. "I'm sure I looked silly, but it didn't matter. Each time I found one, I was so excited, and I just had to find another. Then, with my back hurting, I stood for the first time in hours. There was the most beautiful sunset spreading across the sky."

"And? What happened then?" John smiled as he waited for her story.

She pressed her lips together and took a deep breath, her eyes suddenly misting. "I heard God speak to me. As clear as day, too."

He teased her gently, "In a boom of thunder?"

She smiled. "You can't make fun of this, John. It was in my head, but I know what God said to me. He told me I'd found a lot of sharks' teeth, and I'd been excited over every one. Yet, none of them had satisfied me for long. Quit looking so hard, he told me. The beach I've created is beautiful, and you're missing it. Just walk the beach, and if you're looking, I'll show you the sharks' teeth."

"How does that apply here?"

"God gives us life to enjoy. The special things don't come along as often as we wish sometimes, and that's okay. God wants us to enjoy the time in between. Walk the beach to enjoy the sunset, not to find the sharks' teeth. The blessings of God will be there when he has them ready, if we're just looking."

He smiled. "So, I shouldn't worry about the van, and I

should just enjoy my ostrich burger."

"Well," she said. "You can enjoy one other thing, too."

He wrapped his fingers around his tea glass and wiped the moisture off. "What, Frankie?"

She winked. "Me."

He stood and stepped to her side of the table to put a kiss on her cheek. "I always do."

"Good answer," she said with a grin. "That was the perfect thing to say."

KAREN PULLED in the parking lot at Ostrich Bar and Grill, and she was very disappointed. "Children, everyone in Austin's here. Are you sure you want to stay? Besides, this looks like a real bar." Touching the gas gently, she began to search for a parking space.

"Mom." Lissie tapped the windshield to point to the sign on the side of the building. "Don't you pay any attention at all? Grill. It's the Ostrich Grill." She put the side of her finger back into her mouth.

"Lissie? What is it with your nail today?" That chewing was about to get on her last nerve, if the child's attitude didn't get there first.

Lissie cut her eyes to her mother and frowned. "Oh, it has a rough spot. I'm filing it down."

"With your teeth?"

From the back seat, Dylan called, "Use your razor sharp wit. Oh, you can't. You don't have one."

"Dylan, leave your sister alone. We all need a little space today." He was grinning wickedly as Karen glanced in the rearview mirror to frown at him.

He leaned over to put his finger in Chipper's hand and spoke to him in a baby-like voice. "Your mommy's got plenty of space, doesn't she, Chipper? It's just that it's all between her ears."

"Ooh!" Lissie groaned, and she grabbed her purse and threw it at her brother. When it hit him, it showered the back of the van with all her personal items.

He leaned to the floor and picked up one item that was clearly very personal and obviously carried for emergency purposes only. He held it high in the air and barked out an evil laugh.

"I wonder what this is for, Sis? Why, you must be worried about starting puberty. That's my motto. Always be prepared." Then he giggled insanely. "Oh, I forgot, we already have Chipper. He's proof of puberty. You do need this."

"Give me that, Dylan!" She grabbed for it, but he held his arm towards the back of the van, keeping it thoroughly out of her reach. "Mom!" Then, frustrated beyond her capacity to contain it, she hit her seatbelt button and threw it back from her torso. With a frenzied twist, she scrambled between the seats and aimed right for Dylan, yelling, "Weasel!"

In the melee, the item in its white paper wrapping was fumbled through the air, landing in Chipper's car seat. Once Lissie had Dylan in a headlock, he cackled with laughter and held up both hands to show he didn't have it. She rubbed her knuckles hard across the top of his head.

"Where's it at, worm?" Her fist ground against his scalp.

"Mom," he cried. "Lissie's gone crazy! Tell her to let go."

Karen tried. "Lissie, let your brother go. This is not the way to solve your problems."

"Did you see what he had, Mom? He was waving it around for everyone to see."

Karen slowed for a car as she cautioned, "Not quite everyone. You and me, maybe. I'm not sure Chipper would know what it was if you tried to explain it to him."

"Still, Mom. You know what I mean. I'm so embarrassed."

Karen drove past a very big window that dominated the front of the bar and grill, and then she tapped the brakes, searching for a parking space on the side of the building. She could see the area with the picnic tables, and it was outside under a covered porch. She did not want to eat outside, not in the heat. Then Dylan yelled again at his sister, and she decided she had to get their attention.

"I found the picnic tables. Is it okay to park here?" She called to her children, raising her voice when they didn't seem to pay any notice. "We won't have air conditioning if we eat here."

Lissie groaned, finally letting her brother free. "They have ceiling fans, Mom. Grow up and smell the roses. The rest of us do. You might even like it."

She might, she wistfully pondered. Still, with two children, a grandbaby, an unfinished pool in her backyard, and her picture on the front page of every newspaper in Austin, who had time to smell the roses? It was all she could do to keep her nose above water. One more thing today, and she was certain she would sink beneath the waves and drown. She drew in a deep breath before speaking.

"That's okay, sweet daughter of mine. You can smell them and tell me what it's like. My sniffer's gone sour. Maybe I've just smelled too many rotten things lately."

"Mom!" Dylan called. "Don't be gross." He leaned over to see what the baby had found to play with, and he drew back in disgust. "Has anyone noticed that Chipper is starting to stink? Talk about gross! He needs to be changed, and in the worst way."

"Worse way?" Chipper's little voice called his words aloud as he beat his new, white, paper-wrapped toy against the arm of his baby seat.

JOHN CHOSE rhubarb pie once he'd cleaned his plate of ostrich. Rhubarb and ice cream, he'd told Barry. Frankie decided on chocolate cream pie.

They both had orange-cinnamon coffee.

"Not bad, Frankie." John stirred the conversation. With stomachs full of ostrich, they had taken their time ordering their desserts. There were plenty of empty tables since the bar wasn't open, Barry told them, so they didn't need to rush. Relax. Enjoy the afternoon. Have coffee and a dessert —or two, he'd suggested.

When one hefty boy went by, wheezing as he walked, Frankie nudged John. "The middle Broady's eldest," she whispered. "They'll probably all visit the restroom before we get away. In Sunday school, they make a steady stream anytime one of them is in a class I teach."

John's eyes followed the boy. He was probably about

the age of Karen's boy. This one took up twice the space, though, and there was a permanent scowl on his face. John guessed he'd have a permanent scowl, too, if he had to work so hard just to maneuver across a room. He'd never thought about the Broadys envying him when they were kids, just because he was thin.

Then, a few minutes later, a boy carrying a baby, little more than a toddler, walked past. He had that vaguely familiar look of someone John might have seen before, and he wondered if he was the same boy he had seen in church that morning. However, it was the difference between him and the earlier one that caught his attention, and he smiled. The first boy could hardly walk, and the second one carried a toddler with ease. In that moment, he felt real sympathy for the Broady clan. He laughed when he heard the baby call out, "Os'rich! See os'rich, Dilly!" It was equally amusing when the boy put his finger to the baby's mouth, whispering, "We ate the ostrich. It's all gone."

Taking a sip of her orange-cinnamon coffee, Frankie touched John's arm, chiding him. "You would want two of those?"

He dropped his eyes, realizing he had actually been studying them. "The last two, maybe. I think so, anyway, if they came in a package with Karen. Of course, I only saw her son in the dark, and I've never seen the baby, except when she was putting it in her van by the condo. Those could be hers, for all I know."

He sighed, looking out the window. The squirrel twitched its tail, as if it knew he was watching. He nodded at it and smiled to see it dart up the tree. He looked back to

Frankie.

"I guess I really don't know her, either." He felt he did, though, ex-husbands, parakeets, and all. "I'm trying to live the beach, or however you said it. I really am, even if it has only been half an hour. Everything makes me think of her, though. Kids, cars, this pie."

"Pie, John? What about pie makes you think of her, and rhubarb, especially?" Her eyes twinkled.

"I don't know." He looked embarrassed at the question. "I just wonder if she's ever made pie before and how good a cook she might be. I don't cook. You know that. She might, though. That'd be nice."

Frankie touched his arm. "Don't look over. It's another Broady. The eldest."

The man was muttering to himself, "Wanted three burgers. Waitress only brought two. Don't know if I'll leave a tip or not." Then he was through the doorway as he turned to waddle down the hall towards the restroom.

"That was Rick, the oldest?" He was beginning to recall bits of information about them. It was Rick, then Jeff. Jeff'd be the father of the boy who had come by. Next was Bobby, and the youngest who had hated John most was Bubba. He probably had some real name, but Bubba was all John had ever heard.

Frankie nodded. "They married sisters, you know. Four brothers married four sisters. All the kids look the same, almost interchangeable. I'll have to bring in some of their barbeque to the office next week. It's rich but tasty."

"Their barbeque? What do you mean?"

"I told you, four restaurants, very successful." She

laughed. "You don't eat out much, do you? Their restaurants are famous, and all over Austin, too."

"How come I've never heard of their places if they're so successful?" He picked up his coffee cup and twirled the napkin underneath with his little finger. He looked back into the restaurant to locate the rest of the Broady clan and discovered them dining in a very disorderly way. Two of the children were throwing wadded napkins at each other.

"You have. You just didn't know." A bite of pie was on her fork. Looking at it longingly, she placed it in her mouth and chewed. "Next to the burgers, this place should be famous for its cream pie."

"So, Frankie. What places do they own? Are they a national chain, or unique to Austin?"

"B-B-B-Barbeque." She smiled and waited to see if he'd get it.

"Stutters?" He laughed. "So, old Stutters Barbeque is really Broady's. Who would have thought? That's brilliant, you know. Four Broady brothers, a 'B' for each."

Frankie sipped her coffee. "Stutters? I've never heard it called that."

"It's the way the sign lights up and blinks at night. The three 'B' letters light up one at a time, and then the word barbeque flashes. When they put the first one up on I-35, it always looked like the sign was stuttering to me. So, that's Broady's Barbeque. I've eaten there."

"It's just not called Broady's. Stutters, either." She cautioned him with a frown. "So be nice today. I know them, so they'll probably stop by the table."

"I always am, Frankie. You know me."

She laughed at that one. "That's what I'm afraid of. I remember a few black eyes that came from you being nice to the Broadys. Especially that first time you stood up to them, and it wasn't the last black eye you brought home, either."

"MOM, DON'T be mad." Dylan seated Chipper into the high chair at the end of the picnic table.

"Why would I be mad?" She took another bite of her ostrich burger. Now that she'd eaten something, she felt much better. The food had taken the edge off her nerves, and she'd needed the edge taken off.

"I saw one of the Broadys in the restroom. He was the oldest, I think, Rick. Anyway, he was talking to one of the little Broady boys, but not his."

Karen licked her finger and looked at her son. "Dylan, an uncle can talk to his nephew in the restroom. No law says he can't, unless you've heard of one I haven't."

"They were talking about you, Mom."

She felt the events of the past eighteen hours wash over her, and it swept a rock into the pit of her stomach. She knew the Broadys from Wayside, but not well, and mostly by reputation. This did not sound good to her at all.

"About me, Dylan?"

"Lissie's gone. Where to, Mom? I need her to watch the baby."

She grabbed his arm. "Rick Broady was talking about me in the restroom? Focus, Dylan."

Picking up his burger, he sat. He bit out a chunk as he began a narration with his mouth full. "Well, it was sort of

183

about you but mostly about the man with you in the picture in the newspaper." He swallowed, then bit into his burger again.

"Dylan, and?" She wasn't entirely sure she wanted to hear this, but it would come out sometime. It might as well be now.

Dylan shifted uneasily in his seat. "You said he was working on the pool when you fell in, right? I mean, I was there." His voice told his building nervousness.

"What is it?" Karen looked him in the eyes, wondering just what he wasn't saying.

"I think Mr. Broady said a bad word about that man." He looked down. "And maybe about you, but he couldn't know it was you, not unless he had one of the papers at church." Those words came out really fast.

Karen breathed in and held it for a moment before releasing it. Her attention was now focused on what Rick Broady might have said, and she pushed her burger away. She sometimes wished Dylan could get to the point, instead of wandering carelessly like a fifteen-year-old. She needed him to be twenty at this point. Still, she had to appear calm in front of her son.

"What did they say about him?" She pressed her lips together firmly, holding her feelings in check. She wouldn't ask what they said about her.

"What's a pimp?" Karen's face turned white, and she looked away from her son. "What is it, Mom? Are you sick?"

"They called him a p-i-m-p?" She spelled the word out. She didn't even want to say it.

"Sort of—"

Karen was suddenly short of patience with her son's half answers, and she barked at him, "What *did* they say, Dylan?" She turned her eyes to glare at him.

His eyes teared up, and he looked shocked. "Mom, I didn't call him that. It was them. Don't be mad at me."

She put her hand on his and tried to smile. "I'm sorry, Son. Just tell me what was said, please. Can you do that?"

In a quavering voice, he mumbled out, "I think Rick said you were being held by your pimp. Then he laughed."

She looked away, her heart burning. The situation couldn't get any worse than this. The Broady brothers might be Christians and fellow attendees at Wayside, but they were rough and crude. What Dylan had heard Rick say was proof of that. There were three of them, too. From experience, she knew that what one said would be times three before it could even get to the door. They would also twist the facts into something that appeared much worse than it had been in the first place.

"Mom, where's Lissie?"

She closed her eyes and felt them burn. "The restroom or something. Tricia is working here, she told me, and maybe she's visiting with her. Go look for her."

"Do I have to take Chipper? He wants to play when I'm carrying him. I can look quicker without him. Can you watch him?"

She bit her tongue. His request was innocent enough, but it was almost too much for her to bear. She wanted to spit back that she had been exposed to ridicule through no fault of her own. She wanted to stand and scream that it wasn't her fault, that she didn't even know this man, and that the Austin police department needed to keep their cameras out of her backyard.

That was the answer she wanted to give her son. She didn't, though.

"I can watch him. Go find your sister, and you can get money from my purse for that video game you've been eyeing." She looked away, her eyes burning with impending tears.

His expression brightened, and in a flurry of digging, he had enough quarters to fund his game. Karen watched him dash off, aware of just how innocent he was. No matter how bad things were, all it took was a video game to make his world right again.

Karen didn't know what to do, except not fight back. She hoped that was enough. Maybe he didn't even read the paper. He was a construction worker, after all. Maybe construction workers didn't read, just comic books or television guides or hot rod magazines instead of the Austin Statesman.

Chipper called, "Mimi cry?" He banged his fork on the table.

She smiled at him, reaching two fingers to run them along the bottoms of her eyes. They came away wet. However, enough was enough, and she pulled herself together.

"Not any more, Baby."

She was glad no one else was sitting in the heat on the porch. Without this bit of peace and quiet around her just for the moment, she was certain she would go under for the last time, and no one would be there to rescue her. If she did, she was certain it would be her moment to drown.

Then she reached to the baby and patted his cheek. "Do you love me, Chipper? I need someone to."

"Wuv Mimi." He grinned and slammed his fork even harder.

She smiled at him and wiped her eyes again. Not everything had fallen apart for her. Chipper still loved her, and that was a whole lot of good in her life. To her, the scales just tipped in her favor, and the Broadys could go and find someone else to humiliate.

"Chipper," she whispered to the baby, remembering a weekend trip the family had taken the previous summer, back when Brad had at least pretended to be a part of the family, "At least we have Paris." She looked into his innocent eyes, and he laughed his high-pitched child's laugh.

They would always have Paris, too, even if their Paris had been no farther away than a weekend trip to Paris, Texas.

Chapter 12

THE SQUIRREL scampered halfway down the trunk of the tree, and it froze with its paws at two, four, six, and eight. Dark eyes surrounded by cinnamon fur looked in the window of the dining establishment. The only sign of life was in the occasional flicker of its bushy tail.

Then, as a car drove past looking for an empty space to park, the glare of the sun off a piece of chrome flashed across the tree trunk. With an unparalleled quickness, the small animal snapped its tail back and forth once for balance, and in a blur of moving limbs was on the ground, sitting with its nose high in the air. Seeing that all was now still, its two front paws dipped into the soil, and dirt flew. A small nut dropped in the hole, the hole disappeared, and the squirrel was off across the drive with its tail held high in the air.

On the other side of the glass, the animal's activities went unobserved. The remains of cinnamon and orange coffee were drained, and the last of sweet desserts were scraped from white, ceramic plates. A pretty teen girl who had surprised John with her similarity to Karen passed by on the way to visit the restrooms. His eyes following her as she walked past, Frankie touched his arm.

"Do you know her, John?"

His eyes flicked away, and he ran a hand over his hair roughly. "No." He sighed heavily, and then he smiled ruefully.

"Well, I might. I believe she's been in one of my Sunday school classes. I can't recall her name at the moment. The boy from earlier looked familiar, also." She smiled encouragingly.

"I'm still trying to walk that beach of yours. It's just that everything I see reminds me of Karen. In this case, it's everyone. That girl. When she first walked up, I was certain it was Karen. Then I could see not. In my mind, however, I was watching Karen walk by. Maybe it's time for me to get home. I might go to the office later and try to get my mind busy. You know, idle hands and all." He rubbed his eyes and looked outside for the squirrel, but it was gone. He laughed at that. "Even my little friend has abandoned me."

Frankie set her coffee cup in her dessert plate and laid her fork beside it. "Your little friend?" Picking up her napkin, she folded it and placed it beside the plate, and she looked at him for a response.

"There was a squirrel out earlier, and it seemed he was watching us as we ate. He's gone now." John glanced up at a clock by the neon restroom sign. "Are you ready to leave?" Then he saw her napkin already folded by her plate and remembered his own in his lap. Pulling it up to place it on the table, he grinned. "I guess so. Do we pay here or at the front desk?"

She reached in her purse and pulled out the company credit card. "*I* pay up at the front desk. You get the car. I want it at the front door with the air conditioning running. It's already hot out there."

As they swiveled around, preparing to stand, Jeff and Bobby Broady crowded the path to the restrooms, talking in coarse tones to each other. When Frankie saw them coming, she put her hand on John's arm and shook her head.

"Wait, John."

He glanced behind him to see the two men approaching, and he twisted his legs back under the table. Then, just as the two big men wheezed past, the youngest brother, Bobby, recognized Frankie. He stopped and smiled at the familiar face. Breathing hard, the round-faced man spoke.

"Miss Frankie! You should be eating at one of our places instead of this dump. Barbeque's best, and B-B-B-Barbeque's better than the rest." He stopped and caught his breath before turning to his brother. "Jeff, you remember Miss Frankie?"

His older brother paused, and when he glanced down and caught John's face off to the side, his expression darkened. "John? John Springfield?"

John's eyes caught Frankie's, and he dampened a grin when she subtly shook her head at him.

"You got me," he said to the bulk of a man at his side.

He looked up to the big man standing there, and in his face, he could see the effort it took for him to simply hold his balance. The girth he wore was almost more than he could manage. John reached out his hand. "Hey, Jeff. How're you doing these days?"

"Good. Got four places. Barbeque, you know. Making money, too. Lots." He shook with a meaty hand, but his voice was rough with hard emotion. He started to say something else, but his eyes flicked to Frankie, and a vivid range of emotions wracked his face. Finally, he settled into a frown, letting go of John's hand.

John saw the storm threatening to come out, and he made a point to be especially courteous. "I've been to your place on I-35. You do serve good barbeque."

"Yeah. Our first restaurant. That one was Bubba's." The big man turned to look away, his eyes suddenly red. "Belongs to his boy, now."

John nodded. "I heard, and I'm sorry about Bubba. I'm sure it was hard for you."

Bobby looked at his brother and elbowed him roughly. He snorted his response to John's sympathy as he looked down a reddened nose at him.

"I'm sure you're real sorry. I remember how Bubba used to hit on you some." He snickered, and it came out rough and blubbery. His eyes narrowed. "Your daddy still got that big house outside of town?"

John could see how this was going to go, and it wasn't any different than it had been fifteen years ago. "He's still there, mowing his grass and cleaning his pool." He glanced at Frankie, hoping she'd rescue him from this. She just made a neutral face and pursed her lips.

Jeff broke in, his voice harsh, "He still building pools? Seems I heard he retired, but I see the signs about."

"I'm Springfield Pools now." John knew he needed to downplay his image here. These men were still in junior high mode, and they needed to feel they could one-up him. "Dad retired several years back, and I'm trying to keep the business up."

"Making money?" Jeff's voice growled his question, as he reached to wipe sweat from his forehead. "Your daddy sure did."

John chuckled. "A bit. Enough to keep my rent paid at Carriage House." He could see the competition ramping up, and he had no desire to reveal too much to these men. He had nothing to prove to them.

About that time, Rick came lumbering out of the restroom. He stopped behind his brother and wheezed, looking puzzled until he caught sight of John's face. His expression went hard, and he looked away.

Bobby snorted and grinned. "Carriage House, huh? Here that, Rick? Pool business must be off, John. You should'a gone into food. Barbeque in particular. We built Momma a new place south of town, near to Canyon Lake. Twenty acres. She got a pool, too. Bigger than your daddy's, I bet."

John nodded. "Congratulations." He couldn't resist one little gibe, though. "When my pool company goes under, I'll be sure to get out with enough to buy into barbeque."

He looked at Frankie to see her grin. She knew how conservatively the pool company was run, and there was no danger of it going under. She made sure of that.

John turned to see a half-sized Broady walk up. There was a big woman with him, and she panted as she pulled on Rick's shirt. "Rickie, she's here. Outside at a table with that baby."

Rick frowned at her and hissed, "Not here, Carlita."

She wasn't ready to be put off, though. "Stinky here says you told him she was the one that pimp was holding in that picture. From church this morning, remember?"

"Excuse us, Rick, Bobby. Frankie? Shall we?" John stood, ready to exit with the turn of conversation. She shook her head, pursed her lips, and began to refold her napkin; and she nodded toward the exit. The brothers had their way blocked, and all she and John could do was be patient.

Jeff intervened between his brother and his wife. "We're talking, Carlita. Rick and me, we're talking to an old chum from the church. John Springfield."

Her eyes narrowed. "Springfield Pools John?"

John smiled and offered his hand. "Yes, ma'am."

She didn't bother to shake. "I know about you. Jeff tell you Rickie's built their momma a big house on acreage down south? Nobody's is bigger. You remember that."

John drew his hand back. "I will remember that. Thank you, Carlita." He felt Frankie's hand on his arm, and he glanced at her to see her narrow her eyes at him. *"Don't,"* she mouthed. He chuckled. He didn't intend to. This wasn't the time or the place, and the Broadys weren't worth it. Frankie must surely know that.

However, the Broady boy grabbed Rick's arm, determined to get him to listen. As Rick shifted his position to lean down, the effort it took was clear on his face. His worked his mouth, and his breath panted from between parted lips. Just that small move seemed to tire him.

"Uncle Rick, you gotta come look. That woman in the newspaper is here, the one you said was being held by her pimp. I'm certain of it. I want you to see, make sure it's her."

Jeff put his hand on Rick's shoulder, his own face sweating with the pressure of his physical needs. "The bladder's gotta go, Rick. I can't get past ya, and the toilet's on the other side. You go see the trash out there with Stinky if you want, but I've got water to pass. It's either you or me, but one of us has got to back up here. Nobody makes aisles wide enough, ever."

The four big people jostled and maneuvered and rear-ranged their space until Jeff was able to make his way heavily down the hall towards the restroom. Rick pushed at his son to start him back into the restaurant, and he paused before walking away from Frankie and John's table.

"Sorry, Miss Frankie." He nodded in a semblance of gentility. "The boy needs me. That was a shame about that Wycliff woman in church this morning, her picture in the paper with that pimp of hers. You think people like that'd stay out of church and quit setting a bad example for my kids. Then we have to eat lunch with them." He took one step and paused, his hand on the table for balance and support. He glanced at the man across from Frankie, and he rapped the table one time with his knuckles. "John." Then he lumbered off with obvious effort.

John sat with his eyes closed, breathing heavily. This

was no longer about teenage competition and one upman-ship. This had turned into an attack on an innocent woman's honor.

Frankie cautioned him, "They might be talking about someone else. There mustn't be any black eyes today, John."

"Wycliff. You heard him." His voice was ragged and low. "She was there at church, and I missed her. I looked, but not hard enough." He was also furious about what the brothers had said about her. Himself he didn't care about, but what they said about Karen wasn't true. She had fallen into the pool, and then he had left. They hadn't made contact since, not really, except maybe outside that condo building, if that had really been her. This was all his fault.

Frankie stood. "John, I can see you, and you do not want to let yourself get angry over this. For me, John, let this go. We'll find her. We'll make this right. Now is not the time."

Her words struck home. Find her? They didn't have to find her. She was here. The man had said so.

"She's here, Frankie. I saw her van outside, and she's here. I heard what the Broadys said. Right now is when I know where she is." He made to move when Frankie grabbed his arm and held it tightly.

"You're angry, John, and with good right. Those Broadys can be crude, and everyone knows that. Can you separate anger and concern? For Karen's sake?"

He let out a heavy breath, and he looked at the hand on his arm. In his head he knew Frankie was right, but in his heart, there was no limit to what he would do to defend Karen from these brutes.

195

However, before he could move, Jeff lumbered heavily back from the restroom. Without looking at either Frankie or John, he passed them, forcing Frankie back into her seat, his hands touching each table he passed for support. It was the words Jeff mumbled under his breath that were John's last straw.

"Her posing with her pimp on the cover of a Christian paper! Going to tell that trash to get out of places where respectable people eat, her and her trash kids."

John yanked his arm from Frankie's hand and threw himself from his seat. "Jeff!" He stood and barked the man's name with a level of authority he'd never been able to master fifteen years ago.

The big man turned around and worked his heavy jowls. "John?" He frowned as he looked at him, almost as if surprised to see the scrawny boy he'd helped pick on as a teenager was no longer scrawny.

"I'm that pimp, Jeff, and you don't know the story. You need to back off and leave Karen alone."

Jeff's expression changed, and he snorted a laugh. Then he loudly rapped a table at his side to get his brothers' attention. "Rick! Bobby!"

John barked out, "You don't need Rick and Bobby. You just need to leave Karen alone. She didn't do anything wrong, and you know it." When he felt Frankie's hand on his arm, he shook it off. These bullies were out of line, and someone had to rein them in.

About that time, two additional bodies filled the space behind Jeff, and John realized what he was up against if this went further than just words. However, the hair on his neck was rankled, and he was determined to make a stand for this innocent woman.

"Jeff, what's up?" Bobby called over his brother's shoulder.

The eldest brother, Rick, laughed, and as it wound down, it wheezed in the silence of the restaurant. The music had long since quit, and everything being said echoed throughout the building.

"I saw you earlier." Rick snorted his derision. "John 'Pretty Boy' Springfield. I didn't know you were even still in Austin. Been laying low, huh? I'm not surprised with the way we set you in your place back when you used to come to church with Miss Frankie."

Frankie made her presence known, and she cleared her throat. "Boys, this doesn't need to happen here."

Rick smiled, and it was not pretty. "Hello, Miss Frankie. What doesn't need to happen?"

"Three men against one." She put her hand on John's shoulder, and she leaned in to whisper quietly, "John, don't do this."

However, his reply was determined, "Frankie, I can't let this continue, and you know it."

Her arm dropped away, and she sighed. "I hate it, John, but you're right. Do what you have to do. However, there are three of them, and you're giving them an opportunity they were looking for fifteen years ago. If you don't mind, I'll sit down and pray for you."

He growled back, "This isn't about me, Frankie. This is about Karen."

She whispered, "To you it's about Karen. To them it's

about bringing you down."

Jeff barked with a hint of a wheeze, "Enough, John. What are you going to do to stop me?"

Rick nudged his brother. "What's going on, Jeff?"

He laughed. "You know that picture yesterday?"

"That trash posing with her half-naked pimp?"

"Yeah. The one in the cowboy hat—"

"—with the Hooters pin." All three brothers were talking as one, finishing each other's sentences. It was obvious they had spent a good deal of time discussing this among themselves.

"So, John," Jeff continued, breathing heavily in the close quarters. "What do you intend to do to stop us from throwing that trash out onto the street, you pimp?"

Rick leaned in as best he could around his brother's massive bulk, "Pimp? John's the cowboy pimp?" He laughed at the very idea. "John 'Pimp' Springfield. Ha!"

John's face was red, and his words were iron. "Leave Karen alone. She's done nothing to you. That picture was a mistake, and it shouldn't have been in the paper."

Rick leaned a meaty arm over Jeff's shoulder to point to John, and as his lungs labored to draw in each rough breath, his voice was cruel. "You're right about that. It was a mistake, and we're going to make sure good Christian people don't have to be around her or her kids."

The bulky arm extending out over his brother's shoulder vibrated with intensity, and it became the symbol of all the abuse John had taken from four bully brothers a decade and a half before. In an explosion of fury, he leaped to tackle that arm, and he slammed into the person standing in front of it to do so.

As soon as John threw himself into the melee, Bobby tried to get his ham of a hand in his face, and in a flurry of fists and flying blood, a brawl to defend an innocent woman's honor was underway.

ONLY FRANKIE noticed the girl who looked so very much like Karen as she crawled over tables and chairs to get back out of the restroom and into a calmer part of the restaurant. Frankie prayed for her, too. She knew John would be a casualty, although he would probably inflict a few injuries of his own, but she didn't want the girl hurt. She was innocent of any involvement in all this, and Frankie was relieved when she managed to get by without intersecting any of the flying appendages.

Dear God, Frankie prayed, I know that all things work together for the good of those who love the Lord, but I can't see the good in this. Please God, help John out.

It didn't look like God was listening, though, because with three Titans against him, John was soon on the floor, and when a man's enemies weigh at least three hundred fifty pounds apiece, on the floor is a very bad place to be.

"MOM, DON'T be mad."

Karen looked up from playing with Chipper to find Lissie at the table. Not again, Karen thought. "Mad about what, Lissie?" This was twice in one afternoon, and anyway, it was about time to head home. She had thought this place might be an oasis of calm and peace, but obviously, she had been very wrong.

"Issie?" Chipper reached his hands for his mother, but she pushed them away.

"Not now, Chipper. Something important's happened."

Karen reproved her daughter. "Lissie, dear. Nothing is more important than your son. You would do good to remember that." Her daughter's eyes were wide, though, and her skin was flushed. Obviously, something *was* going on. "What is it, Lissie? Spit it out."

She put her hand on her chest to calm her breathing, and then she began, "Mom, I was trapped in the restroom—"

"You were locked inside?"

"Don't be silly, Mom. I don't get locked in restrooms. Just listen. Anyway, the Broady brothers from church, the ones with the barbeque places, were going to the restroom. I didn't want to try to squeeze past them, so I was waiting, and they started a fight."

Karen frowned. "With you? Surely not. All three Broady brothers? At once?" She knew they were rather rough, but to start a fight in a public place—and with a girl—wasn't like them. They were more likely to torment people privately.

"Mom, smell the roses! There was this man, and he jumped up and defended you." Lissie stopped there, a pleased expression on her face, even if she hadn't told more than the bare bones of the story.

Karen was appalled. She hadn't been able to get what Dylan said earlier off her mind, but what in the world had the Broadys said that was so bad someone would start a fight over her? Standing, she asked, "Where are they, Lissie?" She looked to the game console where Dylan had been playing and didn't see him there. It seemed her kids were never where they were supposed to be.

Lissie sighed and sounded exasperated. "I just told you, Mom. I was in the restroom. They're right there at the neon sign."

"Lissie!" Karen barked her frustration at her daughter, her patience worn to the breaking point for the second time in one afternoon. "I have never been to this place before. I have no idea where the restrooms are. Please tell me, or at least show me if you can't."

"Mom," Lissie huffed. "I didn't start the fight. You don't have to be angry at me. I thought you'd want to know, since it was about you."

Karen sat and put her hands over her face. "Good heavens, Lissie! All I want is for today to go away. I am at the end of my rope, and I cannot take any more. Please help me or take your son and go away. There is nothing worse that can happen to me today, not even being abandoned by my own children."

Lissie sighed dramatically. "Okay, Mom. If you're going to be melodramatic, I'll take you there. I don't want Chipper to see it, though." About that time there was a crashing noise that carried through the wall.

Karen's head jerked up. "That's the fight? How bad is it?"

Lissie sighed again. "Mom, I told you already. All three Broady brothers were there, and they were fighting this tall man in a gray shirt and a black tie. He was really good-looking, too, and he stood and said, 'Leave that Karen woman alone. She hasn't done anything to you. That picture should never have been in the paper.' I don't think he was winning, though."

"Why not, Lissie?"

"Mom, you know the Broadys. They're huge. The man who was fighting them was on the bottom, and there was blood everywhere."

"You've got to take me in there, Lissie." Karen leaped up, frantic. "Now."

"Let me get Chipper. I can't leave him here."

Just then the wail of a siren cut through the warm Austin afternoon, and an ambulance pulled into the parking lot. It disappeared around the front of the building, and after a moment the siren stopped.

"Mom, I have Chipper ready."

Karen was frozen, though. Someone in all the fighting must have been killed. With an ambulance here, she just knew it. That awful picture had appeared in the paper, and all of Austin had seen it. She knew the Broady brothers, and she knew their rough reputation. The one person in all Austin who had tried to stand up for her had been killed.

In her sudden and overwhelming devastation, she could not break through her despair to respond to her daughter's entreaties, even when Lissie let the baby stroke her face. On this one day, the most miserable of her life, she was now convinced God had abandoned her, and there was no point in going forward. Not even little Chipper could buoy her out of her depression.

It was when the sirens began to wail again that Karen stood and pulled her keys from her purse. "Find your brother, Lissie. It's time to go." Turning, they could see the ambulance as it sped out of the parking lot and onto the main road.

"Mom, we have to pay for lunch still."

She tossed her purse on the table and reached for Chipper. "Pay, Lissie. I'll be in the van. Don't forget your brother." With red eyes, she turned and walked from the table with the baby in her arms.

Chipper raised a small hand and brushed her hair. "Wuv Mimi."

She pulled his head to her face and whispered back, "I love you, too, Chipper." She did, too. It was the rest of the world she couldn't deal with, and she knew the day was far from over. If she could simply get home, then she might just be able to make it through.

If. That was the challenge. If.

Chapter 13

"YOU DON'T understand, Mom. I was there. I watched it happen."

Dylan leaned over the car seat, and his fifteen-year-old enthusiasm bubbled over. The traffic around them was a cacophony of colors and sounds. Karen cringed at every word, especially since it was all so clearly her fault. She felt horrified, and she wished he would find another topic to talk about. Any other topic.

"That man stood right there and told Jeff Broady off, and then he jumped right into the three of them. Just like that, Mom. He dived in with both his fists swinging." The boy fell back into his seat and looked out the window with a smile. "That was the most thrilling moment of my life. No one messes with the Broady brothers, but he did."

"How badly was he hurt?"

"I don't know. He was on bottom. All I could see was the first punch, then the Broadys covered him up." He grinned with the excitement.

Lissie quizzed her brother, "Did you think he was good-looking? I saw the fight start, you know."

He made a face at his sister. "I don't know if he's good-looking or not. He was tall, and he wasn't fat or ugly. I could tell that. He was mad, though. His face was red, and whatever he said, Rick Broady didn't like it. Rick stuck his arm out, and he was so mad at the man, his fat shook. Then the man attacked him."

Karen ventured, "Who was in the ambulance?" She hated to ask, but she really wanted to know.

"That man, Mom. The one who jumped Rick and Jeff."

"I thought he jumped all three brothers." Lissie snorted with contempt.

He laughed. "Bobby Broady is a chicken. He wants to bully people, but only if he's safe. He punched then stood back and waited until he could kick. He was in church with us, Mom."

"Of course he was, Dylan. All three of the brothers are there every week." She pushed her hand through her hair, letting it catch her fingers, trying to fight back tears. "Thank God, or they'd terrorize the city."

"No, Mom. The man who jumped them. He sat right in front of me."

That got her attention. What had Lissie said earlier? Gray shirt and black tie? Hadn't the man who sat in front of her son worn just that?

"Do you know his name, Son?" She glanced to the

rearview mirror to try to catch his eye. The man in the hat. *Oh, God, please let Dylan know his name. Oh, God, don't let it be him.* It had to be him. Oh, she didn't know what she wanted.

"Sorry, Mom. He was new. Remember the guy with the funny hat? He was beside Miss Frankie, and she introduced him."

"Miss Frankie?" Karen had a sinking feeling inside. She might not know Miss Frankie by name, but she remembered the man in the funny hat and the woman who sat beside him. It had been a black fedora, and he had worn it pulled down over one eye. When he had smiled, he had squeezed her heart until she thought she was going to burst. Dear God, not that man. Not that man who had pulled at her heart and made her want to cry.

"Are you sure it was the same man, Dylan? It's important."

"Mom," Lissie pushed. "Can't you ever just believe us? We're not children. We pay attention, unlike some people in this van."

Karen looked at the girl in the seat next to hers. Lissie didn't always pay attention. Karen knew that, even if her daughter didn't. However, she didn't have the strength to argue with her at the moment.

Dylan leaned forward and pointed over his mother's shoulder. "You know you're speeding. Look in front, you're even catching up with the ambulance." Sure enough, not far in front of them they could see the brightly marked vehicle. The siren was off, but the lights were flashing. "Look at that. I can tell he's not dying, at least."

"Dork," his sister shot at him. "There's no way to tell that. You're not inside the ambulance."

He gloated. "Can, too. They go slow and run just the lights if it's not life threatening, or sometimes don't run the lights at all. I bet he's injured but not going to die. We learned that in driver's ed."

"Dylan," Karen said. "You haven't signed up for driver's ed."

"Zack has, though, and I read that in his stuff. Can we follow it?"

Lissie goaded him, "Did you also learn that it's illegal to follow an emergency vehicle?"

"Maybe we're just driving to the hospital, Lissie-Prissy. Did you ever think of that? People do drive to the hospital, you know."

"Yeah," she sneered, "and people get tickets, too. Did you ever think of that?"

Karen had heard enough. "I want to drive to the hospital, and I'll take my chances on getting a ticket. Now, both of you, be quiet."

"Mom, look!" Dylan slapped the back of her seat.

"Dylan," her voice was stern. "I said to be quiet."

"But, Mom. There goes Miss Frankie. She's following the ambulance, too."

Karen looked in her mirror at her son, focusing on the fact that she seemed to be the only one who was unfamiliar with this woman. "How do you know Miss Frankie?"

Both of her children looked at her and said together, "She was my Sunday school teacher."

Karen looked ahead and murmured, "I never knew

that."

Lissie looked sideways at her and whispered, "You would if you paid attention. I hope you invited her to the party."

Karen kept her mouth shut. Maybe Lissie was right. It seemed there were a lot of things she didn't know. In the back seat, Chipper finally perked up. "Pay 'tention, Mimi. Pay 'tention."

Lissie just laughed.

JOHN LAY in the ambulance, and one eye was swollen shut. He knew his lip was busted. He could feel it, and the iron taste of blood was in his mouth. When the paramedic reached to dab at his face, John tried to shake his hand away.

"Sir, you need to let me help. Those were big guys who attacked you, and we uncovered you at the bottom of the pile." The man grasped John's chin and forced him to hold still while he patted the eye carefully with a damp cloth. "This is gonna be black for a while. Yep, you got socked pretty good."

"I can't see out of it. Is it blinded?" John considered what the paramedic said, that the other men attacked him, and he would have laughed, if he didn't hurt so much. That wasn't exactly the way it had gone down. They might have said things that provoked him, but none of it was aimed at him until he'd jumped up and called himself a pimp.

However, even with his injuries, he wasn't sorry he'd done what he'd done.

"Blinded? Probably not. We won't be able to tell until we get you to the hospital, though. Sometimes damage is more than skin deep. You've got plenty of the skin-deep sort, though. What caused all the trouble, if I may be so nosy?" He pulled his cloth away, and it was soaked with blood.

John reached his hand to scratch his head, and he realized his fingers were wrapped. "What's with the hand?"

The paramedic laughed. "I think you must have gotten in a few really good punches there. That's what's left of your fingers." He checked some readings and marked a few items on a paper chart. Turning to input information into a laptop keyboard, he said, "You don't have to tell me, you know. I'm just curious. Not everyone we get in here is conscious."

"Tell you what?" John worked his good eye, trying to focus.

"Ah," the paramedic laughed. "The memory is already gone. Severe brain damage. I'm marking that for the surgeon. Seriously, what was the fight over? I saw the Broady brothers there. They tend to stir things up."

"It was over a woman." Looking away, John licked his lips.

"I see. Something very romantic. This story I could enjoy hearing." He looked away, his hands busy, as he adjusted one of his machines.

John chuckled, and it hurt. "Ooh," he groaned. "My side."

"Sorry," the paramedic cautioned. "I forgot to mention a possible cracked rib."

"Any other forgots?" John smiled, but it was strained. He hurt, and badly in a few places.

"We're trying to find 'em. When it hurts, you tell me, and I'll tell you if I know about that one yet."

"Very funny." John tried to shift positions, and he groaned with the effort.

"Back to the woman. How's the romance?" The medic pulled a fresh cloth and pressed it to John's mouth. "Hang on a minute before you try to talk. This cut's starting to bleed again."

When he was finished, John drew in a breath. "Not much romance. She doesn't even know about the fight."

The paramedic made a sympathetic noise. "Ouch. So, what was the fight for?"

"Her reputation. The Broadys called me her pimp."

"Pimp?" The paramedic's eyes opened wide at John's revelation.

"Yeah. There was a picture in the paper of me holding her in my arms. Front page. It wasn't like it looks, though."

"Cowboy hat with a Hooters pin?" The man smiled.

"That's me, the pimp." John grinned, causing actual tears to flood his eyes.

"She was pretty in the picture. What's the real story?" The siren kicked on. "We're almost there, so make it quick." He started prepping John for arrival at the hospital emergency room.

"My company is building her pool. She slipped in, and I caught her."

"In the dark? I read the captions, you know."

John grinned again, although it quickly took on a pained look, and he groaned.

"That one hurt?"

"Yeah."

"Back to the pool. In the dark?" The medic thumped a small bag and set it aside. He paused, looking expectantly at John.

"Yeah, in the dark, but that's the long version. Her son was holding a flashlight for us to get out, and I guess that's why the helicopter targeted us."

"She's a lucky woman to have you defend her honor. I hope she finds out." The ambulance stopped, and the back door opened. The medic shifted his position, readying for John's exit.

As he was wheeled away, John whispered, "I hope she doesn't. I feel like a fool."

However, the paramedic was still in the ambulance, and he didn't hear.

"ARE YOU the spouse of the injured party?"

Karen looked at her two children and the grandson in her arms. She didn't even know the injured man's full name. James, she thought, or maybe John. She only knew the man had just been brought in, and she needed to see him.

"I'm sorry, but no," she said. "The fight was about me. I'm the reason he's here." She winced when she said that. She'd never had a man get in a fight because of her before, except Eddy back in high school. "Can I see him?"

"I'm afraid he is in surgery right now. If you call the main number, you can get his room and visitation hours. Here, at the top." She handed Karen a card with several contact numbers and a web address. "You can go online, also. I must warn you, however, he may be on restricted visitation with the extent of his injuries."

Karen took a deep breath. She hated to ask this next question. "Could you please give me his name?"

"I'm sorry, ma'am. I can't give out that information. Hospital information about patients is confidential."

"Thank you." Karen felt frustration well up inside her, and it was only with effort that she bit it back. She turned and glanced at a newspaper on a side table, and there was the reminder of why this man was in this hospital, right on the front page, exposed to the world. She stepped forward, pushing Dylan aside, and she grabbed the paper. Turning to the hospital receptionist, she held it up and shook it as her aggravation snapped inside of her.

"This is yesterday's paper. Don't you people know that? Yesterday's paper. Don't you take the Sunday edition?" Shaking with the adrenalin coursing through her blood, she folded it and dropped it into a trashcan. "Come, children. It's time to go."

"Mom?" Lissie looked at her. "Are you okay?"

Karen stepped to the door, and with her hand on the handle, she turned. "Yes, Lissie, dear. I am just fine. I am forbidden any information about the one man in this city who has stood up for my moral integrity. I am absolutely fine. Please come to the van."

Inside, however, she wanted to grab the receptionist and yell at her, tell her that the man in that surgery ward had fought for her honor against impossible odds, and she needed to see him, to know who he was, and to thank him. She wanted to do that, and all for a smile she had seen for the first time in her life only hours ago.

Pushing through the door into the warmth of the Austin afternoon, she stood with Chipper in her arms and waited for her daughter and son to join her. Turning to look towards the sky to take in the face of the building, she couldn't help but think that he was in there. He was that close, and she had no way to find who he was.

A hand touched her shoulder, and she jumped. Turning, she saw Lissie, and she put a very firm smile on her face before facing the parking garage. However, her daughter did not turn her loose.

"Mom?" There was an uncharacteristic tenderness in that word, and Karen placed her hand on her daughter's. "I know this is important to you. Miss Frankie would know who he is."

Karen stood for several breaths, and then she turned to see a brand-new daughter at her side, with her son, Dylan, just behind. This was not the critical, demanding girl who had tormented her mother since her father had run away, leaving the family to face the past three months alone. There was a tone of concern in that seventeen-year-old voice that Karen wasn't sure she had ever heard offered toward her, and she let herself smile. Then she felt her eyes begin to burn, and she turned away, blinking to retain her self-composure.

"Thank you, Lissie." Her whispered words were for her daughter, but they carried equally well to the ears of one much closer to her.

"Thank 'oo, Issie." The childish, high-pitched voice of a toddler repeated her sentiments.

In that moment under the bright Texas sun, Karen some-

213

how felt she had found the strength to go on, even if she didn't know the next step to take. At least she could take one, and that was the important thing. Take one more step after that, and eventually it would lead her somewhere. She didn't know the destination, but with her children at her side, she was certain she could find wherever she needed to go.

"YOU ARE an all-American baby, do you know that?" The nurse in the examining room with John slapped him on the bare shoulder. Then she winked at him. "I bet you were good looking before you got yourself beat up. What'd you go and do that for?"

"Who, you should ask." He rubbed the place on his shoulder where she'd hit him.

"Lift your arms," and she looked at her chart for his name, "John." He winced as he did so, and he inhaled a deep breath as she began to wrap a compression bandage around his torso. "This is bruised, not broken, but you need to keep it wrapped if you want to be able to sleep without pain. Live with the pressure. Also, keep that hand in that support until those broken bones heal, and you don't get to decide when. You come back in, and we'll decide then if it needs a cast. Your face? Just live with that. I could keep you until the swelling starts to subside, but I suppose you'd rather come back when your eye reappears for us to check it then. I see no problem with that. Your good looks will have to come back gradually without much help from me, though. Sorry. Other than that, I'm done here." She turned to mark several items on a clipboard at his side.

John sat for a minute with his arms in the air, and then he asked, "Can I put my arms down? They're getting heavy."

The nurse looked at him and said, "With that finely-muscled torso, I'm surprised you didn't win that fight. A fighter like you should be able to keep those arms up a while, but you can put them down if you must."

"The reason I didn't win is because the other three were twice as big as me." He grimaced at twinges of pain as he slowly eased his arms down.

She crossed her arms over her clipboard, and she smiled at him. "I take back what I said. I'm surprised you're alive if there were three of them bigger than you. What motivated all this?"

He coughed out his laughter, grimacing in pain, and looked away in embarrassment. "A picture." His chest still hurt, and the laughter made it worse.

"Oh," she said. "You're him."

"Pardon me?"

"Shawn's already telling your story. I think half the hospital staff knows, and probably just as many patients. We saw the picture yesterday, you understand, and while it was funny, no one could figure it out. A man in a cowboy hat was holding a woman in a muddy pit, while off to the side a kid was shining a flashlight on them. It was comical to those of us here at the hospital."

"Not to me." He gently touched the skin around his swollen eye. "Or to Karen. Who's Shawn?"

"Shawn was in the ambulance with you. I guess Karen was the woman in the picture who slipped into your arms as she fell?" She had a smile on her face.

John growled. "Please. It was ten feet down, and I was standing in six inches of mud. I nearly dropped her." He chuckled. "Actually I did, but only after she told me to."

"You dropped her in the mud?" The nurse was interested now.

John laughed, and then he caught his side and groaned. "Yes. Her son had the flashlight, and she didn't want him to see her in my arms. Well, that didn't work out."

"It was dark, though. What was with that?"

"I'm the contractor building her pool. The crew ran short on rebar. I was calculating for a delivery the next morning. I'd been in the yard working all day, and I was just finishing up. I should have left five minutes earlier, and then I'd have been safe."

He knew he wouldn't, though. He'd have still remembered that yellow parakeet and the way she called to it in that soft whisper, her dud of a whistle, and the way she thanked him before going inside. Even now he wasn't sorry. Sure, she'd turned his life upside down, but maybe he'd needed his life turned upside down. Frankie sure seemed to think so, and Karen had certainly been the one to do it.

The nurse winked as she handed him his shirt. "For want of a nail. Still, all's well that ends well. You, sir, are free to go. Someone named Frankie has already paid for your stay, and she is outside waiting on you. I believe she said all this is on your credit card."

He stood and looked at the shirt helplessly. When she saw him standing there, the nurse took mercy on him and offered to help him dress. Even then, his bruised rib was more painful than just about anything he ever remembered happening to him.

When he stepped to the exit, there was his Frankie. She reached to his face, and closing her eyes, she sighed. "John, John. You've paid a steep price. Was it worth it?"

He paused as if thinking about his answer, and then he asked a question of his own. "How did my opponents fare?"

She looked at him and laughed. "You did some damage. When the paramedics were loading you up, those bullies had their wallets out handing over wads of cash to cover the damage to the restaurant. At the same time, their women were fussing over more cuts and bruises than I thought were possible on any three people. They even paid for our meal. They were more worried about the police and bad publicity than anything else, I think."

He smiled. "You know, Frankie. I think I got off cheaply even with my injuries. Thank you for waiting on me."

She slapped his arm and snapped at him. "Don't you thank me, John. I didn't do it for thanks. I did it because I love you." Then she licked her lips, pausing, and she told him more gently, "I was frightened when I first got here. There was some confusion when another ambulance came in just after you. I went to ask about you, and they told me you were undergoing emergency surgery for life-threatening injuries. It was fifteen minutes before I found out differently."

He carefully put his arm around her, only grimacing once when a sharp pain lanced through his side. "I am so sorry. You know, I don't think I'll be eating at Stutters again. I think I'm over barbeque for a while. I might just fall in love with fried chicken."

"Ostrich burgers, John? Are you giving up on them?"

He sighed and thought about it. "Can I send you for takeout?"

"I've got the credit card."

"Done." He leaned over to give her a kiss on the cheek, and he did his best to cover his latest wince of pain.

Frankie saw it, however, and she patted his chest. "I saw that."

"What?" He looked away and sniffled, his eyes moist.

"You hiding the pain, and trying not to let me see. The fact you tried to hide it makes me love you even more than I thought I possibly could."

"Did I hear you say you love me?"

She cleared her throat. "What I said was, I love the way you tried to hide it."

"Ah! I just misunderstood."

"That's my John." But she had a smile on her face.

JUST DOWN from the parking garage where Karen and her brood were coming to terms with their need for each other, a woman and a man walked slowly out of the emergency room entrance. His hand was wrapped, and to judge by his face, he could very well have been in a traffic accident. However, his uninjured arm was around the woman's shoulder, and her hands rested in front of her on her purse. Neither family saw that they were within feet of each other. Instead, in the brilliant Austin afternoon, they walked away in opposite directions, never realizing just how closely God had brought them together.

Chapter 14

KAREN GLARED at the swimsuit lying on her bed. It was bright, colorful, and sunny, and the total opposite of everything she felt inside. She supposed she should be glad she was able to fit comfortably into her new two-piece, but losing ten pounds because of depression wasn't the way she preferred to slim down.

A flash of yellow fluttered into the room, and it was followed by a cry of excitement. "Junie! Here, Junie! Come here!"

Karen swooped up the small boy. In the past three weeks, he felt like he had grown heavier, and she thought that might also be part of the reason for her weight loss. Picking him up so often, she must be building muscle mass, also. She had held him a lot, too, since that incident at the Ostrich Grill.

Ostrich Grill. She could barely make herself say the full name of the restaurant, Ostrich Bar and Grill. She hadn't been back, either, there or to church. Dylan had, and Lissie. Karen had gotten up the past two Sunday mornings, and it had just been too much. She would think of the Broady brothers or the man she had put in the hospital. Then she would put the keys to the van on the kitchen counter and tell Lissie to drive carefully. Karen would climb back into bed with Chipper until her children returned, and only then would she deign to face the day.

"Mom! I can't find—oh, there's Junie. Chipper opened the cage, and he just flew out." Lissie called the little bird and began to whistle.

Karen sighed. With the party tomorrow, she'd taken a day off work and let the kids stay home from school. Maybe that had been a mistake.

"Don't, Lissie. I want him to fly in here. Chipper likes it, and it seems rather nice that he's free. I don't want him caged today. Please." She reached down to rub the baby's head. "So, Chipper's finally learned to open the cage. I guess we'll have to move it off the floor."

Lissie's voice was less forgiving. "Or get a lock. Mom, the last three weeks Chipper's been into everything. I can't control him."

Karen looked at her daughter with sympathy, but she knew it wasn't all Chipper. Karen had been very distracted with the three men she'd fallen in love with, most of all with the one from the bar, or rather from the grill. She'd also been back at work the past three weeks—thank God for that distraction. She hadn't been home to watch the pool progress at all. Chipper had run wild, and she hadn't cared. For the first time in his short life, Lissie was being forced to step up to the plate with him.

She had gotten Lissie to call the hospital, but there had been no one there by the name of James or John, at least that had been admitted on that disastrous Sunday afternoon. All the hospital had been able to tell them was that the man who had been in surgery that day was still in the critical care ward, and no visitors were allowed. It had been three weeks, and just the thought of it kept Karen in turmoil.

"Mom? Are you okay? Are you sure the baby's safe with you?"

Karen smiled and waved both her daughter and the baby toward the door. "Take him to the park, Lissie. That always tires him out. Try the one on the south side of the river, Town Lake Park. It's over off Lee Barton. Take the Camp-mobile." That made her think of the man she'd seen there, and the glass-walled lofts her construction worker lived in. It also made her butterflies flutter once again as she sat watching her grandson play with his fingernails.

Lissie sighed, and it was loud and dramatic. "I know where Town Lake Park is, Mom. That's where Kenny and I first . . . ." She let her words die off.

Karen had heard, though. She just couldn't feign any interest. After all, she had put a man in the hospital, and she was in love with two others, besides. What else could be worse than that? Nothing, and that was the problem she could not put out of her mind for even one instant.

JOHN'S DOORBELL rang. He sat by the window looking

out at the brilliance of an early Austin summer, and he didn't care about the doorbell. He was watching for a red VW Campmobile van to pull up at the curb, and he wanted to see a beautiful woman climb out to take her baby for a stroll in the park.

The bell rang again, and this time very insistently. Drawing in a deep breath, he called out, "It's unlocked." His eyes never left the street and the parking place where he had last seen that van.

Frankie's voice called out, "You let any old strangers in?" She laughed brightly and closed the door after her, making a point to lock it. She set a bag on the kitchen counter. "I have a key, you know. You don't have to leave the door unlocked for me."

"It's too much trouble to lock it. No one wants anything I've got. You know that. They don't even want me."

Frankie walked up to sit on the leather ottoman beside his feet, blocking his view of the street. When he shifted to see around her, she moved back into his line of view. Finally, he sat back and leaned his head against the top of the chair.

"I give, Frankie. What?" His eyes were closed, and his voice was flat with lack of emotion.

"John, three weeks ago you gave up on life. You sent me out with a checkbook to buy this place, and now you're here. Your things are still boxed up in the extra bedroom, and all you do is sit in front of this window on the only piece of furniture you have in this condo. I don't even have to ask why, do I? You know where she lives. You don't have to do this."

He put his hand on his forehead and ran it through his hair. "Just waltz into her life and announce that I'm her knight in shining armor? The pool's at least finished now. Maybe I can put her behind me."

"You could go check on the pool, you know. You could do that, John. Call her up to make sure she's home, and go by to take pictures for our new sales brochure."

"We don't have a new sales brochure. I'm not going to lie just to go see her."

Frankie took one of the company's most recent brochures out of her pocket, and she held it up between them. With a flourish, she ripped it in half.

"Oops! That was the last one in our files. I guess we have to make new sales brochures."

John finally smiled. " I happen to know that was not the last one. A new box came in just last month."

She patted his leg. "You know that new shredder you bought me?"

He frowned. "New shredder? You got that last year."

"No," she said with mock seriousness. "I got a new one yesterday. It's one of those big, bulk models. You need to get into the office and see it. Anyway, I had to try it out." She paused for emphasis and then continued, "On that box of brochures. That really was the last one."

John chuckled and ran his finger over the leather on the arm of the chair. "I cannot go over there to take pictures. You see my hand? It's still in a cast."

"Yes, I see that hand." She reached to pick it up when she noticed a stack of newspapers on the floor beside the chair. "Been reading?"

"Not really. They're all the same. That retraction, that's all. I keep hoping that helped Karen out." He reached and handed her one. "Here. Have a copy."

She took it and told him, "I have a copy at home. If you'd come see me, you'd know that. It's been two weeks since you came over." She squinted her eyes and read the type aloud. "Amorous Assignation Not as It Seems. Pool contractor catches woman after ten-foot fall into unfinished pool. A RealImage police photo mistakenly made it appear a tête-à-tête in the dark, but hospital sources have confirmed the situation to be entirely innocent. Our apologies to the unnamed couple."

"Thank you, Frankie. I've read it often enough to memorize it. Do you think Karen's seen it?"

"She would if you took her a copy."

His eyes rolled to look past her out the window. "And have her see me like this?" The swelling around his eye had gone down, but the side of his face still sported a grapefruit-sized bruise. The eyeball was laced with bright red blotches of blood. "She'd know me for a ruffian. I was no better than those Broady bullies."

"You were protecting her honor, John. I thought it was very sweet."

"She doesn't know that. It looks like I was in a bar and got in a fight."

Frankie laughed and patted his leg before standing. "That was exactly what happened. That was a bar, and you did get in a fight. You started it, as I recall, not that it wasn't deserved." Walking to the counter, she pulled out several Styrofoam packages. She carried one to him and held it out.

"What is it?"

"A burger." She smiled.

"What kind? It smells good." He took it and opened one side.

She laughed out loud. "Ostrich, and on your credit card. I have rhubarb and chocolate cream pie, too." As she turned, she called back, "We need to get you a dining table. I get tired of trays in my lap."

When she returned with two drinks in her hands, John was holding the opened container with his good hand, and tears were running down his face. He glanced up at her and reached with the back of his injured hand to wipe his eyes on his arm.

"What, John? Talk to me." She placed his drink on the floor beside him and took her spot on the ottoman.

He held up the burger, and then he said, "Rhubarb, too. I can't stop thinking of her. I need to find a shark's tooth, Frankie. God may want us to enjoy the sunset, but I really need to find a tooth."

She looked at the drink in her hand, and she touched the straw to swirl the ice. After a moment of silence, she began to speak.

"When Herbert died, I cried for weeks. I had three little girls, and I couldn't see the end of it. One day God took me to the jar where I keep those sharks' teeth I found all those years ago, and he told me just to walk the beach. He had a special blessing coming up, but it wasn't ready yet." She looked up to catch his eyes. "The next day your daddy brought you to work with him for the first time. John, you were my shark's tooth. You were the blessing God had for me, and you just weren't ready yet."

He looked out the window and smiled through his tears, but he couldn't hold it, and it quickly faded. "Thank you. It's hard, though, you know?" He turned to look back at her, and his smile brightened. "You brought rhubarb pie?"

"On the counter. Just for you."

He took a deep breath and let his eyes rove the ceiling. "It makes me think of her, Frankie. Of course, then, everything does."

"God's got your blessing coming. It might be Karen, and it might not. You just keep walking, and it'll be there for you to find if you're looking for it."

"I guess so. Maybe."

She smiled. "I know so. Right now, though, let's walk the food part of the beach. I'm hungry, and I'd hate to think this bird died in vain."

John reached for his burger with his one good hand. "Those rhubarbs, either."

Then the room was quiet except for the small sounds of good food being consumed by very hungry people.

JUST OUTSIDE, a young girl, not yet eighteen, who looked very much like Karen, pushed her toddler in a stroller to the park. She didn't mind walking, but she did mind parallel parking, so the van she drove was parked two blocks away.

When a small bird flitted out of the bushes, a child's voice from the stroller cried, "Junie?" However, the day was hot already, and his mother didn't answer. She wanted shade, and she would have to reach the park for that. In the heat of a Texas summer, everyone wanted shade, and Lissie was no exception.

THERE WAS a yellow flash outside her bedroom window, and Karen felt a surge of panic. She would tolerate Junie enjoying a taste of freedom in the house, but he could not be allowed to fly free in the yard. The bird might fly away, and she couldn't bear another loss at this time.

"Dylan!" She called out her door. "Junie's outside."

He would have to be the one to whistle for him. When her son didn't answer, she walked across the room and pulled the sheers aside. Her heart caught in her chest as she saw him standing on the roof. His skin sparkled with iridescent water droplets, and all he was wearing was one tiny yellow Speedo swimsuit.

In a panic, she grabbed the handle to the window and began to twirl it open as quickly as she could. When there was enough of a gap for her to call outside, she yelled, "Dylan! What in heaven's name are you doing?"

He looked at her and waved. "I'm practicing my can opener. The diving board's not high enough."

"Into the pool?" She was incredulous. They had only filled it with water two days before, and the chemicals were probably still adjusting themselves. The irrigation system had gone in just that morning, but the landscaping company wasn't due to be there until early in the morning. Dylan would track in mud everywhere!

He looked at her and shrugged his shoulders. "There's plenty of water, Mom. Look. It's perfect. Besides, I have to practice for Uncle Eddy. Why else did you let me stay home from school today?" He took two running steps and leaped off the roof into nothing.

"Dylan!" She gasped the word, and she watched him disappear beneath the water, sending a cascading spray onto the surrounding deck. It was only when he burst above the surface laughing that she felt her heart begin to beat again. She waved at him and watched as he pulled himself up on the side, the water from the pool streaming down his body. Without hesitation, he ran to the gutters and began his ascent to the roof for another leap.

She closed the window and turned back to her room, breathing heavily. Was he going to be just like his father, never minding the rules, always leaping when he should be looking? Could she stand another five years of that? It might even be seven or more if he lived at home during college. Some U.T. students did.

At least the little yellow bird she had seen outside wasn't one she needed to catch. However, she didn't need to watch, either, not if he was determined to kill himself jumping off the roof into the pool. If nothing else, all that swim practice with his team was counting for something.

The phone beside her bed jangled, and she jumped. Laughing nervously, she called out, "Lissie? Can you get that?" It was probably one of her daughter's friends, and besides, Karen didn't feel like talking to anyone today, anyone except her brother. That was the one thing she thought might make the day better. Eddy hadn't seen the pool yet, and Dylan was anxious to show it off. He was supposed to be on his way.

The phone jangled again, and she glared.

"Lissie?" She groaned and snatched the receiver from its cradle. "Karen speaking." For once, she wished her daughter could be responsible and do as her mother asked. However, she would not heap abuse on her caller, and she kept her voice bright and friendly.

"Mom! Thank goodness you answered." It was Lissie, and she sounded near to tears. "I have Chipper with me. How could you forget to stop by the station and then loan me the van? How can you expect me to put gas in your van and watch my baby, too? Am I the only responsible person living in our house?"

"Lissie," Karen growled, her mind racing. She *had* stopped by the station. How could the van be empty? "Are you sure? Did you check the correct gauge?"

"Mom!" She wailed her distress. "I'm here at the station now, and the needle points to the E. How can I watch Chipper and put in gas, too?"

Karen immediately understood the problem, and she berated herself. How had she been so lax to let her daughter get to be seventeen and not know how to manage a baby and fuel a car at the same time?

However, that was not the problem today.

"Lissie, are you listening?" She thought she heard sobs from the other end of the line. "Lissie? Are you still there?"

"Of course I am." She gasped out the words in between her sobs. "The van's out of gas. How could I go anywhere? I think Chipper's hungry, too. Oh, Mom! How can you be so irresponsible?" Chipper's voice was bright and cheerful in the background. He was talking to himself, and he didn't sound especially hungry.

"Lissie, listen to me. The gas gage is on the top, remember? Your father had the shop put in a digital one. The one with the dial doesn't work."

"Oh." There was a pause, and she took several ragged breaths. "I remember. I see it. But, Mom, it doesn't show any gas, either." At least her sobs had finally slowed to sniffles. "What if Chipper gets hungry? How will I get him any food? I'm stuck here forever."

"Stuck?" That was Chipper. "Issie stuck?"

"At a gas station, Chipper," Karen heard her call to him. Then, "Mom? Are you going to help? Can you call someone to bring your grandson some crackers or something? I didn't bring anything with me for him to eat. I didn't know I would run out of gas."

You're at a gas station, Karen thought. Go inside and buy some food if your son gets hungry. She didn't say that. Instead, she offered her daughter a simple suggestion she must not have tried yet.

"Lissie, turn on the key. See if the van has gas then." There was the sound of a starter turning over the engine, then it roared to life, quickly settling into a background purr. Karen prompted her daughter, "Lissie, how does it look?"

"Oh, Mom! That was so easy. I have a full tank. I didn't know it could be so easy to fill up the van. I didn't even have to get out. Thanks, Mom!" Then, with a click, the line went dead.

"Thank you, too, Lissie," Karen murmured as she returned the phone to the holder. She knew one thing. She was getting too old for this. Her big brother had never minded the years when they rolled by. He still didn't. She did, though, especially with two errant kids, a grandchild living under her roof, and that yellow, feathered nightmare she could never control.

That made her think of Dylan jumping in the pool, wearing only his yellow Speedos, and she felt the tension in her head ease. She did love that boy, and he was adorable running around in his brightly colored suit. No matter what he did, she could always find it in her heart to forgive him. That forgiving nature of hers was probably why Brad had walked over her for all those years, why he was with that bimbo even now. At least those wasted years were over and forgotten.

However, this birthday was thirty-nine for her, and that was too close to forty for comfort. Eddy said the high side of forty felt just like the low side, but she doubted that. There a sound to the word that ran up and down her spine like cold chills on a hot summer day, and she did not mean that in a good way, either.

Until Lissie punched out little Chipper, she guessed she hadn't really minded birthdays, either. She had always been the twenty-something from college with just a few more numbers added to her collection of birthdays. She even remembered looking forward to them. Now? Never!

She looked at her bed. There was a swimsuit spread out, almost as if its owner had laid down for a rest, then faded into the bedding, leaving the suit to fend for itself. Even before the pool was started, she had one picked out. Not this one, but a one piece, very conservative, in black. Then she'd had to return it by way of her daughter for a smaller size.

Now she had this brilliant two-piece in a much smaller—and much more revealing—size.

Stress. Stress will do that to a person. She had been so excited three weeks ago, her upcoming party her springboard into her chance at a new life, but she couldn't even think about it now. She might have to wear the suit for the party come tomorrow, but for now she left it on the bed and headed downstairs. Her brother was coming, and that was better than a new swimsuit any day.

With a smile of anticipation, she recalled how he always liked coffee when he showed up for a visit. She had to have a pot on when he arrived at the door, and she headed to the kitchen. She was barely to the living room, however, when she jumped, startled, as water splashed loudly against the windows.

"Dylan!" She called, even though she knew he wasn't listening. She couldn't see him outside with the blinds shut, anyway, and he was probably still under the water. Even so, the pause as she listened for his reply gave her heart time to settle. She laughed, her nerves still jangling. Perhaps she didn't want to see outside.

After her run-in with the construction worker in the pool that disastrous night, she had been religious about leaving the blinds closed. To her chagrin, as much as she had enjoyed being held in the pool worker's arms, it was that man from Wayside who had really snagged her emotions. He had stood up for her honor, even if he wasn't standing at all now. No, she had left him in the critical care unit at the hospital, and there had been nothing for her to do about it.

Her windows had remained closed because she simply didn't need another incident with anyone who had anything to do with her pool's construction. That little tryst—how she hated that word—splashed all over Austin had been a bit too sensual for comfort.

The blinds being closed, however, didn't exactly block out the sounds of Dylan's antics off the roof. Every time he hit the water, the memories washed over her: Dylan there with his flashlight; and a helicopter that wantonly snapped pictures of private dalliances in very private pools. Dalliances? No. A better word was disasters. Disasters of the heart. Hearing Dylan out in the pool reminded her too strongly of a pool she did not want to see until after Eddy showed up to fortify her underpinnings.

She shivered, hating the ragged reminders, yet admitting her son had to be allowed to have fun sometime. She just didn't have to watch.

She also hadn't been back to Town Lake Park. One evening, Chipper had gone with her to Lakeshore where they had braved the bigger crowds, because she didn't need to see that man from the loft, either. He was surely the brother to that man from inside her pool, or at least his smile had made it seem that way. Surely it was a sign of God's favor seeing that black-tied, fedora-wearing man at church with her children's Miss Frankie, wasn't it? She hoped so, anyway. He must have some sort of religious background, and she would insist on that in any man she hoped to be involved with. Then, it was as if God had seen how his smile had toyed with her heart and taken a giant flyswatter and squashed it all, before anything could even get started.

It was more than that wonderful smile, however. It was the way he'd stood up for her against the Broadys, taken a stand for a strange woman he hadn't even met. How special did a man have to be to do that?

Now she hoped to rectify the hadn't-even-met part if possible. She just had to wait until he was out of danger in the critical care ward at the hospital. Of course, she also had to find out his name.

As she poured water into the coffee pot, she growled at Lissie and Dylan. They hadn't been much help. The last two weeks they hadn't asked Miss Frankie about her injured champion. Karen didn't know if that was their excuse for teenage laziness, or if each week, Miss Frankie had exited the services during the closing prayers, but they claimed they hadn't been able to find her. All in all, there wasn't much she could do about it, and in her depression, she had chosen to set it aside. After all, she couldn't visit the man if she couldn't find out who he was, and her attempts to learn his name were going nowhere.

As the coffee pot began to burble with its customary chattering sounds, the doorbell rang. Closing her eyes and smiling with anticipation, she knew who this was. Eddy always took care of her, and she needed his company right then.

Opening the door, she smiled at the bulk of a man her big brother had grown into. He'd never been skinny, but as an adult, he'd matured into his frame like he'd been born to sturdiness. He had a barrel of a chest, and while he was thicker than he had been as a youngster, his jeans still looked good on him when he walked.

"Sis!" He dropped the duffel he carried, and he held his arms out. Her eyes teared up, and she threw her arms around him. After relishing the contact of familiar skin for a time, they separated, and Eddy held her at arm's length. "Baby sis? I do believe that's a sad look I see on that pretty face. After four months, are you still grieving for that rotten dog that left you for his secretary?"

She pulled loose to put one arm around her brother's waist and led him into the house. "No, Eddy. Brad was gone long before he ever left, and I just refused to see it. I'm not blind anymore."

"Is this sadness from turning thirty-nine? It does that to some people." He touched her chin to look into her face. "I see my baby sister here, and if I didn't count the candles, I'd swear I'm looking at twenty-eight instead of ten more."

"I'm eleven more than twenty-eight, Eddy."

"Not for another week." He winked.

"You're so nice to me, my favorite big brother. I've needed you here." She put her head against his chest and smiled.

He laughed, and as she leaned against him, the sound of it rumbled through his chest. "Your only brother, but I'll take what I can get. Sis, I'm nice to you, but I'm not just being nice to you about this. Somehow you've stepped off the merry-go-round, and you haven't added one line since you were a girl. You smell good, too. Is that coconut in your hair?"

"Eddy, Eddy. I love you. Come see the pool. The land-scaping will be installed in the morning, but Dylan's swimming now. Rather, he's doing can openers off the roof."

He chuckled at that. "Sounds just like that nephew of mine. I brought a suit. I might follow him in."

Karen pulled away and gave him a stern look. "You use the diving board, Brother. I don't want you on that roof. Dylan's bad enough. Oh, and I've got coffee going."

"I smelled it the moment I walked in the door. Cinnamon roast?" A smile spread across his face.

"Just for you."

"Let me get my things, and I'll be right there. Coffee first, and then out to the pool. Priorities, Sis. Always pay attention to priorities." He turned back to the door.

She thought about that, and she wasn't sure she always had. Brad, and this pool. Then there had been three lost opportunities for love. Now she was celebrating thirty-nine with a party in her backyard. How stupid was that? She had even planned it all on her own, guest invitations and all. She knew one thing. Even with all the *life* her family kept swirling around her, she clearly had entirely too much time on her hands.

She jumped as a huge wave of water crashed against the breakfast room window, and almost immediately, the door into the garage flew open with Lissie complaining about every driver in Austin who had frustrated her on her trip back from Town Lake Park. She started to vent about the gas station, then she caught her mother's eyes and uncharacteristically let it go. She leaned to set Chipper on the floor, and as a flash of yellow darted towards the open door, he cried, "Junie! Chipper want Junie! Chipper eat Junie!"

Karen took a deep breath, just as Eddy stepped past them and closed the door, trapping the bird inside. He

236

stepped to Lissie to kiss her on the cheek, and then he got a cup out of the cabinet. Grinning, he stood at Karen's side and poured himself a steaming cup. He turned around just in time to see Lissie grab the baby without another word and march off upstairs with him.

"Same old madhouse, huh, Sis?" He sipped on his coffee and chuckled. "At least the kid can't eat the bird if it's loose in the house."

She sighed. "Madhouse, you think? Brad being gone hasn't changed that a bit." In that moment, she remembered something. She didn't have too much time on her hands. She had too much *life* on her hands.

Chapter 15

JOHN'S TRUCK idled, the air conditioner fighting back the heat of the day. It was Friday evening, and the cars in the shopping center lot were beginning to thin out. All that were left were several SUVs and an old yellow Camp-mobile. How unusual was that? Frankie had said Karen's wasn't the only one around.

Frankie had suggested, and strongly, too, that he should visit the office for a bit, but he really didn't want to talk to anyone. With his face still so rough, he hated to be seen in public, and this was his first real venture out since the week-end of the fight. He just needed to see something besides that parking space outside his new condo's window where that red Campmobile never seemed to park anymore.

Reaching and killing the ignition, he listened to his truck's diesel engine sputter to a stop The air conditioning fan whirred for a second or two more, and then it was silent. There was music low in the background, and he realized the radio had been on all the time he'd been driving, and he hadn't been able to hear it. Reaching to the dash, he touched the control, and it flicked off.

The residual heat of the Austin day assaulted him as he opened the door. Sitting in that new condo for weeks had sucked away his acclimation to the Texas summer temperatures. He'd have to build that back up, or the rest of the summer would be miserable.

He cringed when he walked up to the building. His reflection in the tinted glass was sharp and clear in the late afternoon light. The skin was still tender where the purple stain ran across his face, and deep red marks still blotched the white of his left eye. On his follow-up visit to the hospital, they were glad to see he still had his vision on that side. He was lucky. Give it some time, and they were sure it would eventually sharpen back to 20/20.

Out for his first time today, he could tell his peripheral vision still suffered. He chastised himself, figuring it was a pretty good reason not to get into fights with men bigger than he was.

With just one good hand, he tossed his key ring in the air, and when it landed sprawled out in his palm, he used his thumb to select the key for the door. Letting the rest fall to the side, he pushed the key inside and gave it a turn. The door dinged as he pushed it open, and he turned to the alarm pad to see it wasn't activated. That irritated him. Three weeks away, and already the office was getting sloppy. He'd have to ask Frankie who had exited last today.

Walking to his office, he flipped a floor light on beside his desk and pulled out a drawer. He lifted out one file folder and placed it on top, opening it and spreading the contents out.

"Wycliff." He sat and flipped a desk lamp on. Locating the original contract, he looked at the signatures and read them aloud. "Brad Wycliff. Karen Wycliff." There was another contract, too, a replacement for this one. The most recent one had just Karen's name on it. It was how Frankie had known about the divorce. To finish the construction, Karen had been required to take full responsibility for the installation, and they'd rewritten it just for her.

He ran his finger over her name, blinking his eyes and looking away for a moment. Then he slipped the paper-work back inside and closed the folder.

Pulling a large rubber stamp from a rack on his desk, he opened a pad, inked the surface of the stamp, and pressed it hard against the outside of the folder. When he lifted it, the words in red said *Installation Complete.* On the line just below it were the words *Final Check Received,* and a blank was inked in for him to write in the date. That would be tomorrow. It would be a small check, just to cover the landscaping, but it would be collected, the folder would be dated, and then it would go into another filing cabinet in the storage room. These folders usually stayed in his desk until the final check was in hand, but he wanted this one gone.

He needed to move on.

He sat and blinked rapidly. He didn't really want this folder gone, and he wasn't sure he *could* move on. How-ever, he could not find a way to approach this woman. He remembered Frankie's idea, and he smiled as he wiped the gathering tears away. New brochures. He wondered if she really had shredded the old ones.

Heading to the storeroom, he twisted the doorknob and was surprised to find the light was on. Another slipup, he thought, as he stepped inside. Then, his heart jumped into his throat as an arm wrapped around his waist.

"John! You know we're closed."

The voice was as familiar as it was unexpected. With his peripheral vision gone on one side, he hadn't known anyone in the room.

"You'll have to come back Monday if you want me to sell you a pool."

He laughed, but his heart pounded. "Frankie! I thought I was alone." He breathed roughly, grabbing the top of a filing cabinet to brace himself. "I think you stopped my heart there for a moment." He leaned forward to rest his head against his arms. When he finally stood, his eyes were wet with tears, but a smile was on his face.

She laughed. "I'm sorry. I thought you saw me. I was right beside you when you stepped in." She rubbed his side where her hand held him, and then with a final pat, she stepped away. "You really were startled, weren't you?"

"You have no idea. My peripheral vision hasn't returned on my left side yet. I was irritated the alarm was off, and then when this light was on, I just assumed someone was sloppy when shutting down the office for the weekend. I had no idea anyone was still working." He glanced toward the window. "Your car, I didn't see it."

"Yes, you did." She smiled, and then she walked to the

back of the room. "Come here, John. I want you to see my new shredder." He laughed when she pointed it out to him. It was waist high and two feet square.

"Did you really shred our brochures?" He was beginning to believe her.

"See that stack on the shelf above the shredder?"

"What stack?" She pointed, and he frowned. "That shelf is empty."

She grinned. "You learn fast, boy. You were like that at six, and I've enjoyed it ever since. Follow me." She led him into the break room, and she reached to a letter tray on the table. She pulled out five folders, and she spread them out in front of him.

"So, is this the mystery sales brochure contest?"

"Open one, John. Any one." She could barely keep from smiling.

His finger opened the first, and he looked up at her. It was a contract of sale for a new pool installation. "Who sold this one?"

She smiled in self-congratulation. "Yours truly."

"The others?" She beamed, and he chided her. "We have sales people, Frankie. You earn twice your paycheck already, you know, just doing what you do. You don't have to sell pools, also."

She held out her hand. "Then pay me twice. I'll take it."

"Seriously. You sold five pools? You didn't even tell me when you were at my place today. Why?"

"What do the young people say today? I've got your back, John. Springfield Pools has been my bulwark for nearly thirty years, and you needed me for three weeks. I stepped up to the plate, and I didn't mind it at all. Now, you get to go out and build them. You know tomorrow's the final day." She said her last statement very casually as she absently picked up the closest of the five folders.

He reached to flip through the rest of the folders, before glancing at Frankie, "The final day?"

Her smirk was obvious. "Karen's pool. We were pushing to get it finished for a party she was giving. Landscaping goes in tomorrow morning."

He gave a small, sour laugh. "I know that. I had the file out on my desk. I've already stamped it, ready to be dated."

"Already? Before the final check clears?"

He looked away. "I need to get on with my life. I want this done."

"Do you really? Someone has to pick up that final check tomorrow. It could be you."

He turned his face to her. "Could it really? We talked about this today. This is my brawling-with-the-Broadys face. Not even I like it."

"John, sit." She patted a spot at the table. When he pulled up a chair, she sat beside him. "Three weeks ago, I guessed this might be the start of love, perhaps a jumping off place. Then you attacked those Broadys, and I thought it might actually be for real. Three weeks of moping, John? Three weeks of this tells me something that first weekend didn't. Don't walk off from this woman like this. Give her a chance. You owe yourself that."

"She doesn't even know me. Do you remember that?"

"She does know you. Give yourself some credit."

"She knows a man who held her in her pool, and who

humiliated her on the front page of the largest paper in Austin." He chewed his upper lip, and he pushed a folder around on the table. "She doesn't know me."

Frankie was determined to make a point, though, and she reached to gently touch the left side of his face. He jerked away at the unexpected pressure, and then he relaxed when he realized it was her hand in his blind spot.

"John, you were nearly blinded to protect her honor—"

"Which she does not know about." He snorted his derision for that reminder.

"She doesn't need to. I know, and you know. What if she feels the same about you?"

He thought about that, and he remembered that night when she had fallen into his arms. She brushed the dirt from his chest, and he never answered her question. She said he might be holding a vengeful Amazon. He said he knew better, and then the flashlight had appeared. He'd never told her how he saw her. Kind. Loving. Caring. Very beautiful. All those things and more. He had seen all that in one yellow parakeet and the way she had tried to call it to her. Still. Still.

"She doesn't know me, Frankie."

She stood, and she reached to a shelf at her side. With a stern look on her face, she slapped an envelope on the table in front of John. "I am out of patience with you, John Springfield. I love you, but I have no more patience with you. Someone has to pick up that final check tomorrow. It goes in that envelope. If that envelope shows up on my desk Monday morning, I'll know you are the man I've always hoped you'd be. If not, then I will still love you, but I won't come babysit you when you mope around about this woman. Make some choices, John. God told me I'd have to be looking for the blessings to find them. It seems to me God dumped this blessing in your arms. Do this, John."

He sighed. "For you, Frankie?"

Tears came to her eyes. She stepped to him to kiss him on the forehead, and she whispered, "Not this time. Do this for you." Then she walked to the door and paused. Without looking back, she said, "Turn out the lights. Lock the door, too." With those words she was gone.

He stood and walked to the window. He wanted to see what she meant about having seen her car. Somehow, when she walked up to the yellow Campmobile and opened the door to climb inside, it didn't surprise him at all.

EDDY SWAM to the pool's steps, laughing, and in the darkness of the Texas night the light from the water's depths gave his skin a greenish glow. He hadn't had this much fun in years. That nephew of his could swim like a fish, but he was no match for his uncle's long arms. Eddy had thrown the boy over his head again and again until he'd cried for mercy.

That afternoon, Dylan and his uncle had balanced the pool chemicals, and then they had assembled the outdoor furniture, setting it up around the deck. The table now had an umbrella for daytime shade, and all the chairs had colorful, striped cushions. Even the settee was outfitted with three tufted, outdoor pads designed to be left out in the weather.

At least they didn't have to put together a grill, Karen

had told him. Brad had done that, or at least paid someone else to do it. It had arrived in their backyard the previous year fully assembled. The pool contractor had poured a special place in the deck to position it, and it sat nicely out of the way.

As he rose from the water, pausing on the top step, Eddy got a surprise. A fifteen-year-old set of arms wrapped around his neck from behind, and with his limbs flailing, Eddy found himself struggling to stay upright.

"Gotcha, Uncle Eddy," the boy cried. He leaned backwards, attempting to overbalance the bigger man. "Cry uncle, or I won't let go."

"Help, Sis! I think he's got me this time." Then the two were gone into the pool, silenced under the weight of the inrushing water.

KAREN LAUGHED and waved as she watched her brother and son tumble backwards into the pool. Tucking her towel around her, she appreciated that Eddy was bringing life to her house in a way that she hadn't seen in a long time. It brought home to her that this house needed a man. This family needed a man. Eddy would be a great stand-in for the weekend, but then he would be gone. She needed someone permanent, someone that Brad hadn't been in a very long time. The only thing was, she didn't exactly know how to make that happen.

When Eddy climbed out the second time, he raised his arms to show acquiescence to the nephew still prowling the pool like a shark waiting for its next meal.

"Uncle, Dylan. I give up. I want to sit and talk with your

mom for a bit. I'll tell you what. You do some can openers, and later we'll fire the spa up."

"Cool, Uncle Eddy." Inside the pool, the boy jumped and pumped his arm excitedly in the air. As it came down, his elbow hit the surface of the water with a smacking sound. Then, in a more subdued tone, he turned to his mother, "Mom, is that okay? The spa? Uncle Eddy's the one who suggested it."

She waved her hand at him. "Of course it is, if Uncle Eddy suggested it." She turned to her brother. "Thanks, Uncle Eddy. I get to pay the gas bill."

He grabbed a towel and rubbed his head as he sat. "I know that deserter husband of yours makes ten times enough to pay any gas bill you might run up. However, if you run short, let me know. I'll pick up the difference."

She smiled at him. "You are good for me right now, Eddy. I should have had you over four months ago."

He laughed. "You didn't have your pool finished four months ago, or I would've been here, even if you hadn't asked."

"In the middle of winter? We had that cold snap, you remember. We were iced in, and then it rained for weeks. Trust me. You wouldn't have wanted to be in the pool then even if it was finished. However, the thought is nice, and I appreciate it."

As he draped his towel behind him and leaned back in his chair, Eddy nodded at Karen's son climbing up the gutter downspout to the roof. "I talked to your boy this afternoon."

She glanced at him, unsure what he meant. She gave

him a moment, watching as the pool lights flickered against the back of the house and lit the second story. Dylan could be seen glistening as he scurried across the roof in the warmth of the night air, his Speedos glowing yellow when they caught the light. He laughed and called to his Uncle Eddy, and then with his lithe swimmer's musculature, he took two fast steps and sailed into the pool, sending water flooding over the coping. Karen pulled her feet up just in time to keep them dry.

"Okay, Eddy. What about?"

He looked back at the house. "I like the blinds open." He had raised them, complaining about not understanding why every blind facing the pool was as tightly closed as it could be. He said he needed the outside to come in. Karen had just laughed, telling him that with no neighbors out on his ranch, he also had no need for blinds. His high-tech argon-filled glass could keep out the sun and heat, and he could enjoy the deer and other wildlife both summer and winter.

However, her blinds were not raised now. She had asked Lissie to put them back down, then twisted the wands so Eddy could see out. That was all she had been able to give him. She at least needed the illusion that her construction worker from the bottom of her unfinished pool would not be looking back inside at her—and she would not be looking outside for him.

Still, they could see everything inside the brightly lit house. Lissie moved through the living room into the kitchen. Chipper toddled along after her, carrying an empty bottle, and finally his mother stopped and picked him up.

He wrapped his arms around her neck and squeezed her tightly.

Eddy whispered, "She's learning, Karen. Just turning sixteen was too young to be a mother, but she's learning. Graduation is coming up. What's she going to do next?"

"I don't know. University work. I'd like that, and the money's still there in her college fund. With Chipper though, I don't know. Lissie was running around in diapers the last two years I was in school, you know. It was tough, both on me as well as Brad. I really wanted that college degree, and I, at least, was halfway there before I had my first baby. Lissie? I'm hoping she has that much drive."

They sat in silence watching Dylan disappear under the surface as he swam repeated laps under the water, only coming up for air when Karen's heart began to pound with worry. She loved that boy immensely, even if he sometimes drove her to the brink of despair.

"What'd you speak to Dylan about?" She closed her eyes. Eddy was one to see things. He was also a doer. He saw things from the outside, and he saw them as they were, not as he wanted them to be. She didn't always have that skill. Actually, she had never had that skill. She saw nuances layered upon nuances, and she would still be unpeeling the onion while her brother had it sliced, diced, and sautéed in the pan.

"Do you look at him, Karen?"

The sound of a soda can opening told her he was planning to discuss something serious. Eddy didn't just sit. He did. With his hands, and his mind, and however he needed to get things done. She also knew it would exhaust her after a while, but not yet. At this point, she was still glad to have his energy and support sitting next to her.

"Okay, Eddy. What am I not seeing?"

"He'll be sixteen in the fall, little sister. You see him every day, so you don't have the perspective I can bring you. It's been three months since I've seen him, and he's filling out. A lot. You're seeing a boy. I see the man coming out. It's not here yet, but close, Sister."

"What are you saying?" She thought she knew, and she really didn't want to deal with it. However, she also knew if she had listened to her brother three years ago, Lissie wouldn't be in there preparing a nighttime bottle for a twenty-three-month old toddler.

"I was fifteen a long time ago, Sis, and at fifteen, a boy's hormones are an uncontrollable wildfire. That's at fifteen, too. At sixteen, it's worse. Do you know he sneaks out at night?"

"He has this friend, Zack. They're inseparable. You'll get to meet him tomorrow. He's spending the rest of the weekend with us. I wanted you to have Dylan to yourself for one night, so I refused to let Zack come until bright and early in the morning. Get ready, Eddy. You think your nephew's a raging wildfire? He and Zack together are an inferno." She laughed. "I love my son. Dylan's helped me survive the last four months." Especially the last three weeks, but she didn't say that.

Eddy took a deep breath before speaking, and Karen could hear it. "He's seeing a girl, Karen. At night." He reached to the back of his chair and dug in his shirt pocket to pull out a small, flat package. He handed it to his sister.

"Do you know what this is?"

"Eddy!" This hurt her feelings. She knew exactly what her brother was giving her. "You want me to give this to Dylan? That's like encouraging him to go ahead."

"You don't understand. That's why I asked if you've really looked at him. He's nearly sixteen. He's not your innocent little boy anymore. I took this out of his wallet. He has more in the house."

Her heart stopped. Her eyes found her son, and she watched him clambering up the downspout and onto the roof. She tried to see in those arms and legs what her brother was telling her. She looked at the package in her hand, and she felt her eyes blur and burn.

"How long, Eddy? Did he tell you that? How long has he been using these?"

Eddy reached for his sister's arm and worked his hand into hers. "He said he hasn't. However, he talked to me quite freely. He hasn't used one, but not for lack of desire. He hasn't used this one because the opportunity hasn't presented itself. He carries it in his wallet so he's always prepared."

"So he's always prepared? For sex?" Dylan was a boy, and he was sweet. He chased the girls, but he never caught them. At least he never had in the past.

"Those are your son's words, Karen, not mine." He stood. "He's heard it from me, Sis. Make sure he hears it from you. Don't wait on this. Now, if you don't mind, I've got me a nephew to drown."

Karen waved him off, and she fingered the package in her hand. When she looked at the bright yellow Speedos leaping into the pool almost onto Eddy's head, somehow they didn't look quite so cute and innocent on him anymore. Perhaps it was time to buy him some baggy trunks. Then at least she wouldn't have to see him and be reminded he wasn't a little boy any longer.

She laid the package on the table beside her and closed her eyes. She smiled at the thought that baggy shorts might solve this problem. "Thank you, Eddy," she whispered as she listened to them roughhousing in the water. She would tackle this, but what her son really needed was an Eddy, a man who lived under the same roof with him to give him a good example, advice when needed, and lots of love.

She chuckled at that. She needed exactly the same thing, except the last part was what she really wanted. Lots of love. Like that was going to happen for her.

She stood and threw her own towel aside, calling out, "Boys, I'm turning the spa on. Come and join me when you get tired of drowning each other." Stepping to the spa, with her foot, she pressed the button set into the deck, and she heard the heater and the jets kick on. Tomorrow evening was her party, and she took a certain consolation that her actual birthday wasn't for another five days. Her friends would all be here, and she would have fun.

Yes, she told herself, she would have fun. She *would* have fun.

Chapter 16

THE CHIRPING of a yellow parakeet awakened Karen. The sound was soft and pleasant to her ears. Then, a voice screamed bloody murder, and she jerked up in bed. When the scream merged into a loud splash of water, she breathed a sigh of relief and fell back onto her pillow. Zack must have arrived to spend the day with Dylan. As sleep began to overtake her again, the doorbell rang.

"I've got it!" Lissie's voice rang out, and Karen heard her thumping down the stairs. She knew it was too early for guests to arrive, but the landscapers were scheduled for the morning. Lissie could send them around back, though. Karen didn't have to get up to do that.

When the knock came at her door, she turned to see her daughter's face peeking inside. "Mom, um, you might want to get dressed. We have company."

"Company, Lissie?" She sat up. Could her daughter be any vaguer? Good heavens, it was Saturday morning! Who comes by on Saturday mornings?

"Mom?" Lissie slipped inside and closed the door behind her.

"Can you be any more specific than just company?" She glanced at the window to see Dylan's yellow Speedos flying through the air; and following him, she knew the blue she saw must be Zack. That would probably go on all morning. She hoped the boys didn't slow down the landscapers.

"Mom. Get ready. It's Dad."

Karen's eyes shot to her daughter's face. "Your father's here? Did he say why?"

"Mom! Have you forgotten?" Lissie peered through the door, then gently pushed it closed again. "You've planned a party today. Remember? You're turning thirty-nine and all? You said it would be your last birthday ever, and everybody had better come to this one. Well, Dad's come."

Karen drew in a deep breath and let it out. "Well, now. That's not too bad, is it, Lissie? He might even have me a present."

"His new wife might have you a present. That's what you should say." She turned to see the door opening and sighed with relief when it was just Chipper. "Come, Chipper. Give Mimi a big hug." She reached to give him a boost onto the bed. "Uncle Eddy's entertaining them until you get downstairs."

"Mimi hug." Chipper crawled over to Karen and put his arms around her neck. "See Junie?" He pointed, and as the bird moved to a new perch in the room, the boy's arm twisted to follow. Finally, unable to hang on and watch Junie at the same time, he lost his hold on Karen and fell to the bed.

"Chipper?" Karen wrapped her arms around him and set him up. "Are you all right?"

"All wight. See Junie." He pointed again.

She smiled. "That's right. See Junie. Keep the important things in perspective."

Lissie frowned. "Mom, you know he doesn't understand those words. You have to say things he understands."

"Then, Lissie dear, I would always talk in two word sentences and never pronounce my beginning r sounds. How would that become a mother who has to work full time to support her high school children?"

Lissie rolled her eyes. "Fine, Mom. I just came up here to warn you. You don't have to make fun of me."

"I wasn't, Lissie, and thank you for your warning. Will you please take your son so I can fortify my beauty? After all, I am almost forty, and I have to face the enemy already gathered underneath my feet."

Mollified with her mother's droll wit, Lissie grinned. "Mom, you can have a sense of humor when you want. That was funny. Face your enemy. Well, you don't have to worry. I just saw her, and she has tons of makeup on. You're a lot prettier. Younger looking, too."

Karen especially appreciated that last remark. She happened to know Brad's secretary, or rather his new wife, if Lissie was correct, was only twenty-six. Brad was turning fifty this year. It must be his money. Why else would a twenty-six-year-old woman marry a man of fifty? Love?

Ha! Karen had lived with Brad, and she knew him. If what Brad had to offer could be called love, then his secretary was welcome to him. She wanted someone who cared about her, not about how much she improved his image of himself.

Choosing her tightest jeans, the ones she could just now wear for the first time in two years, and silver lamé sandals, she slipped a snug tee over her head. Applying a touch of lipstick and patting her cheeks for color, Karen ran her fingers through her hair and decided she liked what she saw.

Walking down the stairs, she paused and listened as her brother's voice carried up to her. "She'd doing well, Brad. Karen's a survivor; you know that. After all, you lived with her for nineteen years." She could tell her ex said something in reply to her brother's remarks, but she couldn't tell just what. Brad was always a bit soft-spoken, and even when told his voice didn't carry well, he never bothered to speak up. However, Eddy had no such problem, and his voice rang out again. "I think finishing the pool's the best thing she's ever done. Too bad you can't stay for the party tonight. I don't know the exact count, but I expect we'll have more people here than we can shake a stick at." She smiled at that, and she wanted to make herself known before she could be accused of eavesdropping.

"Hey, all!" Walking loudly, she continued down the stairs and into the living room. "Brad! How pleasant to see you today! How's your new wife? She is your wife, now? That's what I hear, anyway." She turned to the blonde-haired girl at his side. "Oh, my dear. Bambii? Is that right? How perfectly radiant you look. Being a new bride becomes you so much. I hope that look never wears off. Would the two of you like some coffee? I have toffee surprise, and I'll get a pot going. Give me just a moment. Eddy? I need you to get the coffee pot down for me, please."

She turned, and in her most sultry walk, made her way out of the living room. Once in the kitchen, she leaned against the counter and closed her eyes. She was glad to hear her brother follow her in.

"You need help with the coffee pot?" He laughed softly.

"Morale, Eddy. Morale. It's there beside the stove. The tall cabinet. Please get it out for me so I'm not lying."

"What about toffee surprise?" He set the pot down, then leaned against the island and crossed his arms over his chest. "I've never heard of that."

"Well, you have as of today, big brother. Take those toffees in the bowl behind you and unwrap ten or so. They go in the pot. I just hope the coffee's hot enough to melt them before I take it in to Brad and that bambina he's brought into my house." She slammed the filter into the machine and dumped in way too much coffee. Slamming back the water lever, she let the water run into the reservoir. Then slapping it off, she turned to Eddy with her eyes burning.

"Eddy, she looks nineteen!"

He stepped to her and wrapped his arms around her. "Little sister, you look nineteen, and you just crawled out of bed. That woman's spent hours primping her face just to impress you. I don't think this is a fair fight at all. You win, hands down." He backed up enough to look in her face. "Chin up, Sis." He ran his thumbs under her eyes to wipe the moisture pooling there. "This is your party, so save the tears until they're gone. Show 'em you never crack."

She laughed, and she reached to flip the coffee maker on. Then, seeing the pot on the island surrounded by toffee wrappers, she pushed her brother aside to grab it and slip it inside the machine just as the first drops of coffee fell through the filter.

"Okay, Eddy," she said. "I never crack. I'm nineteen, and I'm beautiful even when I crawl out of bed. Gotcha!"

He smiled. "You are wonderful, Karen. That bozo should have never let you go, but I'm glad he did. He didn't deserve you, not from day one. Keep your spirits up. Someday you'll fall into the right man's arms, and he'll hold onto you forever. I promise."

She put her hand on his chest, and she started to speak. Then she balled her hand into a fist and let it fall. Turning, she looked out the window at Dylan and Zack taking yet another flying leap off the roof.

"You'd think they'd use the diving board at least occasionally."

He walked up beside her. "You'd think, wouldn't you? What were you going to say just a moment back?"

"He did drop me, Eddy. Right in the mud."

"What?" He frowned at her.

She laughed. "Later. I'll tell you all about it. It's the story of my life. Right now, it seems coffee's ready." The smell of toffee had begun to fill the air. Just then the pot dinged, and she laughed, "Let's see if it's more toffee or more surprise."

Eddy laughed and kissed his sister on the cheek. "You

are wonderful, Sis. I wouldn't trade you for all the bambinas in the world."

"Brad did." She cut her eyes to the boys playing around the pool, and she let herself smile when Zack grabbed Dylan's arm, flinging both of them into the water.

"And Brad, my dear sister, is the biggest loser in the world."

"Thank you, big brother. You are my most loyal supporter." She didn't hug him, though, because just at that moment, she wasn't sure the biggest loser wasn't her. After all, she had lost both Brad and that man who had stood up for her out at Ostrich Bar and Grill. It was even worse if she counted the pool guy and his brother.

Turning, she pulled two cups from the cabinet. "Pour, Eddy. I have coffee to serve."

He did, too, and there weren't very many toffee lumps in it at all.

JOHN WALKED in the door, and he smiled at the cashier. She was young, and she smiled back. However, when he turned his head and she saw the bruising on his cheek and the blood in his eye, she blanched and turned away. He cringed, but he should have expected that. It was exactly the reason he had stayed hidden away for three weeks. However, Frankie's opinion of him carried a lot of weight, and he had that envelope in his pocket.

Looking at the signs posted above each aisle, he searched for one that said makeup. This was his first visit to a drugstore in years, and he wasn't good at finding his way around in this one, or any drugstore for that matter. Finally, he admitted to himself that he was lost, and he made his way to the blanching cashier and asked where he could find stuff to cover the marks on his skin.

"Birthmark?" She had a nice voice, but she had trouble looking at his face.

"If you want. I need some stuff, makeup stuff, to smear over it. Do you have that?"

Her eyes finally found his face, looking carefully. "I can't do anything about your eye. You could probably get an optometrist to give you contacts for that." With a change of expression, she found her bright, salesgirl's voice and began talking as if he were a normal customer. "My friend changed her eye color that way. For your, um, birthmark, follow me." She handed him a small basket. "It's called foundation. You look like a summer, so you might want this nice brown color." She pulled a bottle from a rack and dropped it in the basket

"I just smear it on?" He looked with distrust at the little bottle.

"Sure," she said. "To blend it in, you'll want a brush. Powder, too. Otherwise, it might look shiny." She paused, a brush in her hand ready to go in the basket, and she looked at him with a frown. "You're not one of *those* guys, are you?"

"One of those guys?" He looked in the basket at the items she was handing him, and he picked one of them up. "Powder? Does it shake out of the container?"

She laughed. "I guess you're not. If you were, I figure you'd have all the basics. No, you need another brush for that. Do you want some guyliner, too?"

"Guyliner?" When he looked at her, her earlier question really dawned on him. "What do you mean those guys?"

"You know. Sweet." She put her arm up and let her hand flop to the front to show him. "My brother's friend is like that. Sometimes he goes on 'manny' dates. That's where boys date other boys." She shivered dramatically.

"No guyliner, please. I just want to cover my, um, birthmark."

"Consider it done. Oh, and this. You have to have this. It's a finishing spray so your new foundation doesn't come off."

"Finishing spray?" He was beginning to get worried.

She laughed, leading him back to the register. "I see you've never done this before. I could give you a lesson, if you want." She reached behind the counter and pulled out a pack of gum. Sliding a stick out, she unwrapped it and popped it into her mouth. "Sure. I can help you out. Putting on guyliner is more fun, but I like adding the finishing spray. I already put that in your basket for you. It'd be just like at a sleepover." Leaning down, she put her elbows on the counter and smacked her gum once. "You wanna?"

He eyed his package, then he eyed the girl. He didn't think he wanted to do the sleepover thing.

"Um, I'll experiment when I get home. Is that okay?"

She stood and shrugged. "Okay by me." Her gum popped once. "Good luck, and I hope you score."

He had a pretty good idea what she meant by that, but he decided to abstain from answering. Instead, he held up the package and winked. She laughed.

Once outside, he climbed in his truck and started it up, turning the air on high. Breathing deeply, he considered driving by Karen's just to see whether the landscapers were actually finished. After all, it would make a very plausible explanation if anyone stopped him. They had to have the yard completed before he could go by to collect the check. If he went to pick up the final payment when the yard was still incomplete, Karen might be offended that he was asking to be paid with the landscaping still in progress, like he wanted the money before he had done all the work.

Then his heart fell. He knew he didn't need to go by to check whether the landscapers were finished. He could just give them a call. They were the same people his company always used, and their number was in his cell phone. Surely his ruse would be uncovered.

There was possibly another reason to visit that he could fall back on, giving him a valid excuse to drive by. He thought he might be able to justify stopping over to check how the landscape installation was actually progressing. Contractors do that. The best ones do, anyway, and the land-scaping company couldn't give him away. There'd be nothing to give away.

But then he sighed when he remembered that Karen might see him with his damaged face. She would refuse to speak with him, leaving the check on the patio, or she would call his phone and tell him to stay away; the money was in the mail.

He sat in his truck with the engine running and the air conditioner on, and he was sick to his stomach with inde-cision. His leg shook with nervousness, and all he could think was how much he wanted to see her. It would be enough to watch her take out her checkbook and pull a pen out of her purse. Then she would push the clicker, and her fingers would write her name across the signature line. Karen. Wycliff. Then when she handed it to him, perhaps he could reach a little farther than necessary, and he could say excuse me, but his hand would have already touched hers.

Thinking of her in that way, he could already feel more going on in his body than what he wanted to experience while sitting out in public in his truck, and he shook his head to clear those images from his mind. What he needed to do was drive back to the loft—he called it that because he remembered Karen's words—and learn how to smear foundation across his bruised skin.

Setting the bag to his side, it shifted, and the contents tumbled out. He turned to look, and he was dismayed at how much the salesgirl had talked him into buying. In addition to the foundation, he also had to learn to brush on powder and seal it with finishing spray.

In that moment, he hoped Frankie was correct. For him to consider doing all this to his face, he must be in love, either that or turning into one of *those* guys. He was pretty sure that wasn't the case, so he trusted it was love.

"A TRAY, Eddy. The cups must go on a tray." Karen pointed to a cabinet, and he pulled one out to hand to her. "Now we are ready."

"Are we sure?" He touched her gently on the arm.

She put a really bright smile on her face. "No, but the

coffee's ready, and that's a start. Let's go. Follow me." She marched bravely out of the kitchen with her shoulders held high.

"Ah, Karen," Brad began as he stood. "Bambii and I can't stay long. We have something we want to give you."

Karen walked right up to him with her bright smile still on her face, and she said, "Sit, Brad." She heard Eddy chuckle when he did as she told him. "I have made my special toffee surprise coffee for you, and you must try it. In fact, I insist. You, too, Bambina."

Brad cleared his throat. "It's Bambii, Karen." He looked at his new wife and smiled in apology, but when his eyes caught Eddy's, his expression soured. Eddy wasn't smiling.

"Oh, what did I say?" Karen drew back, taking the tray with her just as Bambii reached to take a cup of coffee, leaving her hand grasping at the empty air.

Brad sighed. "You called her Bambina."

Karen giggled, and while some of it could be attributed to nerves, she made sure her laughter was bright and irritating. "Bambina? Isn't that Italian for little girl? How appropriate of me!" She turned her attention to Bambii. "I'm sure you won't take offense. You look so young and innocent. I'm sure you had no idea Brad was a grandfather when you took up with him." Then she turned to Brad. "You did wait until your high school-age daughter gave birth before you started, um, showing your affection to Bambina?"

"Bambii, Karen. I know what you're doing." Brad was turning red around the ears, and his words were sharp.

"Oh, yes. I certainly know what I'm doing, Brad. I'm serving coffee, and you haven't tried any yet. Have you seen Dylan since you've been here?" She finally set the tray down in front of Bambii, and she walked to the window. "See? He has a little friend over. I think Dylan is taking after you, Brad. Eddy found an insurance policy in your son's wallet last night. Dylan said he carries it just in case the opportunity, um, pops up. After all, he just might see a pretty sixth grader. You never know what these youngsters will do." She smiled sweetly at Bambii, who had just taken a sip of the coffee. Bambii tried to smile in return, but she coughed, glancing into her cup with dismay, before stifling a gag and setting the cup aside.

Brad stood. "Bambii, I think we should go. Karen's having a moment, and this isn't a good time."

Karen wasn't through, however, and she held up her finger. "No, no, Brad. You cannot leave without saying good morning to your son. Out, sir, to the backyard. Besides, you haven't seen the pool you picked out back when we were still married." She giggled and called to her brother. "Oh, my, Eddy. I almost said back when he was an honest man, but then I saw Bambii there, and I knew I couldn't lie in front of a child. Now, out, Brad, and you, too, Bambii. Am I getting that right? It is Bambii?"

Brad's new wife smiled. "I was named after the deer, just with two i's."

Karen patted her on the back. "And what nice eyes they are, too, dear. Maybelline?" The girl looked at her with a mystified expression. "Come, come," Karen called. She waved the crowd off the porch, and they could see Dylan and Zack up on the roof.

"Karen, should the boys be up there?" Brad finally

looked concerned.

Karen called to them, "Boys, are you safe up there?"

"Sure, Mom," Dylan called. "Hi, Dad. Are you staying for the party tonight?"

Brad looked at Bambii and back to his son. "Sorry, Son. Bambii and I have reservations in San Antonio for dinner. On the River Walk."

"Zack," Karen interrupted. "I have to check your safety, too. Are you safe on my roof?"

"Yes, Mrs. Wycliff. We've been doing this all morning."

"Good. Now, pray tell, just what have you been doing, Zack?"

"Cannonballs. Oh, and can openers."

"Which ones make the best splashes?"

The boys looked at each other, and they both chimed in at the same time, "Cannonballs!"

Karen turned to Brad and Bambii. "You have to see this before you go. They are quite good. Both boys." She leaned in to speak to Brad in a stage whisper. "I don't know that Zack carries protection in his wallet, but that's neither here nor there."

She caught Eddy's eyes, and they twinkled. It was clear he was very amused at the way she was handling this visit from her ex-husband and his new wife on the day of her big party.

Brad sighed. "Just have them show us, Karen. It's two hours to the River Walk. We have to get on the road. We won't need to go back inside. What we brought is on the table. You can open it after we're gone."

"Sure, Brad. Would you like to see also, Bambii with two eyes?" Brad narrowed his eyes at Karen while Bambii smiled tentatively. "Good," she continued. "This will be a special treat for both of you, from our family to yours. Stand right here while I walk over to give the boys special instructions to make this as spectacular as possible. Don't move, now." She smiled sweetly at them.

When she got underneath where the boys were standing, she winked as she spoke softly, "Both of you boys. Jump at the same time. They want to see a really big splash."

"Mrs. Wycliff, they're standing just where our splash goes up and hits the windows—"

"Shush, Zack. You just do your best for Dylan's father. You two, Dylan. He will be so proud."

Just then, Brad, clearly irritated at waiting, called, "Karen, let's get this over with."

She turned, and she smiled at her brother's thumbs-up sign. "Sure, Brad. Ready, Bambii?" At the girl's vigorous nod, Karen turned to Dylan and Zack. "Together, boys, and make it big. Yell, too!"

They did, and the effect was just what Karen intended. When the boys hit, the splash reached all the way to the far window, and Brad and Bambii were standing right in the way.

Chapter 17

KAREN LAID the manila envelope back on the dining room table. She looked at her brother, and there were tears in her eyes. If only she'd known what Brad had come by for, she wouldn't have been so mean to him.

"Karen, are you okay?" Eddy sat across from her, and he reached to take her hand. "You didn't know. How could you? He hasn't contacted you in four months."

She gave a rough laugh. "I've gotten the child support checks."

"Through your lawyer. He's not talked to you, though." He took his hand away.

"I know. I didn't even know they'd married. I was just so shocked, I took aim and fired both barrels. I feel so like a heel." She pulled the paper back out of the envelope and fingered the words there. "The house, Eddy. He just signed it over. He doesn't want any of it. How could he do that? It's not like Brad to give things away."

"I guess he's moving on, Sis. He wants to clear the slate. Had he ever told you the place was free and clear?"

"Never, Eddy. I thought he was making the payments until the dust settled, and then he'd ask me to sell. I've been sick all this time about this pool going in, and I didn't have to be. If it hadn't already been started, I'd never have gone ahead with it. The kids will be glad that we don't have to give up our home."

"Are you ready to move on?"

"I've been trying to. I guess now I have to." Then she chuckled. "That poor woman's hair. It was funny. I feel sorry for her, but it was funny. Bambii with two i's. What mother would do that to a child?"

Eddy grinned. "I thought steam was going to come off Brad's ears. He was furious. I'm pretty sure Bambii saved your hide, little sister. She just wanted to get in the car and leave. I suspect you'll never see those towels again." He took the paperwork and slid it back into the envelope. "Now, Sis. I want to know about this man who dropped you in the mud. Was that reference real or just in a manner of speaking?"

It took the gears a moment to shift, and Karen took her time, soaking in the quiet in the house. She could lambaste Brad all day with aplomb, but to speak of this other man was much more difficult. It wasn't just one man, either. Three men were involved, including the one who had fought in her defense and was still hidden away in the critical care unit at the hospital. That did seem strange to her. She didn't think he could have been injured that badly, not even facing all three of the Broady brothers.

"Eddy, I've trash-talked that woman Brad married, but I'm just as bad as she is." With one hand she worked nervous fingers into her hair and pulled them through before shaking it out. Her eyes danced across decorative items displayed around the space. "I'm really bad, Eddy."

"I've not heard you trash-talk her."

"Trash-thought, then. I have, too, but that's not why I'm so bad."

He tapped the table, then he looked up to see Junie flit across the room to land inside the chandelier. "Your bird's still loose."

She looked at him, and her eyes stung. "We don't care anymore. Eddy, I'm in love with three different men." It was out on the table, now, and she knew she could not take it back. She felt horrible, too.

He exhaled a long breath. "Three men? How long's this been going on?"

"Three weeks, Eddy, and I'm miserable. I haven't even been to church in all that time."

He tried to hide a smile. "You've missed church for three weeks? What will Wayside do without you?"

"Well, I've missed for two weeks. My affairs have been going on for three."

His eyes opened wide. "Affairs? With three men? And to think I was worried because Dylan was carrying one little package in his wallet."

She finally laughed. "I'm sorry, Eddy. I'm not being very clear. Affairs was the wrong word. Involvement might be a better choice."

"Not much better, if you must know."

"Just listen. The kids don't even know." She glanced in the kitchen and laughed at that. "They know part of it. Let me get you the paper from three weeks ago."

She showed him the picture, and she told him of looking for Junie and how the man had whistled to get him back again. Eddy learned of falling in the pool directly into that first man's arms, and Dylan's unwanted flashlight rescue. She described the man and the smile she had seen at the condos by Town Lake Park, but it was when she told of the third man, the one in the church who had worn his hat dipped low over one eye, that her eyes misted and her voice broke. It was the part that happened in the restaurant that brought the sobs, and once she revealed the extent of his injuries, she could tell no more. She loved them all, she said, but the one who had defended her honor the most of all.

Eddy leaned forward across the table and took her hand. "What did you love about the first two, Karen?"

She didn't even have to think. "The smile. They both had this hundred-watt smile. You couldn't miss it across the room. At one point, I was convinced they were brothers."

"So, you love smiles. That's not so unusual. Was there anything about the third man, other than the fact that he attacked three burly men to rescue your honor?" Eddy knew of the Broady family. He'd never eaten at one of their restaurants, but anyone who had spent any time in Austin knew of their reputation for size and meanness.

"That's not when I fell for him, Eddy. I fell for him in church that morning. He was with his mother, and he was talking with her, and he smiled, and I knew. It was the same feeling I had in the pool and at the condo by the park. I sat in that church, and all I wanted was to be with him."

Eddy grinned at his sister's graphic rendition of her man problem. "A smile again, Sis. Are you sure these three men are not one and the same?"

"How, Eddy? It would be impossible." Her eyes locked on his, disbelief on her face. "A sweaty construction worker? Did I mention that? The man in that picture was very sweaty, and you can see he has a straw cowboy hat on."

Eddy looked down at the table and laughed. "No, Sis, you did not mention that. I am most glad you filled me in. Finish your answer for me. Why would it be impossible?"

"The man at the condo was neatly dressed, and I've checked. They cost upwards of a million. He was a construction worker? If so, he couldn't afford to live there. I think not, Eddy."

"Maybe he didn't live there."

"He was up inside one of those units, or someone was. I'm sure it was the same person I nearly backed into. Then, maybe not. I haven't been back to find out."

"This man you saw in church. How are you sure he's not the same as one of the other two? Did he look the same in any way?"

"His smile, but that was all."

"How was he different, then? His eyes, his hair? Think, Sis."

She crossed her arms on the table and laid her head down in frustration. "I don't know, Eddy. I didn't see any of their faces, not really. The man in the pool had that straw cowboy hat on, and the one at the condo, I only saw him in the mirror as I was driving away. At church, that man was wearing a fedora, and he kept it dipped over his eyes."

Eddy grinned in triumph. "So, it could be one man."

"No, you weren't there. It couldn't be just one. I would have known. Besides, I talked to the first two." She had also touched the first one's chest, and very tenderly, too. She had trouble telling that part. It reminded her how much she had desired him, and how lonely she'd become.

"You never talked to the third man, the one at church?"

"I only saw his smile."

He frowned. "You know, I'm still having trouble with this fight thing that went on. How do you know so much about it if you only saw him at the church?"

She looked up and smiled. "You forget I have two way-ward children. They were both there in the thick of it. I got all the latest updates. I was headed inside to see it myself when the ambulance carried him away. He's been in critical care ever since."

Eddy reached and once again placed his hand on his sister's. "Karen, you are simply dealing with a very difficult time in your life. That does not mean you are in love with three men. Be generous with yourself, and don't let anyone tell you you're not wonderful. If one of those three men loves you back, he'll come find you. Just be ready, and enjoy your life. Can you do that for me? Just for today?"

She smiled. However, she knew Eddy was wrong. There had been three men that weekend, and she had fallen head over heels in love with each one, especially with the one she never got the chance to meet.

JOHN LAID out the supplies on the bathroom counter. His shirt was with the envelope for the check on his leather ottoman. The first thing he did was tear open the brushes. Then he looked at the square bottle of brown makeup. Shake Well, it said. He did so as he looked at his eye. Sunglasses might be the thing, so sunglasses it would be. Half the battle was already won.

Holding the bottle in his good hand, he squeezed the glass part of the bottle, grasping the lid with his fingers that stuck out of his plaster cast. He gave it a hard twist.

What he got was not what he expected. Sudden pain lanced through his encased hand, and he knew he had not successfully solved anything.

He turned to sit on the counter. He'd never been one to give up, not even as a boy. When the Broadys had come at him each week, he'd tried ever new ways to avoid them. Of course, there were only so many ways to get from one place to another at Wayside, and eventually he'd used them all. That was when he'd had to stand up and fight.

He wouldn't give up now, either. Getting the little bottle open was on the way to becoming a vendetta. At one point, he tossed the unopened bottle down to head into the kitchen, and frustrated, he threw the bedroom door open harder than necessary. As he moved forward, the door came back and caught his cast, shooting pain through his hand.

He yelled out in frustration, "Good lands alive, and stupid computer motherboards!" He refused to give up, though. He had a check to pick up, that and a woman to see.

"MOM! THE grass is here."

Karen looked up to see her son's face peering in the back door. His hair was plastered to his head, and his skin was flushed with his constant activity off the roof.

Just then, a yellow bird saw his opportunity and took it. With bullet-like speed, he was across the living room and out into the morning sunshine.

"Dylan! Junie!" However, it was too late. The bird was already gone.

The boy glanced behind him and called back into the house. "I see him, Mom. I'll get him." Then, as he closed the door, she heard him yell to his friend, "Hey, Zack! Want to go bird hunting?" Through the windows, the two Speedo-suited boys could be seen stalking the poor, defenseless animal.

Eddy chuckled. "In my day, those words would have had a completely different meaning."

"What words? Bird hunting?"

"Grass. I never would have said those words. 'Mom! The grass is here.' She would have called the police, and I'd have been behind bars on a drug charge."

"Different kind of grass, Eddy." She smiled.

"Mom!" This voice was from inside the house.

Eddy winked at his sister. "That sounds like your other child." He turned as Lissie came down the stairs holding Chipper.

"Junie fly?" The small boy pointed towards the back-yard.

Eddy reached for him, and he looked the child in the

face. "He sure did, Chipper. Do you want to go outside and see Uncle Dylan and his friend on their bird hunt? We might have parakeet stew later."

"Eddy," Karen admonished. "Chipper loves that bird. You cannot eat his parakeet."

He looked up with a look of mock puzzlement. "What did I say? Come on, Chipper. You need some outside time. Maybe fried 'keet after while, crocodile."

"Thanks, Uncle Eddy." A look of relief flooded Lissie's face. Behind her, Eddy rolled his eyes. Lissie turned to her mother. "Is Dad still here?"

Karen sighed. Already, Lissie had managed to stick a poker into the sore spot of the day. "Well, Lissie, it seems your father had an appointment in San Antonio. He couldn't stick around. Something about his plans being flooded out, so to speak."

At first Lissie looked puzzled, and as quickly, her face melted at the news her father was gone. "Mom! He never stays around. First he's in Baja with that bimbo—"

"Watch your words, daughter." Karen's voice was suddenly stern.

Lissie paid no attention, continuing with a vengeance, "Then when he shows, he doesn't even stick around for one little question."

"What question, Niece?" Eddy had reached the back door, and he turned before going outside.

Chipper mirrored his words, "Wha' weston?"

She turned to him, and her look was one of desperation. "Uncle Eddy, I'm graduating this month. I wanted to ask Dad if he'd get Mom a new car for my graduation."

Karen smiled, inexplicably pleased. Her Lissie had suddenly grown kind and considerate, putting others' concerns before her own.

"That is incredibly thoughtful of you, Lissie. I cannot believe you would ask your father to give me a present for your graduation. I see maturity there, I think." She stood and put her arms around her daughter to give her a hug.

Lissie looked puzzled, and then her expression cleared. "I do want something, Mom. I want your van. I always thought that Campmobile was really ugly, but now that you've let me drive it, well, wow! It's like it's got a Corvette engine in it. Dad can get you a new something. I want your van for my graduation present." She smiled and gave her mother a kiss. "Thanks, Mom!" Her feet flew up the stairs with excitement. Her voice called back down, "I'm going to call all my friends!"

Karen looked to see Eddy at the door laughing. "Eddy, did my van just get given away, and without anyone even asking my permission?"

"I think so, Sis. Corvette engine?"

"Actually, I think so. Brad did it all out. That's why I love that van."

"I do still have that old Shelby Mustang in my garage. It's not had 500 miles on it since that frame-off resto. With the new GT-500, I never drive the old one. Wanna take a drive? It's yours if you want it."

She took a deep breath. "I don't know, Eddy. I might. It needs to be my decision, though, not Lissie's." She looked to the stairs and yelled, "Lissie!"

Chipper tugged on Eddy's shirt. "Outside! Get Junie!"

"Okay, bud. We will." Eddy opened the door, and out they went into the hot, Texas springtime.

Chapter 18

"KAREN?" Eddy called from the back door. "Hey, Sis, did you order in for lunch?" Stepping inside, he put Chipper down. "Go find Mimi, Chipper. Uncle Eddy needs her to come outside."

Chipper danced to be picked up again, and then not getting his wish, he turned and ran towards the kitchen, calling, "Mimi! Mimi!"

"Karen?" Eddy followed the baby to the laundry room.

"I'm folding towels, Eddy. Come on in. I'm hiding away, actually." She laughed. "I needed a few moments of peace. What is it?"

"Look out the window, Sis. What do you see?"

There was a pause, and then a gasp. When she spoke again, the laughter was gone.

"Oh, my word, Eddy. It's been four months, and I'd

forgotten all about having scheduled the caterers. Just getting the pool completed has sapped all my attention." She also knew something else had kept her distracted the past three weeks, but she was trying to put that aside. "The grass people are still putting the sod down, and we're supposed to run the sprinklers as soon as they've finished." She turned to him with wide eyes. "What am I going to do, Eddy? The caterers need the lawn for tables, and the party starts in four hours."

"Baby sister, I'll tell you what we're going to do. First, we'll step outside and talk to these people. Then, in four hours, we're having a party, whether the sprinklers have been run or not. How does that sound?" He stepped up behind her to put his arms around her shoulders.

She folded one more towel before responding, and then she set the rest aside. She turned and looked her brother in the eyes, taking a deep breath and speaking firmly.

"Yes, sir. I can do that. I can be tough and not crack in front of anyone." She turned to look back out the window.

He put his hands on her shoulders. "Can you really? There seems to be a lot on your plate this weekend."

"What is it they say, Eddy, about making your bed and having to sleep in it? Well, I guess I fixed my plate, and now I have to eat what's on it." Her voice was overly bright as she spoke. "It's just a little party, you know. Nothing more. A few people will show up, and they'll play in the pool, and I won't even have to do the dishes afterwards. How much easier can it be than that?" She turned with a bright smile on her face. "See? I'm better already." She slapped her hand on the top of the folded towels, and much too quickly for someone who had things under control, exited to deal with her hired services outside.

EDDY WOULD join her if needed, but he stood at the window and watched the beehive of activity in the backyard just for a moment. Two tanned teenage boys were flinging themselves from the roof, green-shirted men were unrolling sod and pressing it down with a heavy, wheeled instrument, and yet more men in white shirts and aprons were standing around looking perplexed. When he saw his sister join them, he also saw the redness around her eyes.

"Not better yet, Karen. You're not better quite yet." With a grin of determination, he set out to offer her whatever support he could. As he stepped by Junie's birdcage, he was glad to see Dylan had been good to his word. The little yellow demon was in the cage for the first time Eddy remembered.

"YOU'RE coming open, little sucker." John picked up the square glass bottle, and wedging it firmly in place, he used his free hand to grasp the lid and twist. With a hiss, the vacuum seal released, and the lid popped off in his hand.

As he set the bottle on the counter, it slipped out of his hand, toppling, and left brown liquid dripping down the doorframe. He grabbed at it only to knock it across the room. As he did, he crashed into the bath counter, hitting the edge along his side, right where his ribs had been bruised in the fight.

Setting the half empty bottle on the counter, he collapsed onto the floor in pain, his good hand holding his side.

Charisse McAuliffe

"Dear God in heaven," he cried. "All I want to do is see Karen tonight. This is my last chance."

A voice answered, "Then we'll see if we can make that happen." However, the voice didn't sound so very much like God. It sounded more like Frankie, and there was more than a hint of amusement there.

"Frankie?" John looked up. Then he closed his eyes again. "I'm in real pain. I don't think I'll survive this."

"Wimp. Where's the man who jumped three Broady boys all at once and lived to brag about it?" She reached for the bottle on the counter.

"I'm not bragging, Frankie. I'm in pain, and I'm wishing I'd never touched a one of them." He held his head against the wall, and he rubbed his forehead with his good hand. "Now look at my bathroom. There's makeup everywhere."

It was, too. It had splattered on the wall and across the mirror.

Frankie kicked the shoe on his foot. "Baby. You know what got that retraction in the paper, don't you?"

He sighed with resignation. "I do. Thank you, Mom, for reminding me. Me being in that ambulance did it. It still hurts, though."

"You're too young to remember, John, but there's an old song out there. It says love hurts, and that's about right. You just have to ask yourself if it's worth the pain. I say it is. Now, about this makeup. Did you buy this?" He nodded. "Land's sakes why, John? Aren't there enough mixed-up people in the world without you going goofy, too?"

"I want to go over there to see Karen, but not like this."

He pointed to his face.

"So, the idea is to disguise the damage. Hm. How does it feel? It's been three weeks."

"Tell me," he moaned. "Three weeks of hell."

"John!" Frankie frowned, then her face relaxed. "I guess the past three weeks certainly have been a kind of hell for you." She reached a hand out, and he cringed when she touched it. "Sore, still, I see. Hm. Well, we can give the makeup a try." When she reached her hand to help him up, he stopped her.

"In the bedroom closet is my compression bandage for my ribs. I think I need it before I can stand."

"John," she said in a matter-of-fact voice, "you will have to stand before I can put on the bandage. Up, Chuck."

He reached to the counter to pull himself to his feet, and before he stood, he paused and looked at her. "Up, Chuck?"

She laughed. "I just always wanted to say that. It'd be even funnier if your name really was Chuck. Come on, let me help you."

She did wrap the compression bandage around his torso, and she slapped his shoulder a few times when he complained. If he couldn't take this, she told him, how could he expect to drive out and collect that check?

She smiled as she helped him apply the makeup. The color the clerk had chosen didn't exactly match his skin, but she assured him she had some practice at this, and at a glance, no one would notice. Still, it needed a finishing touch.

"Powder, John? You bought that, and brushes to apply it?" He dumped a bag out on the counter. She picked up one of the brushes and felt the bristles. "This is a good one. It probably cost you quite a bit."

"The clerk said I needed all this. She offered to give me lessons, too." He chuckled, then groaned as he put his hand to his side.

She looked skeptically at him. "You didn't take her up on it, I hope."

"She said it would be like a sleepover, and I didn't think I wanted any part of that."

Frankie grunted as she picked up a cloth and began to scrub the makeup off the floor and walls. "At least you made one smart decision. That beats no smart decisions at all."

"You think I can do this?" He looked at the brush and the powder, mystified.

"Just brush a layer on."

"Oh. What is finishing spray?" He held the can out to her.

"Beats me," she said. "For your hair?"

He chuckled again, catching his side, and fighting the laughter. "The clerk sold it to me with the makeup. It wouldn't be for my hair."

"Then pay attention to the name. Finishing spray. I guess you spray it when you're finished."

"On my face?"

She looked up from her cloth. "Isn't that what you said she sold it to you for?"

"Sure. Powder first. You sure you don't want to do this?" He held out the brush.

"Rag, John. I'm cleaning. Enjoy." She smiled, however,

and a bit too gleefully for John's satisfaction.

He brushed a layer of the powder on, catching Frankie watching him with a smile on her face, then he took a deep breath and closed his eyes. He squirted multiple pumps of the finishing spray onto his face, wetting the powder he'd just applied.

"Whoa, John," Frankie cautioned. "I've never heard of finishing spray, but I know that's too much. You don't want to lacquer the makeup to your skin. Let me check."

He opened his eyes to see the powder streaked down his features, and he was aghast. "It's ruined, Frankie. What do I do now?"

She let a note of sympathy creep into her voice. "You start over. You take the makeup off, and you just start over. Where's your cold cream?"

He froze. He remembered buying the bottle, powder, and brushes. The finishing spray, too. However, there had been no cream. The girl hadn't even mentioned it.

"I don't have cold cream, Frankie. How important is it?"

"Only if you want to take off the makeup. Otherwise, not at all." She had her hand at her mouth, trying not to laugh, and her eyes glistened with the humor of it all.

"Can you get me some?"

"Sure," she said, wiping one eye, and trying unsuccessfully to be properly glum.

"My keys are on the ottoman. My wallet, too."

She waved him off. "I've got money, and I'll take my car, thank you very much."

He smiled at that. "Don't you mean your Campmobile?"

285

"I mean my car, John. I didn't sell it." She stood and moved towards the front door.

"You were driving that yellow van. I saw you get in it."

She smiled at that. "I have a garage. You just never nose around inside."

"I thought it was Herbert's garage, all his old stuff and such." He frowned. He'd always considered it a sacred mausoleum, and that meant none of his business.

She winked at him. "You're just not very nosy, and I love that about you."

He looked surprised. "All these years I thought it was filled with old junk. You keep that van inside?"

"Among other things you've never seen. The van was Herbert's, and I kept it after he died. I told you that red one wasn't the only one around. You admiring it so much got me thinking, and I had mine towed to the shop. It runs again for the first time in years. Now, if you'll let me, I have cold cream to buy."

"Thanks, Frankie. I be waiting."

"I love you, John. I didn't expect you to be going out like this." She touched his face gently before exiting out the door.

After a few minutes of boredom, he dozed off in front of his glass wall, and while he slept, he was in the bottom of an empty swimming pool. He was holding Karen in his arms, and she gently brushed dirt off his chest. Then, in the barest whisper, she said the three words he so wanted to hear.

"I love you. I love you very much, John."

It even seemed very real to him, and he enjoyed the

experience very much. There was only one troubling thought in that dream.

He didn't think she knew his name.

"MOM! YOU can't let them do this." Lissie was in tears. The caterers were acting as a moving crew, and all the furniture from the living room and dining room was being carried upstairs to be stored in the bedrooms.

Karen stood in the backyard and looked up at her daughter leaning out of the master bedroom window. It was Austin in the middle of the day, and she was perspiring in the summer heat. Parties were supposed to be fun, and at this point, she was not finding this one to be very enjoyable.

A twin flash of color off by Dylan's window caught her attention, and she winced as two wild screams split the hubbub that had been murmuring around the pool. All the landscaping crew as well as the catering personnel stopped and turned to see what was happening. When the boys hit the water, the splash was awesome. Not everyone was impressed, though.

"Ma'am, will it be possible to have the boys hold off on diving?" She turned to see the head caterer. His forehead was creased in exasperation, and it was clear he was close to the end of his patience.

Just then the boys surfaced, and they whooped in exultation.

"Mom!" Dylan put his hands on the side of the pool, and he raised himself half out of the water. Then, in a quick motion, he swung one leg up, and placing his foot beside his hands, he pushed himself upwards in a rush of water to stand on the side of the pool. "Did you see? That was the best splash ever!"

Zack followed his example, flinging himself to his friend's side. "Yeah, Mrs. Wycliff. Do you want to see it again?"

She turned to the caterer apologetically. "The pool is brand new. This is our first weekend to have it open, and the boys are excited." She was glad to have the two of them occupied, too, but she didn't tell the caterer that. "I can ask them to stay off the roof, if you think that would help."

He looked relieved. "With the yard unavailable, half my crew is inside the house moving furniture upstairs. We're already tight on time to have things ready at four. We'll get there, though. I appreciate your understanding."

Then he paused for a moment and looked around at the yard and the trees. "Several of my men have mentioned a bird flying around. Some are afraid of it attacking them. Have you thought of calling Animal Services about getting it picked up?"

"A bird? Yellow?" Her heart sank. She had seen Junie in the cage earlier, and she didn't know how he could be out. She called to Dylan, "I thought you put Junie in the cage earlier."

He looked at his friend and back to his mother. "Zack saw me, Mom. I did put Junie in the cage. Didn't I, Zack?"

"Whistle, Dylan. See if he comes to you."

Just then, Lissie called from the upstairs window, "Mom, I can't find Junie. Has anyone seen him out here? I thought he was trapped in my room, and the movers left the door open. He got out, and I can't find him in the house anywhere."

Karen closed her eyes. Lissie and that bird! She knew how much Chipper loved seeing him fly free, but just for one day, Lissie!

"Dylan, whistle, please." She turned to see Eddy at her side, and he had a smile on his face.

"You're doing okay, Sis. Let me handle your daughter." He turned to the opened second story window. "Crank the window closed, Lissie. Did you notice your mother is running the air conditioner? It's hot out here, and the windows are designed to keep the cool air inside. Thank you, Lissie."

"Mom!" There was a note of petulance in Lissie's voice, and it carried to them over the sound of the workers preparing for the evening's events. Normally, Karen would have let it go, but she was tired, and her brother's expertise in handling her children's idiosyncrasies was giving her the strength to stand up to things she might otherwise overlook.

"Just do as your uncle asks, Lissie. Close the window. Can you do something as simple as that?"

Even from across the yard, the girl's frown could be clearly seen, and as she backed into the room, a high-pitched voice could be heard calling to her.

"Junie? Where's Junie?"

Dylan's whistle pierced the air, and everyone in the yard stopped to see what was going on. A yellow fluttering in one of the trees drew their attention, and twenty sets of eyes watched the parakeet fly directly onto Dylan's upheld finger.

Karen glanced up to see the window was finally closed, and she looked across the pool to where the bird had been.

Then, she spoke to herself quietly and with exasperation, just before she turned and walked firmly back to the house.

"There's Junie, Chipper. He's right there on your uncle's finger."

Dylan called after her, "Mom? Do you want Junie? Zack and I want to get back in the pool."

She didn't even turn around. "Stay off the roof, Dylan. Tell Zack, too. Please." Then she disappeared into the house.

"LET ME take him, Nephew." Eddy chuckled to himself. The little bird chittered at the unfamiliar hands, but he held it firmly. "Go back and swim, son. Just stay off the roof."

"Okay, Uncle Eddy." Dylan turned to Zack and yelled, "Cannonball contest. I can make a bigger splash than you!"

Zack's voice hit back, "No way, loser. I can make the bigger splash."

Eddy shook his head. He thought being on the roof might be better. That way, they at least knew which direction the water would fly. However, now he had the bird, and he would tell his niece to make sure the animal stayed in the cage for the next twelve hours. Surely the girl would do that for him. A high school senior should be able to do anything for twelve hours.

Eddy would be more confident if Lissie weren't Karen's daughter. However, he loved Karen very much, and he would give the girl the benefit of the doubt. He'd do that for his sister, as well as for her kids. He loved them, even if he considered them a little on the wild side.

Chapter 19

THE POOL sparkled in the mid-afternoon Texas sun, and Dylan and Zack lounged on pool floats as they munched on potato chips. There were long tables lining the pool deck, stretching off onto the lawn where extra tables and chairs provided additional opportunities for outdoor dinner seating. The tables in the direct sun had cloth canopies stretched over aluminum frames protecting them from the heat. Others were placed where the afternoon would provide encroaching shade from the overhead trees. Beside the house, two massive heat pumps hummed against the wilting heat of the Austin sun.

Karen's kitchen buzzed with catering personnel, and cloth-covered tables were set up throughout the downstairs living area. Each one had a summer flower arrangement in the center. Cool air blew from the ceiling registers, and sun filtered in through opened window blinds.

In the two-story entry hall, Chipper sat on the bottom stair, and he reached out to touch the yellow parakeet in his mother's hand.

"Hold Junie?"

"Shush! You can't let Uncle Eddy hear." Lissie took the baby's wrist and held it firmly. "Easy, Chipper." Then she set the bird on the boy's finger. "Hold him easy. Don't let Junie get away. We aren't supposed to have him out."

Chipper grinned in excitement, unable to sit still. "Junie! Fly, Junie!" He shook his hand, and his voice screeched with joy to see the bird take to wing.

Lissie hissed at him, "No, Chipper. We have to get him back." She stood and let out a little whistle.

"Back, Junie!" Chipper jumped up and down. "Come back, Junie!"

Lissie whistled again louder. Then she looked up and saw Dylan open the back door. He had a towel in his hand, and his wet hair stuck straight up on one side.

"Dylan, you have to help me. Uncle Eddy said I couldn't get Junie out until after the party, and I did anyway. Now he's loose, and he won't come back."

Her brother looked at his nephew dancing on the bottom step, and glancing up, he saw the bird fluttering along the side of the room.

"Sorry, Sis. Zack's here, and we're enjoying the pool. The bird isn't my responsibility. I just came in for more chips."

"More chips? You had a whole bag already!"

"Zack ate 'em all. Anyway, who cares about your bird?

If Junie's out, it's your fault. You get to catch him."

"Yeah, and Mom's going to be furious when she sees water all over her floor."

He glanced down and saw the water running off his legs and dripping to the floor. He looked up, disgusted. "Okay, a compromise. Will you get my chips from the pantry if I get Junie for you?"

"Dylan, you are a dork. Just call the bird. You know you're better at it than me. Please."

He hung the towel on the back of a chair and shook his head. "Have fun, Lissie." Then he darted across the room to the kitchen door, only to find it had been taken over by the caterers. He turned to his sister, "Are they going to be in there all day?"

She looked up to see Junie heading upstairs. "Dylan, is your window open?"

He had to stop and think. "Maybe. Why?"

She put her hands together to plead, "Okay, I'll get your chips. Just please call Junie. Deal?"

"Deal, Sis."

He let out a warbling whistle, and holding out his hand, the bird came fluttering from somewhere upstairs to rest on his finger. With his other hand, he wrapped his fingers around the animal's body and held it out to his sister. "Where's the cage? It can't still be in the kitchen. There was no room with all those people in there."

"My room. They moved it up there. If you'll go put him up, I'll get your chips." She headed toward the kitchen. "Take Chipper with you, though. You can't leave him alone."

293

"Lissie, take him to the kitchen with you. He's heavy to carry upstairs."

"You are such a baby." She turned to her son. "Chipper, sit down. Be good. Uncle Dilly Bar is going upstairs. I'll be right back. Okay?" She smiled at him. Then, to her brother, she frowned and barked, "Hurry, Dilly Bar. Put the bird away and get back down here."

He paused and glared. "I could just turn him loose, Lissie-dork."

"No!"

"I won't. You just get my chips for me."

A small boy's voice echoed, "Junie go bye-bye?"

"Junie go bye-bye, Chipper." Dylan looked at his sister and continued in baby-speak, "Lissie get Uncle Dilly chips, too. Aren't you, Lissie?"

She growled. "Just get back down in a hurry so Chipper doesn't get into anything."

Dylan vaulted up the steps, and Lissie disappeared into the kitchen. Chipper stood and walked over to one of the tables that had been set up. When he couldn't see what was on top, he attempted to climb up. Grabbing the tablecloth, he pulled hard. Before he could blink, the fabric slipped on the table's slick surface, and the baby fell onto his backside.

Dylan came darting back down the stairs, and Lissie stepped into the room, chips in her hand, just in time to see the table topple over right on top of the baby. As it did, it brought the two neighboring tables down with it. Chipper let out a wail that brought Eddy out of one upstairs bedroom and directly to the landing. Karen stepped out of another.

"Eddy?"

294

"Karen."

"That sounded like someone just died."

Eddy laughed.

"That sounded like Chipper, Eddy. Do you have any idea what happened?"

He winked. "Your children, probably." He leaned to see what was downstairs. "Ah, Chipper it is."

"Is he okay?" She stepped to where her brother blocked the stairs.

"Your party might be ruined. It's not pretty," he teased, as he tilted his head over once more. "Ouch."

She pushed at him. "Chipper's the important one. Who cares about the party?"

"Who cares about the party?" Eddy grinned.

When she saw her brother's look, she backpedaled. "You know what I mean, and don't give me that look. I've had about enough of this. If I could simply go away and let this party run itself, I'd consider it. Probably no one would know I'm gone, and they'd all have a good time, anyway."

"Sis, you mean that?"

"I'm concerned about the baby. Move so I can take care of him. He needs me."

He stared her in the eyes, his feet still planted, blocking the steps. "Sis, you have Chipper's mother down there, and his Uncle Dylan is with him also. If you don't let them handle this, they'll never be able to grow up and do it on their own. Chipper doesn't seem hurt, and sometimes we need to back off and wish them luck."

She wrapped her arms around her waist, thoroughly irritated. "They're kids, yet. I can't just wish them luck."

"No, you can't, not in everything. Pick your moments, Karen. Let them grow up in small ways, safe ones if you can. They do have to grow, though." He peered over the rail again to see that the baby was out of the pile of debris, and the tables were mostly righted and reorganized. "Now, go down and act as if you weren't concerned. Congratulate them on taking care of the mess, and go on past as if being responsible is normal and expected."

He stepped aside and watched her descend the steps. She stopped and told Lissie that one of the tables wasn't aligned just right, and she told Dylan to take only a handful of chips. The rest of the bag was going back into the pantry, and she would take it. When she turned and winked at Eddy, he shot her a thumbs-up sign.

It was progress, at least.

"JUST BECAUSE I'm the boss doesn't mean I've forgotten everything I know." John didn't bark into the phone, but he had felt useless the past few weeks, and he needed to get out of the house.

"I know, John, but I can call one of the crews in." Frankie was calling from her mobile phone. She hadn't even made it back with the cold cream yet. "It's most likely just a recirculation pump start capacitor. I don't have any of the crews' home numbers with me, though, and every cell phone I've tried has gone directly to voice mail. I'll need to swing by the office and check my files for some home numbers. I might be a while, though."

"No, Frankie. Let me be the one to do this. I've been stuck inside for three weeks. I need to get out. What's the address? Directions, too." He wrote down the information. All his crews had been swamped lately. The brutal winter had put them all behind, and everyone wanted their pool done yesterday. This was the first free weekend for some of them in a month. Besides, he was feeling the idiocy of his first try at makeup, and it made him feel like a fool. Who could fault him for not heading out to pick up that check if he had another job to do, a real pool-repair job. He'd been determined at first to make this last try to see Karen, but now with the failed attempt to cover the damage on his face, his enthusiasm was drained. To top it off, his arm throbbed, even after taking a Vicodin.

"Your bruise, John? Have you forgotten that? That's not taken care of yet."

"I'll just be outside at the pool. If it's more than just a start capacitor, then I'll worry about calling someone in. How does that sound?" He wouldn't, though. If it was more, then it would definitely relieve him of his vow to meet Karen. He could blame Frankie, and he could mope about all he wanted. Then, when his face finished healing . . . well, that was a long way away.

He looked in the mirror. With his earlier efforts, the bruising was mostly hidden, but the bloody eye sure stood out. He was Batman's Scarecrow on a bad day. He wet a towel and patted at it only to find that indeed, it would not come off. It hurt too much to rub it much harder, so he tried something else. Taking the makeup bottle, he dabbed a bit more on the places where it was especially blotched, and then he did the powder thing again. He glanced quickly into the mirror to see if his efforts passed muster, but the look

297

was very quick. He hoped more than believed. He dropped the finishing spray into the trash.

Pulling on a clean, collared shirt, he opened his closet, hoping to find something to wear on his head. There was his straw cowboy hat sitting up on the shelf. Frankie must have brought it in.

He pulled it down, and he rubbed the brim with the tips of his fingers. He was ready to get back to work, even if it was too hot outside for someone who had lost his acclimation to the heat. However, that was how he was going to get it back.

Slipping the old straw hat on, he grabbed his keys. He kept his sunglasses in his truck. He was certain he had capacitors there, also. That was always a first step when checking pool pumps that wouldn't come on, and all his men kept at least half a dozen spares with them at all times.

He hadn't paid that much attention to the street names when he had written the directions, just jotting them down as fast as she threw them out, but now he was surprised at the convoluted, roundabout path Frankie had given him. It was when he pulled off at the final exit to head to the repair location that he realized he would need to drive within two blocks of Karen's house. That riled him a bit.

He picked up his phone and triggered it to call Frankie. After three tries, he realized she didn't intend to answer. He began to suspect there was a bit of a ruse going on, and he wondered if he would even have a repair to do when he got to his broken pool capacitor. Probably not, he suspected. Frankie liked to manipulate him, and normally he accepted it in the way she intended, as love. However, she seemed to be finding it especially enjoyable to do so in dealing with this current lack of romance in his life.

When he arrived at the address she'd given him, there was no one home, and the pool was not running. Rather than find out that Frankie had indeed sent him on a wild goose chase, he simply cut the power to the pool, set his sunglasses on the breaker box, and swapped out the capacitor. Flipping the breaker back, he hit the filter button and was pleased to hear it kick on. Looking at the used capacitor, he knew he could check it back at the office, but he wouldn't. Instead, seeing a trashcan, he simply flipped it inside and exited the gate. There were some things he didn't want to know, and occasionally, things that were better not known. This was probably one of them.

Getting back in his truck, he grabbed a napkin from the glove box and pressed it to his forehead, drying the sweat threatening his eyes. He tossed it in the floorboard, and in that moment, it slipped his mind that he had applied makeup to nearly a quarter of his face. After all, he had more important things to think about. He was only blocks from Karen's, and there was still a check to pick up. He had to decide what to do, and this was really big for him. He had no one to turn to for advice, either.

Somewhere deep inside, however, he knew that wasn't entirely true. He had turned to someone for advice, and she had given him some that was very good. *"Make some choices, John. God told me I'd have to be looking for the blessings to find them. It seems to me God dumped this blessing in your arms. Do this, John."*

He didn't know if he could follow all of Frankie's

advice. However, that check was right on his way, and it would be ridiculous for him to *try* to avoid driving by Karen's. If he saw no one there, then he could tell Frankie he'd gone by, and he had seen no one home. It'd be the truth, too. He wouldn't look too hard, either, just a glance, and if she wasn't in the yard, then he couldn't be expected to search her house, could he? He would just mail the final bill to her. Yes, he could do that, just mail the final bill.

Satisfied with his solution, he started the truck. It had grown very hot inside the vehicle, and it didn't occur to him that part of that could be from his heightened anticipation. No, it was just a very warm Saturday, and thinking of Karen had nothing to do with it.

He thought he was deceiving himself very well, but the telltale was the thumping heart in his chest and the flush on his arms. To judge by that, he wanted to see Karen very much, indeed.

Chapter 20

THE PARTY was ramping up. Karen had climbed upstairs to slip into her suit, wanting to at least show it off, even if she didn't get in the water. Besides, her jeans and tee from that morning had grown stale.

Slipping a lightweight shift over her suit, she admired herself in the mirror. Eddy was right. There wasn't a wrinkle one on her face. There might be a bruise or two on her heart, but her face sure didn't show it. Just for tonight, all the stress of the day would be put aside, and the people around her would distract her from her problems.

Besides, she owned her house, now. She had the paperwork to prove it locked away in the house safe.

Stepping to Lissie's room, she was relieved to see Junie was actually inside his cage. He chattered his frustration at her as she stepped past to look out the front window, and she smiled at the view. The neighbors would probably call the homeowner's association to complain. The cars filled the street as far as she could see. She didn't care, though. Now that everything had come together, she was ready. It was her birthday, after all, even if it wasn't for nearly another week.

Then she saw something that caused her good mood to melt away. She knew many members of her church had received a general invitation, but she could not believe the car she saw driving up. It was a black stretch Lincoln, and written in reverse across the top of the windshield was the name B-B-B-Barbeque. It pulled up right to the front walk, and all the doors opened at once. She closed her eyes when she saw the second stretch appear. She paled to know the Broady clan and all their progeny would be climbing out to join her in her backyard. She understood why they had two cars. They wouldn't fit in one vehicle.

She turned as she heard the door open, glad to see it was her brother. "Eddy," she cried, hearing the desperation in his name. "The Broadys are here."

"The Broadys? That means?"

"They started all this. Remember? How can they show their faces after what they said about me? I am so mortified to have them here. I haven't even been to church for two weeks, and all because of them."

"They said . . . um . . . help me out, Sis. They're part of your church. Surely they're welcome."

"The fight, Eddy. You can't have forgotten."

"The fight. They're the ones who put your boyfriend in the hospital."

"Eddy!" She was suddenly furious. She recognized it was as much from Eddy's use of the word boyfriend as it was from the Broady brothers. She needed to distract herself from that, though. Running ninety-to-nothing all day had done that for her, kept her distracted, and now that the day was slowing down, she was feeling the past three weeks rushing back at her. It was rivulets only so far, but she could tell it was growing stronger. *Boyfriend* was not what she needed to hear.

"What?" Eddy's eyes twinkled.

"He is not my boyfriend. I don't even know the man's name."

He smiled. "Which one, Sis? There were three, as I recall."

"Ooh," she cried and turned to face the window. Then she called him to join her. "This is a sight. They're all in giant Bermuda shorts and sandals. Or . . . oh, my, Eddy. I think those are swim trunks. Do you think the pool will hold them?"

He walked to stand beside her and put one arm around her shoulder. "I don't need to see them. You are a kind and generous person. They must have hurt you more than you let on." He smiled at her. "Be charitable tonight. You have a lot of your church people here. Go ahead and show your ugly side in here with me, but out there they need to see the sweet woman who follows the Golden Rule."

"Do unto others *before* they can do unto you?" Her words were bitter. "He was defending me, Eddy, and they crushed him. Three weeks, and he's still in the critical care ward. I know. I called today."

He kissed her on the forehead. "That is not the Golden Rule, and you know it. I'll tell you what." He reached into a pocket and pulled out a small card. "I got you a present you'll really appreciate. You've put this wonderful party together, and every person you know is here, or will be by dark. Even the food, Sis, will knock people's socks off."

She laughed as she wiped her tears away. "Let me have that. I need something good to happen to me right now."

He pulled it out of her reach. "I want to tell you about my present first, little sister. This is special. I know how much you love the Beatles. Do you still have all those 45 singles from junior high?" He smiled when she nodded.

"They're in the garage in the storage closet."

He nodded knowingly. "Well, my birthday present to you is a night of Beatles music by a professional deejay. He's already down by the pool setting up. I gave him the small porch by the kitchen window. He'll take requests, but only from your favorite Beatles songs."

She laughed at that. There were hundreds of Beatles songs, and while she loved them all, her favorites were limited to a couple dozen. How would the deejay know? She loved it, though.

"My card, Eddy?"

He winked. "Your card, Karen? What do you mean by that? Who said you get a card?"

She grabbed for it, and opening the tab, she drew out the contents. Looking at it, tears filled her eyes. "How did you find this? August 15th, 1965. This is from the Shea Stadium Beatles concert. How did you ever find an unused ticket? It must have cost you a fortune."

He put his hand beside her face. "Sis, it was no more than you deserve. Besides, I'll never get to buy you another present, so I had to make it a good one. After all, it's your last birthday. You said so."

She laughed and swatted her hand at him, and then she brushed tears from her eyes. "You know me too well, my big brother. I will treasure this always."

"Then, come on down, Sis. Your party needs you. Just be nice, especially to the Broady clan. Make Wayside Christian Fellowship proud of you."

"Only God could make that church proud of me, Eddy. You should have been there at morning service three weeks ago. They prayed me back from the gates of hell."

He snapped his fingers and motioned for her to get a move on. "Then they're fans of mine, Sis. Hell's no place for a great girl like you. I've always thought so."

"Oh, Eddy. Take my arm and let's go party."

"Like it's 1999?" He winked at her.

She laughed. That line was from a CD he'd given her once. She tiptoed to kiss him on the cheek. "No, even better, let's party like I don't have a care in the world. I'll even be nice to the Broadys."

"That's my sister. Let's show 'em a Conley never cracks, even when she has to go by the name Wycliff."

They marched down the staircase together, and together, one brother and one sister brought down the house.

JOHN UNDERSTOOD just what Frankie had done, and he knew the most direct route home took him by Karen's house. He'd have to go out of the way to avoid it. Even so, he drove a very circuitous pattern to have time to build up his courage. His stomach was jittery, and he stopped at a food joint to order at the drive-through. Then, when he couldn't eat any of it, he threw it away in a city garbage receptacle.

After a couple of hours burning through gas and driving the same roads over and over, he knew he couldn't postpone it any longer, and he found his truck taking him closer and closer to his destination. Before he even turned on the street, cars lined the curb. At one point, he saw the infamous B-B-B-Barbecue logo on the windshields of two black stretch limos. His hands began to sweat. He had no idea what they were doing here.

When he saw the house, he was floored. Frankie hadn't known the extent of this party. Through the windows he could see people sitting at linen-covered tables, and there were still more outside visiting on the porch. There were two catering trucks by the back fence, and a crowd of people was gathered around an enclosed car hauler taking up a good portion of the street. A barrel-chested man was directing the removal of what looked like a pristine Shelby Mustang. It even had a big bow attached to it.

As he eased his truck past, he saw the barrel-chested man turn and look directly at him. After his experience with the Broadys, that gave him the willies, and he decided this was not a place he could stop tonight, not to pick up a check, or for any other reason. He'd tell Frankie his reasons, and she'd surely understand.

As he eased his truck past several more parked cars, a

hand slapped the fender of his truck, and he turned to see the barrel-chested man waving for him to stop. He rolled down his window as the man hailed him.

"Hey, Springfield Pools. How are you doing? Eddy Conley." The man stuck his hand to the window to shake.

"John Springfield, owner of said company." He returned the shake. "I see you've got quite a party here. Everybody in Austin invited?"

The man named Eddy chuckled in response. "Almost. You, too, if you like. Maybe especially you."

For some reason, that made John laugh.

"SO, JOHN Springfield. You the one who built the pool here?" He nodded towards the house where all the partying was going on. When Eddy had seen the truck, that had set him to thinking. Karen's story. Now here was the driver, wearing a straw hat. There had been a straw hat on the pool man. There was a straw hat on this man.

"Yes, sir. I mean, my company did."

"Well, that's Karen Wycliff's house. You ever get the chance to meet her?" Eddy grinned. He suspected he already knew the answer.

John nodded. He swallowed, and then answered, "It's been a few weeks since I've been here, though. Tonight I was out this way to service a customer's pool, and I just happened to drive by. I knew we were asked to finish by today because there was a party planned, but this is no ordinary shindig."

Eddy nodded. "No, sir, it's not. My sister, well, we won't mention her age, but this is her last birthday ever."

John jerked his head behind him. "That Mustang her present?"

"Maybe." Eddy had considered offering it to Lissie. He knew it was too much, but it would ruin in his garage. Now that the girl wanted her mother's van, well, Eddy hoped to give the Shelby to Karen and let her decide which one her daughter should get.

"Lucky sister. This is her party, then."

"Yeah. Her last one. Your eye. What's with that?" The blood in the man's eye stood out to him. A fight, he guessed. Maybe with three oversized brothers. At a bar. And grill. And his face, like he'd tried to hide the evidence.

John ducked his head and groaned. Then he glanced up and laughed. "I should have remembered to put on my sunglasses. You have two black limos down there. B-B-B-Barbecue. Friends of yours?"

"Maybe. Why?"

"If they are, maybe you don't want to know about the eye." He reached and tugged the hat lower, just now remembering the makeup.

"Maybe I do." Eddy put his arms on the door, and he leaned in. "Especially if B-B-B-Barbecue is involved."

"You sure about that?" John pursed his lips and let out a long-held breath.

Eddy slapped the windowsill of his truck, more suspicious than ever that this might be his man. "You want to get out for a while? Everybody else's here. I suspect one more will be invisible. Besides, I do want to hear this story."

He also wanted Karen to meet this man. He might be the one to pull her out of herself. First, there had been the hat.

Now, the Broadys were involved. Karen thought she had met three men. Eddy suspected otherwise. He thought he might have just found two of them. He didn't know about the third, but as the singer of an old rock song had once warbled, two out of three ain't bad.

"You sure?" John didn't seem convinced. "I only came this direction to collect money on the pool, and it can wait. After all, tonight belongs to your sister."

"You need to see the Mustang. Full frame-off. Come on. We have Beatles music out back, and the biggest steaks you could ever want are cooking on the grill. In fact, let me get the driver to move the trailer, and you can park right in front of the Mustang. How's that?"

"Well, better than I deserve." John pulled his hat lower, reaching for his sunglasses. "You know, I can walk. I don't mind parking down past the crowd."

"Get away, you mean. No, you sit right here."

He wasn't going to let this man get away, not if he could help it.

Karen needed him.

AS JOHN sat in his truck with the engine idling, waiting for the car hauler to move, he quieted the nerves churning his stomach. He studied the dash clock for the time. It was nearly seven. He didn't know when this party had started, but it seemed these people had been here some time. It couldn't hurt much for him to see the car, and he might even get a glimpse of Karen through one of the windows.

As far as food, he wasn't sure he could eat, even if he wanted. His stomach was all torn up, and now he was

309

nervous about the way his face looked. In his condo, his *loft*, rather, it had seemed plausible to put on women's makeup. Now, it seemed ludicrous to have done this to himself.

However, this woman's brother hadn't mentioned his face, just his eye, and there was nothing that he could have done to hide that. He had his sunglasses on now, but in an hour it'd be too dark for them. He'd just make sure he was gone by then.

He had his hat pulled low, anyway. That might help. He'd just keep it pulled snugly over his eyes, and besides, according to Frankie, he looked dapper that way. More attractive to women, wasn't that what Frankie had suggested? He didn't know if it worked with that way with straw cowboy hats, but he'd certainly take his chances. After all, when you've got nothing, you've got nothing left to lose, and tonight was one of those times when he felt like there was nothing he could lose that would make any difference.

The only thing he cared about was Karen, and he didn't have her. She didn't know who he was, and that made his chances pretty slim, indeed.

A PAIR of yellow Speedos darted across the crowded pool deck as *Yellow Submarine* danced from the speakers the deejay had run to various parts of the yard. The yellow Speedos were followed by a pair in blue, and then a splash disrupted the shimmering surface of the water.

Chipper caught a glimpse of the action and yelled, "Junie! Chipper want Junie!"

Karen patted his head. "No can do, pumpkin. That little

birdie's not Junie. That's Uncle Dylan. We're looking for your mommy."

"Uncle Dilly? Want Dilly!"

She put her hands underneath his arms and lifted him up. Kissing him on the cheek, she said, "Uncle Dilly Bar wants you, too, Chipper. However, he's very busy right now."

"Dilly has Junie?"

Karen laughed softly. "It's more like Dilly Bar's wearing Junie, but no, Dylan doesn't have Junie. Junie's in his cage upstairs."

"Go see Junie?"

She didn't respond to that question, because standing on her freshly-laid grass, just across the yard, laughing it up with her daughter, were Brad and Bambii, and after she'd totally humiliated them just that morning. They both had on brightly colored swimsuits topped by collared and pocketed Hawaiian overshirts. At that moment, as if on cue, Lissie pointed, and they turned and looked directly at her.

"THAT'S A mighty big bow." John ran his hand down the drip rails.

"That it is. Guys, can we take the bow off for a while?" Eddy flipped the keys to the Mustang in his hands. "John Springfield, let's you and me take it for a ride."

John shrugged and nodded. He wasn't sure just why he was being given this offer. Surely Eddy had more than enough friends here who would be excited to be out in what seemed to be an original Shelby Mustang. He saw the cool factor in the old car, but he'd be more interested if it were a

Wrangler with six-inch lifts and Mickey Thompson wheels.

However, the man seemed to have taken up with him, and as bad as his day had been, he needed a few emotional pats on the shoulder.

Four clips were released from the drip rails, and the bow was placed on the grass. Eddy popped open the door and grinned, "Watch that hat when you climb in." Then, before disappearing inside the car, he turned to the people standing around and called to them to clear the street.

John pushed through the people admiring the car to grab the handle on the passenger's door and push in the button. The door released, and the heady smell of new vinyl flooded out. Ducking his hat and falling in, he closed the door.

"Smells new. Reproduction?"

Eddy laughed. "Seriously? No. I spent nearly a hundred grand pulling this apart bolt by bolt. That's what frame-off means, by the way."

"Ahh!" John rubbed his hand along the upholstery. "You didn't put in leather?"

"These had vinyl originally, so that's what went back. However, a Shelby's all about this." He turned the key, and the car roared into life. Backing up, he shifted gears and punched it, swerving around John's truck and down the street. "Doesn't compare to my GT-500, but it sure fits the bill for nostalgia."

"So," John began, "why me?"

Eddy downshifted into a corner, and working the clutch, he burned a bit of rubber before letting the car settle into a flying scream. Then, almost too quickly to be seen, his hand snapped the shifter into the next gear, and the engine quieted into a throaty burble.

"Why you what?" He had a grin on his face.

"In this car. You had twenty people back there who would kill to ride in this. You don't even know me. Why am I here?"

"It is a cool car. You have to admit that." He turned the dial on the old AM radio, and a display dropped down underneath the dash. "Satellite radio. I did a few upgrades. I just kept them hidden. Also cool, huh?" The staccato beat of a nineties' song filled the car.

"Sure. What about the other, though? Me, here?"

"Broady brothers. You mentioned them back there." Eddy saw a light change, and he downshifted. The exhaust burbled and popped as the car slowed to a stop. "I heard a story about them, something that happened about three weeks back."

"Me, too." John took a deep breath and closed his eyes. It wasn't an especially good memory. He'd never really thought about it having gotten around.

"My sis, the one with the party? She knows this man who got trounced by the Broady brothers out at Ostrich Bar and Grill, except the man she knows is in the hospital, critical care ward." The light changed, and Eddy eased the car out, waving to a patrol car that had pulled up at the side street angling off the road they were on.

"He's not in the critical care ward."

Eddy looked at him. "That's the answer I'd hoped to hear. But tell me how he's not. My sister sure seems to believe he is."

"I'm the trouncee. An ambulance took me to the hospital, but there was no critical care. Bruised ribs, broken fingers. This eye. Oh, and you probably saw the makeup. I'm embarrassed about that. I didn't expect to see anyone back there." He chuckled, looking out his window. "At least I hoped I wouldn't."

"Bruised pretty badly under there?"

"Grapefruit size. Doctor told me when I went back in that I was lucky not to lose the eye."

It was a bare stretch of road, and without warning, Eddy hit the gas and spun the wheel, sliding the car around 180 degrees in the middle of the pavement. He looked at John.

"Time to head back. We have a birthday cake to cut. My sis does, anyway. I don't want to get too far away with this present of hers, either."

"Yeah. You've also got a crowd of Shelby admirers waiting on you back there." The lights of businesses and homes flickered by outside the window.

"So, the brothers picked on you? Is that what the fight was about?"

Eddy's question brought back the moment when Jeff had threatened to throw Karen and her kids out of the restaurant. John didn't have to get involved, but he'd felt like he was, already. He'd gotten involved when she had fallen on him in the pool. No, they hadn't picked the fight, not physically. He'd jumped them. All three of them. John laughed softly as he said exactly that to Eddy.

"I jumped them. One against three."

Eddy laughed aloud. "I saw them around the pool earlier. I don't know that I'd fight even one of them, much less three. Can I ask the motivation?"

Don't Eat the Parakeet

Karen. It was Karen, John wanted to say. However, he couldn't. This man was being very friendly, but he was an unknown. Those feelings were too intense and too private for him to lay them out there so easily.

"Defense of a woman's integrity. That's all." He looked away, feeling his eyes moisten. He didn't want to be seen crying in front of this man.

"Did she appreciate it?"

"She doesn't know."

EDDY SMILED. This was the man his sister was looking for, and he had him in the car at his side. Was she ever going to be surprised! The Shelby wasn't the best present his sister would receive tonight. He would make sure of that.

Chapter 21

A GURGLING sound from underneath the newly laid sod caught Karen's attention. Chipper bounced in her arms, and in his high-pitched voice, he called out, "Water, Mimi!" Then, in a sudden eruption of hissing fountains, sprinkler heads all over the yard burst from their hidden sleeves, and pandemonium erupted.

"Brad! Not again!" That was Bambii-two-eyes as she ran for the deck.

It was already crowded with laughing partygoers, though, who were themselves dodging the attacking jets of water. A number of people in swimsuits laughed and grabbed plates of steaks from cloth-covered tables, running for the drier climes off the grass. One woman got too close to the edge of the pool, and losing her balance, barely had time for a man near her to grab her plate from her hand as she went crashing backwards into the water.

Chipper struggled to get down, and when Karen released him, he ran to stand beside his mother. "Water, Issie! Water!" He yanked at her hand until she laughed and turned to her father, who had just come out of the spraying water with a frown on his face.

"Chipper loves to play in the sprinklers." Lissie grabbed his hands and did a little dance in the water glittering against the early evening sun. "Fly, Chipper! See the water fly? It's fun!" She turned to her father. "Dad! Lighten up! It's hot out here, and the water feels good. Don't be a sour puss."

The quartet of Beatles' voices from the speakers was lively and bright, and the conversations continued unabated. Those who had been caught in the sprinklers were laughing, and none seemed upset at the unexpected shower, that was except for Brad and Bambii.

Brad put his arm around Bambii's waist and pulled her farther off the grass onto a drier section of the pool decking. Taking an offered towel, he patted his wife's hair.

She pushed his help away.

"I'm okay, Brad." She batted her eyes and gave a forced smile. "I think that's my signal to get in the water. Pardon me. My suit's inside." Her eyes red, she stepped away and headed to the house.

Brad watched her go, and he called to Lissie. "Sour puss? That's how you see me?" When she walked over to stand beside him with Chipper still in her arms, he pushed his wet hair back from his forehead. "I'm a sour puss?"

She kissed the baby on the forehead and looked away. Her words to her father were not kind.

"Dad, you haven't been fun to be around since before Chipper was born. Everything makes you angry, and you never want to spend time with your family. We are still your family, you know." She walked away from him, telling the baby, "Chipper, let's go get you dried off."

He turned to see Karen still watching. "Am I that bad, really, that my kids don't even like me?"

She looked at him. "Are you?"

A splash caught their attention, and they turned to see one of the Broady brothers surfacing in the center of the pool. Karen sighed and turned away. Glancing at Brad, not caring if he followed, she walked to a chair and sat down.

"What, Karen? What is it?" Brad sat beside her. "That's Rick, isn't it? At least I think that's Rick. It seems to bother you that he's here. Did you invite him?"

"I invited the whole church. They attend there. Anyway, at the time I sent the invitations, I didn't have a problem with them."

"So, what's the problem now?"

"You don't know, do you? The picture in the paper?" She looked at him, surprised. She smiled sourly.

"What about it? We saw it. Bambii and I thought it was funny."

"Funny? Being caught in the pool in that awful picture for everyone to see? It wasn't like it seemed, and at church, everyone believed it was true. The Broadys were especially ugly about it." She ran her finger along the bottom of her eyes, trying not to cry in front of the entire party. This was supposed to be an evening for merriment, for forgetting the troubles of the past three weeks.

"The paper ran a retraction. What's the big deal?" He leaned forward and touched her chin, the familiarity of eighteen years of marriage making this moment a very easy one for a safe display of public tenderness. "You do know about the retraction, don't you?"

"Retraction? What retraction?"

She didn't know, and his words caught her off-guard. She didn't take the paper, and she'd refused to read another one since. She hadn't been to church, and at work, well, at work she'd been catching up on a backlog from two weeks of vacation. She hadn't had time for little more than casual conversation and friendly quips with her coworkers.

None of them had said anything about the picture to her, though. Not a one. And she had refused to quiz them, either.

"It was in Monday's edition. Oh, that's right," he said with a smile, teasing. "You don't take the paper, do you? You should get out more, Karen. Have you been brooding over this for the past three weeks? My God, life isn't all about you. It happens to other people, too." He made an attempt to look contrite, but it wasn't very convincing. "However, this is your party. Bambii and I came back to help you celebrate. So, celebrate." He stood. "Do you even know if the Broadys have tried to apologize, or have you been so preoccupied with this party and your pride that you haven't tried to find out? Talk to them, Karen. They wouldn't be here so obviously having a good time if they were still upset at you. Talk to them." He laughed and turned. "I need to find Bambii. Two drenchings in one day are a bit much for her, I think."

"Brad?" Karen had something else to say. The deejay's

music had slowed, and the pulse of the song was long and sweet. It was a moment before he turned, and when he did, she said, "Thank you for what you did for me this morning. The house. You didn't have to do that, and I appreciate it."

He nodded. "Just so you know, that was Bambii's idea. She thought you deserved it." Without waiting for her reply, he headed towards the house.

Now Karen felt really bad. After what she had done to the woman that morning, what she had said, how could she face her ever again? She had told Eddy that she could party like she didn't have a care in the world, but the fact of it wasn't proving as easy as the promise.

Then, Chipper came running up to her, his arms in the air.

"Water gone, Mimi. Back, Mimi. Bring back."

She looked up and sure enough. The sprinklers had turned themselves off. She patted him on the head. "Not now, Chipper. Not just now." There was enough water coming from her eyes, and she grabbed a stray towel to press to her face.

Then, she looked at him and brightened her features. "Okay, Chipper, before I lose my resolve, let's go find us a Broady, and let's see if we can make peace." She brushed her fingertips along his face. "I have a Bible verse to live up to. I can't hide from this. I have to be the one to make it right."

Off to the other side of the pool, the remaining Broady brothers sat digging in to yet another of the caterer's steaks. She started that way, carrying Chipper as her bodyguard. He couldn't do much to protect her physically, but emotionally, he could be a lifesaver, and she needed one at the moment, and very desperately, too.

"I REALLY should go. Thanks for the ride in your car, but this is your sister's party, and I'd just be intruding." John waved Eddy off as several of the men reattached the bow to the Shelby's drip rails.

Eddy grabbed his arm before he could get away. "Not so fast, good friend, John. I want you to meet my family."

"I give. I'd hoped the sun would be down if it came to this." He held his hands up. He pointed. "My face."

"It's close enough to down." Eddy grinned. "It's almost eight, and the hill is about to shade the yard. We'll saunter slowly. I'll introduce you on the way to a few people I know from my sister's church."

"She must attend one of the big ones here in town, I guess."

"Wayside. You probably know it, the one you can see from 35. It has that tall steeple—closer to God, and all that, I think." Eddy chuckled. "It's good for her kids, that's for certain. She started attending about the time Chipper was born, although her kids might have turned out better if she'd started going about fifteen years earlier."

"I was there a few weeks ago for the Sunday morning service." John thought of Frankie. "Chipper is your sister's baby?"

That brought a guffaw. "Hardly. My niece's boy. My niece still lives with her mother. However, she graduates this month, and maybe if she moves out on her own, my sister can get the family back on track."

"Sounds like a crazy life. Mine has been, too." The past three weeks, anyway. "Just got a new place out across from Town Lake Park. Thought a move might help. I'd hoped so, anyway. Sometimes maybe not, I guess." His hadn't, anyway. The van—and Karen—hadn't returned.

"Across from Town Lake Park, huh? Where, exactly?"

"Bridges by the Park."

"Been there long? Like, about three weeks, maybe?"

"Two weeks." John looked in the garage as they walked past. There was the van he remembered, and he glanced down at the bumper. A paint mark, just like that one at the church.

"Two weeks, you say. Not three? I mean, were you at least looking three weeks ago?"

John turned to Eddy, surprised at the depth of the questions. "Three? Sure, I guess, taking a tour, maybe. After that fight, I had to hole up for recovery, so I went ahead and took the unit." He laughed. "I refused to look at anything else." He touched his cheek to show why. He also knew it had been what Karen had said in that pool that had decided him. "My face was pretty bad, worse than this if you can believe it. My eye was swollen shut."

"Yeah, I could see earlier where you tried to cover the damage." Eddy's face brightened. "Hear that? Paul McCartney."

"Beatles? Didn't they have a reunion concert or something once upon a time?"

"You know them, then."

"Only something someone said once while we were at the bottom of her pool." John actually chuckled this time.

He realized how funny that sounded.

Eddy glanced at him, his laughter barely concealed. "Well, my sister loves them. I borrowed all these from her junior high collection, and I've got a deejay at the back taking requests. You should meet her, you know."

"The deejay?" John wanted to meet Karen.

"My sister, man. I've also got a nephew and a niece to show off. And Chipper." Eddy nodded to the back gate.

"And the Broadys? They did this to me, remember."

Eddy laughed. "You let me worry about the Broadys." Then he pushed through the backyard gate where the real party was taking place.

BEFORE KAREN could make it over to the Broadys, Lissie came running up to her, stopping her in her tracks.

"Mom, look who's here." She bounced as she came to a stop. "My Sunday school teacher, Miss Frankie."

"Miss Frankie?"

"Mom, you remember. That day at Ostrich Grill? Dylan and I told you about her." She pulled her mother over to meet a woman with graying hair.

Dylan also came bounding up with an equal amount of excitement in his eyes. "Miss Frankie! You came." He grinned. "This is Chipper." He reached to take his nephew from Karen.

"Wet Dilly. All wet." Chipper brushed his hand along Dylan's chest and then shook the water off.

Frankie held out her hand to the boy. "Hello, Chipper. I know Lissie and Dylan from Sunday school." When he didn't stick out his hand, she reached and pulled it into hers

323

to shake. "Glad to meet you."

Lissie grabbed his free hand to wave it at her one-time Sunday school teacher. "Say Frankie, Chipper. Frankie, Son. Say it."

"An-kie, An-kie." The music was playing brightly in the background, however, and he was hard to hear.

Frankie smiled. "That's right, Chipper. Frankie." She turned to the birthday girl. "Your day? Karen, I believe, right? You've been at Wayside several years, if I'm not mistaken. We've never actually met, and I'm glad to do so now. I'm afraid your children know me better than I know them, but that's par for seeing my students only a few times a month. I'm always glad, however, to match parents with students."

Karen held out her hand to shake. "I understand perfectly. My kids speak highly of you. I'm so glad you could come. You must meet my brother, Eddy. He's around somewhere." Then she laughed. "I hope you like Beatles music. That's what the deejay's playing all evening."

Frankie laughed. "Dear, I was at the Shea Stadium concert back in 1965. I most certainly do like the Beatles. Wasn't that terrible about John Lennon? Poor Yoko Ono." Then she winked. "I still have my ticket stubs framed and on my wall, even though I've grown fond of George Strait in the years since."

Karen motioned for her kids to go play, and she guided Frankie to the serving table. "The cake's coming out after the sun goes down. However, there's steak and sides. Ice cream's being served inside. Feel free to see the deejay for your favorite songs, Beatles, of course. There's a list of the ones he has on the white board on his table."

What she wanted to say was, *Do you know the name of the man who stood up for my honor? He sat by you in church. How badly was he injured?* That was what she wanted to say, but she couldn't get it out.

Chuckling, turning to Karen, Frankie put her hand on her arm. "Your pool was built by Springfield Pools."

Karen frowned. She had no idea what that had to do with anything. "Yes. It was to be done months ago, but it ran behind schedule. The landscaping just went in this morning. You missed the sprinkler debacle."

"Sprinkler debacle? What happened?"

"The grass was supposed to be watered after it went in, and I guess the landscapers set the timers to come on automatically. We were all just sitting around and whoosh!" Karen smiled at the chance to retell the story. It had been funny, especially her ex and his new wife.

"I work for John, you know." Frankie busied herself with a raw carrot. When there was no response, she glanced at Karen. "John Springfield?"

"John Springfield?" The name didn't register for a moment. "Oh, you must mean the owner of the pool company. Of course."

"He's been out here a few times working. Do you remember seeing him?"

"Seeing the owner?" Karen thought for a moment. "Maybe. I don't remember."

"I thought he might have come by today. I really thought he would." Frankie seemed disappointed.

Karen shook her head. "Not that I know of." She turned

at a touch, and when she saw who it was, she felt her breath ripped away. It was Carlita Broady. A shiver ran down her spine.

"Yes, Carlita?" Karen steeled herself. She could do this. It was her birthday party, and the Broadys had been invited. She would be the good hostess. "Are you and your family having a good time? We should have the cake out soon. It's almost dark."

The big woman looked at Karen, her glance dancing back and forth from one of Karen's eyes to the other. She took a deep breath before beginning.

"Karen, my Rickie and his brothers don't want to apologize, but I have to." She turned to glance at her husband talking and having a good time on the far side of the yard. She looked back at Karen, and her eyes were red. "I don't care if he sees me. I know you weren't there, but after that picture came out, me and my family said some ugly things about you. Your kids, too. My Rickie and his brothers told me to let it go, but I can't. They hurt a man because he said that picture was wrong. The next day the paper came out saying it was all a mistake. My Rickie and me are really sorry, and I just had to tell you, even though you didn't know. We was wrong."

Karen smiled, surprised at the generous admission. "Oh, Carlita. That is so sweet of you. You don't know how much that means to me. Let me give you a hug."

Carlita returned her hug, and she patted her on the back. "You throw a really special party, honey. I'm so glad we came." Blowing a kiss to her husband, she stepped away, turning to wave to Karen before disappearing across the yard.

"I saw it, you know." Frankie reached for another carrot. "The fight."

"At the Ostrich Grill?" That surprised her. She knew other people were there, of course, but no one had spoken to her of it. Then, she froze. Of course this woman was there. She'd been at church with the man in the black tie and fedora. Then they'd seen her on the way to the hospital. "So you know the man in critical care?" *Dear God, say yes,* she prayed.

"Dear, I don't know anything about anyone in critical care. But you should know this—"

Before she could continue, however, Dylan ran up, sending water splattering everywhere. Just behind him was Zack, and excitement was all over them.

"Mom, you have to let us. Please. The roof?"

Zack leaned in over his shoulder. "Please, Mrs. Wycliff. Everyone's here, and we want them to see how big a splash we can make. Lots of people are asking us to. Please."

Karen glanced around for her brother, and Eddy was nowhere to be seen. The boys' enthusiasm was so intense, she could not tell them no.

"One time, boys. Do you hear me? You may jump off the roof one time, and then if you come to me again, I'll tell you no. Understand?" About the time the music changed from a ballad to a bright, punctuated beat. The sound was loud and driving, and Karen called louder, "Boys? Once!"

A flash of yellow and another of blue tore across the decking, dashing around people casually visiting with each other. As the two splotches of color attacked the downspout, people who had noticed the flight of color turned to look. It was only moments before there was a mighty scream of intent, and the boys were flying through the air.

It was when they came down that events took a brisk turn for the worse. Flying through the air anterior first and limbs spread, they dive bombed like B-12 aircraft holed and without flight capabilities. When they crashed, water went flying everywhere, and one cascading wave in particular headed directly towards the breakfast room windows. However, two boys instead of one were expelling the water from the pool, and the stream of water was shifted slightly from its usual trajectory. Instead of hitting directly on the breakfast room windows, the water took out the small porch just off the kitchen. In that moment, the entire party heard the speakers fill with static. Then there was a buzzing sound followed by a popping noise. Finally, all was quiet.

When the boys rose from the water, hooting in success, all around them was silence. That was the precise moment when the fully lighted cake exited the house, and leading the procession was Bambii. She was belting out in a surprisingly good voice the very peppy Wayside Christian Fellowship version of the birthday song, and with gusto, everyone else began to sing along.

Good times had arrived, and it was all about Karen at that point. She might not be thirty-nine for several more days, but this day was the one destined to be her day of celebration. It was to be so grand and so very special that she would never need to have another birthday ever.

It would be, too. She just didn't yet realize how special it would turn out to be.

Chapter 22

THIS WAS John's first time to see the pool completed, with full landscaping and actual water inside. The last time he had stood in this backyard, the pool had been a dirt hole, Karen had tumbled down the side, and he had caught her in his arms. That event had also been recorded for posterity in the local Austin American-Statesman.

Now the scene was a lively if somewhat dizzying group of happenings that vied to attack the senses. The only people he recognized immediately were the Broadys. They stood out like a series of rocks on a flat lunar plain.

As he and Eddy stepped forward, they saw a flash of yellow and blue from the top of the porch, and in a dizzying spray of water, the music fizzled and stopped. The deejay could be seen off to the left grabbing towels and attempting to dry the electrical equipment.

Charisse McAuliffe

"I think that was my nephew and his friend," Eddy snorted. "My sister can't keep them off the roof."

As a vivacious rendition of *Happy Birthday* started up on the back porch, they turned to see a procession exit the house led by a very blonde woman. Immediately following her was an enormous cake lighted with slowly rotating miniature spotlights. The center was a red bull's eye festooned with shafts of arrows embedded in the cake, directly in the center of the bull's eye.

As the cake drew nearer to its intended victim, John was surprised to find Frankie standing right by Karen. Seeing Karen made his face warm, and it also made him want to hide. She was as beautiful as he remembered. However, he had a pretty good idea what she'd think about his looks, and he didn't want to hear her tell him to go away. As far as Frankie being at her side, that was a mystery to him. Why she would be here he didn't know, unless she didn't trust him to come by to pick up the check on his own.

"Your sister," he turned to Eddy. "Which one is she?" Lights had already begun to click on all over the perimeter, as well as in the trees. The yard was packed, and the party-goers in the distance were becoming difficult to see.

A toddler came running up to them followed by a high school girl, and in his little-boy voice, he called out, "Hold Chipper." His arms went out to Eddy, and he grabbed him around the leg.

"Sorry, Uncle Eddy. He got away." Lissie made to pull him off her uncle's leg.

"I've got him, Niece. He'll be fine, and besides, I've got to introduce him to my friend here." Picking up the small

330

package, he kissed him on the nose. "Hi, Chipper."

John recognized the boy, and he smiled. "I thought your niece's son was named Chipper. Surely there aren't two of them." When Eddy glanced at him, he clarified, "This is Karen Wycliff's house. Isn't this her baby?"

"That's a good one, but no." Eddy laughed, while reaching to tweak the boy's nose. "Lissie is Chipper's mommy, isn't she, Chipper?"

"Issie," the boy cried. "Mommy!"

John was now lost. "I was certain Karen told me Chipper was hers. There was something about a canary, no, a yellow parakeet. It was out, and I helped her catch it one afternoon."

There was a loud popping in the sound system, and with a whine, the music came back up. The speakers sparkled with a Beatles rendition of *Birthday*, and after a few moments there were more than a few people dancing, with several sashaying right into the pool.

Eddy turned to John. "Let me introduce you to my sister. You'll really like her, I think. I'm certain she'll like you."

However, as they stepped around a bobbing Carlita Broady, Carlita bobbed just the wrong direction. When she bumped Eddy, he overcompensated to keep Chipper balanced, and in doing so, he jostled John just where he had hit his bruised rib against the counter earlier that day.

"Not again!" John grabbed his side. Streaks of lightning shot behind his eyes, and he felt his knees give.

"Hey, man, sorry." Eddy tried to steady him, just as Chipper yelled, "Want Issie!" and he tried to wriggle out of his great-uncle's arms. Eddy stumbled and released his hold on John. Now completely unbalanced, John's feet went out from under him and took him right into the pool.

EDDY SAW John's hat floating on top, and he immediately yelled for backup help. "Man in pool! I don't see him coming up! Where's Dylan?" He struggled with Chipper, patting him on the head and telling him to hush.

Chipper squirmed harder, calling, "Want Issie!"

"Oh, my!" Carlita looked in the pool and froze. Then she yelled, "A man's in the pool." She pointed to the only one fully clothed, now resting on the bottom. "I think he's drowning!"

Eddy saw Karen, and he called, "Sis, take the baby." He began kicking off one of his boots. He was going in, as it appeared that his new best friend didn't intend to come back up.

Karen snatched Chipper from his arms, gasping when she saw the fully-clothed form at the bottom of the pool. "Good heavens, Eddy. Who is that?"

"John," he cried, working off his second boot. When he saw Dylan and Zack back up on the roof, watching the events unfurl, he yelled and pointed, "Nephew! Jump in and rescue this man. Your mother's happiness depends on it."

Karen looked at him in a funny way. As *Birthday* punched the air around them, the two boys came crashing into the pool, and like the fish they were, they soon had John lifted to the side. Eddy was grateful to see he was still breathing, if somewhat waterlogged. John rolled to one side and began coughing, then harder, until he retched. He spat into a planting bed and wiped his mouth on his sleeve. Once they handed him a towel, and he began drying his face, Carlita called for Rick Broady to join her.

"John Springfield. Am I glad to see you!" Rick reached to shake his hand, holding his out expectantly. His wide face was red with embarrassment, either that or exhaustion from walking over. He heaved a deep breath, and he managed to get out, "I feel so bad about what happened at Ostrich's place. We didn't want no trouble, so we took care of everything out there; but when that retraction came out in the paper, then we felt real sorry you went to the hospital and all. I want to apologize to you official like. If I'd known you was here, I'd already come over. We were wrong, John, and you were right to make us stop what we wanted to do." He leaned his bulk further over, placing a hand on Carlita's shoulder for additional support. "Shake? Please, before I fall." He grinned at the soggy man.

John reached with his injured hand first, and groaning with the effort, he switched to his good one. "Apology accepted. You have mine, too. Can you please help me up, Rick?" Their hands clasped, and Rick let go of his wife's shoulder.

"Sure, John. What's with your face, there? I know we hurt you bad, but all around your eye. There's brown stuff coming off." He looked at his wife, as if this might be further damage caused by John's inadvertent dive into the pool. To the side, Eddy wore a smile. Everything was working out to his satisfaction just fine.

"Here, John. Have a fresh towel." Eddy offered him one from several that had miraculously appeared.

JOHN GLANCED at his towel as he handed it off, and he had indeed begun to take off part of the makeup. He ducked his head, quite mortified, but unable to rectify the situation. To face it head on was his only option at this point. "I tried to cover up the bruises. I couldn't fix the eye, though."

Carlita stepped to him with tears running down her cheeks. "Honey, I'm so sorry about all that happened to you that day at the restaurant. Now look at you here today." She turned to Rick. "See this, Rickie? And to think I said those things about him." She turned back to John, reaching her hand to his face. "You didn't want to make my man feel bad for hurting you, and you were hiding the pain. Oh, you poor thing. I said such bad things about you, and I am so sorry." She put her arms around him, patting him on the back. "You're not really a jerk after all."

Rick slapped her on the back of the head. "Carlita. Don't say that."

"Say what, Rickie? I think I like John. I should never have listened to you all these years." She kissed John on the face before she was tugged away by her husband. "A dance, John. Save one for me," she called back.

"Carlita. Stop making a fool of yourself!" Rick pulled her to her seat as his brothers laughed.

The space around John didn't remain empty, though. It seemed he was a magnet, although a very wet one, attracting attention from all over.

"How'd we do, Mom?" Two boys wearing blue and yellow Speedos jumped from the pool to stand at John's side, drenching the pool deck and a number of people around them.

"John," Eddy interrupted, "meet Dylan, and there's Zack, his best friend. They're your rescue team."

"Thanks, boys." John held a hand out to shake.

Dylan wasn't through, though. "I heard Rick. You're that guy from the bar, aren't you? I was there and I watched. You jumped all three Broadys at once. That was so cool. I want to be brave enough to do that someday."

Zack poked him. "You want to fight the Broadys?"

"No, stupid. I want to be brave enough to. There's a big difference."

John rubbed his hand over his wet hair, and he turned when Zack offered him his cowboy hat. Shaking it out, he slipped it on, deciding this might be a good time to make his exit. He wasn't an invited part of the party crowd, and he hadn't managed to remain in the background by any stretch of the imagination. If he left now, maybe he wouldn't have to endure being kicked out when the invited guests realized he had crashed their good time.

KAREN WAS breathing hard by then, and she felt as if Lizzie's parakeet had taken flight—in her stomach. She finally noticed who was standing in her backyard, and he wasn't fresh from the critical care ward. She had been calling about the wrong man all along.

"You were at the restaurant." Karen could barely speak. "I heard that from Rick, but now with that hat on—" She paused, breathless. She was certain it was the man from the pool. His hat was the one from the picture in the paper, where it had been plastered all over Austin. "You surely can't be the same man who rescued Junie." She felt her skin flush in the heat of the night, because she was now sure it was. "Did you or did you not catch a falling woman in this very pool three weeks ago?"

With a deep breath and an embarrassed smile, John spoke, and his words were in that same melodious voice Karen remembered from that dark night.

"Sort of. There wasn't a pool here, then. Just a hole. It was you I caught, though. I didn't think you knew who I was." He paused, and then he chuckled. "I bought that loft you told me I lived in."

"Loft?' Loft? What in heaven's name was he talking about? She looked for Eddy, only to see him raise his shoulders in equal confusion.

It seemed that nothing made sense to Karen, and she hardly dared try. If she did, she thought her head would explode.

Either that or her heart, because something had to give; but please, God, not in front of the Broadys and the world. Please, God, not here.

KAREN'S BIRTHDAY party was far from finished. It had hours yet to wind down. Frankie stepped behind Karen and invited her into the house, motioning to John and telling him to find a dry change of clothes. Once inside, she pulled Karen to a chair and sat across from her.

"I see you two know each other." Frankie smiled. "I expected you did. After all, John installed your pool. Now I see what's been going on the past few weeks."

Karen's eyes were glued on the wall of windows and the

action going out just outside. She searched for a familiar hat. She heard Frankie's question, but she couldn't focus enough to form an answer.

"Karen, right?" Frankie moved her chair closer and put a hand gently on Karen's knee.

Karen nodded as she looked at her. "I, well, I thought he was someone else. A man in town by the park—"

"Town Lake Park?" When Karen's face twisted with recognition, Frankie nodded sagely. "I pay attention more than John thinks. I knew there was a reason he had to have that particular loft. It was you he saw. I see that now."

"I thought . . ." Karen remembered the glimpse of the man she'd seen near the park, and she overlaid the look of his jeans with those of the workman in her pool that day; and as if a puzzle began to fall into place in her head, it all made sense. He'd seemed familiar because he was familiar. She had watched him secretly from behind her blinds, and, and . . . she felt stupid. How could she not have known?

"I'm surprised you didn't see him the Sunday he attended with me at Wayside. We were in the balcony together. I remember your son sitting right behind us." Frankie fought a smile.

"The balcony?" Karen slumped in her seat. She couldn't go outside and meet this man again, no matter how attractive she might find him. She'd not recognized him at the park, she'd ignored him at church, and now he'd fallen in her pool. Gads! How horrible could this be?

And still, she could barely think for the image she remembered of him working in her backyard, sweaty and without a shirt, then coming to her rescue at the restaurant, and she'd never thanked him for championing her cause.

Frankie brought her back to herself, as she leaned forward and whispered, "He bought it for you." She laughed a small laugh. "So he could look for you at the park."

"For me?" Karen jiggled her collar to try to cool down, and she looked for him out the window again. She found him off to the side, pulling on a dry shirt, one she recognized as one of her brother's. It was far too large. What really caught her eye was the bare shoulders he exposed just as he slipped it on. Those she recognized.

"You never came back, though." Frankie stood and held her hand toward the door. "Would you like to meet my John? He's like a son to me, and I think you'll find him a very nice man."

"He doesn't hate me?"

"Oh, oh, my dear." That brought a real laugh from Frankie. "He hates not getting the chance to get to know you. Before tonight, he thought he'd offended you. Thank God you invited the Broadys. Rick's apology was the very thing to get my John to see the error of his ways. Now he knows you aren't offended at all, or he will when you go outside and tell him."

Karen stood and took a deep breath. "I faced down the Broadys. I guess I can face down this." She wasn't as sure as she sounded, but it wouldn't hurt to give it a try. At least Eddy would be there for her if she needed his shoulder for a good cry. She smiled at that and braced herself.

"Go on," Frankie encouraged. "See how his arms feel around you. You might like it."

When she stepped through the door, Chipper hit her leg

first. Lizzie put her arm across her mother's shoulder, asking, "Mom? Are you okay?"

"Take the baby," she replied, her eyes on John, now laughing at one of her brother's jokes. She picked Chipper up and handed him to her daughter. "He's yours. You need to keep an eye on him."

"Mom!"

"Do it, Lizzie." That was Brad, and he pushed his daughter on the shoulder, ignoring her when she pulled the boy's face to her shoulder and marched off. "I spoke with him, Karen. He seems to be a nice guy." He nodded with his head John's way. He smiled. "Black eye and all."

"That's my fault."

"So I heard." He chuckled when she looked at him. "You need someone. I'm sorry it can't be me, but I think he'll make a super stand-in." Bambii was standing meekly off to the side, and Brad motioned her over. "We both do."

"I've been so wrong about you, Bambii. I'm sorry." Karen's eyes began to tear up.

"I want us to be best friends." She flashed a brilliantly bright smile. "That's all, if you want to be."

Karen wasn't so sure about best friend, but she smiled, and before long, to the cheers of those around them, she did make it to John's side.

"Hey, beautiful," he said to her, tipping his hat underneath the glow of a glistening leaf-muted floodlight. "I guess I made quite a splash at your little shindig."

"You did," she whispered, barely able to contain her voice. "I'm glad you wore your hat tonight. I wouldn't have recognized you without it."

"No? How about if I do this?" He put his lips together and tweeted a little parakeet song.

Karen bit her bottom lip to keep from smiling so wide her face cracked. Her song, her parakeet song. Everything else happening around her meant nothing, the pool, the crowds, not even the blasting of the sound system. In those few whistled notes, she remembered how she'd been attracted to him that day, and she was certain her dreams were turning out just the way she hoped they would.

"I'm so glad you fell into my pool." She wrapped her arm in his, and she smiled when he worked his fingers into hers.

"I'm more glad that you fell in on top of me." John chuckled.

Somehow, it seemed just the right thing for him to say, and Karen knew she had found three special men tonight, and they were all holding her hand, all at the exact same time.

CRYING, WAITING, Hoping, started to come out through the speakers, and Karen didn't show up to cut the cake.

No one could find John, either.

Bambii stepped in, calling everyone forward and saying all sorts of kind things about Karen, and expressing her appreciation for everyone showing up at Karen's party. Then she removed the rotating spotlights, cut the first piece of cake, and took Chipper from Lizzie as she handed her the knife.

Karen's lack of participation in cutting the cake was soon forgotten with the rousing beat of yet another song.

Eddy didn't even mind that his gift to his sister had to wait. After all, it would still be there after the party wound down. Anyone should know that the real gift he'd managed to rustle up for her was better than any Shelby Mustang could ever be.

JOHN AND Karen were taking the time to get to know one another. They were out in the drive leaning against the Shelby, taking advantage of the warm night and the star-studded Texas sky overhead. They had progressed from holding hands; and as John held Karen in his arms, he shared his feelings with her about how he'd thought she'd hate him. She laughed, not quite willing to admit to her confusion in figuring out who he was. It was working out, however. A fresh start, John called it, and Karen agreed. He told her he'd ridden in the Shelby, gently rapping the fender with his knuckles.

"With Eddy driving?" Karen looked aghast.

John laughed, pulling her tight. Eddy's driving had left him unnerved and breathless, but it couldn't compare with the woman he held in his arms.

"It's mine, you know. He's giving it to me."

"So I've been told. He must be some brother. I like him." The rest of the package that came with the woman he had fallen in love with? Kids and a house and a pool? Well, if it came with Karen, it was just icing on the cake, and that was all right with him.

"He is, and thanks. I like him, too."

They laughed together, just happy to be in one another's arms.

Epilogue

JOHN FIRED up the Shelby. His truck sat on one side, and the yellow Campmobile that had been Frankie's sat on the other. The old van had a new engine in it now, thanks to Eddy. It also had new paint and a new interior, thanks to John. It was Karen's favorite vehicle.

Dylan still jumped off the roof into the pool, and Chipper loved to come visit on weekends. However, now that Granny Frankie was only working part time at Springfield Pools, she kept him when Lissie was at work. Having another daughter and a baby in the house had given Frankie a new lease on life, as if she needed it. She said she was having fun, though.

"John, er, Dad, can I drive the car to swim practice this time?" Dylan was already in his Speedos, and he dropped into the car on the passenger's side, tossing his bag in the back.

John just laughed. "I saw the paint on the back of your sister's van. I want your mother's car to stay pristine. Get in, and I'll drive you. Someday you can buy your own."

Karen called from the open kitchen door, "You boys be good. Are the two of you staying the weekend in the loft?"

"Are you coming to visit if we do?" Dylan turned to grin at John's question.

"Can I bring Junie?"

John reached up and waved his hand to show her to come on.

Karen blew them both a kiss. "You go ahead to swim practice, and I'll come in later tonight." Then she pointed to her son. "Dylan, I'm still checking that wallet. You stay away from those girls."

"Mom, I never did anything. Didn't Uncle Eddy tell you that?" He ducked his head and glanced at John.

John reached and grabbed his leg. "Dylan, just say, yes, ma'am. I promise. That's something we all learn."

"I heard that!" Karen's words were filled with laughter. "Just stay off the roof!"

John looked at Dylan and winked as he shifted the Shelby into reverse and let it burble out of the garage. Then, putting it in first, he played with the clutch, and the back tires screamed to the end of the driveway.

John's eye's glowed. "I could get to like this."

Dylan couldn't keep the grin off his face. "I already do."

John glanced at his new son as the car danced sideways into the street. "Me, too, Dylan. Me, too."

About the Author

CHARISSE "Chrissy" McAuliffe grew up watching her mother's soap operas. She began writing her own at age 11, but it took another ten years, two failed relationships, one eaten bird (not a parakeet!), and a newly wonderful husband for this story to come to life. Today Ms. McAuliffe lives in North Georgia in the Blue Ridge Mountains near a waterfall. She sleeps with her windows open during the summer so she can soak it all in. She claims she has another story or two percolating in her head waiting to find their way onto her computer. She appreciates receiving reader feedback through her publisher at www.ThreeSkilletPublishing.com.

www.ingramcontent.com/pod-product-compliance
Lightning Source LLC
Chambersburg PA
CBHW071046250626

47159CB00002B/381